Praise for Rajaa Alsanea's *Girls of Riyadh*

"Be warned: This book will rearrange your priorities for the rest of the day so you can finish it." —*Pensacola Independent News*

"*Girls of Riyadh* is so juicy it's been called Saudi Arabia's *Sex and the City*." —*Glamour*

"A taboo-breaking novel." —*The Washington Post*

"*Girls of Riyadh* . . . is one of those rare books with the power to shake up an entrenched society." —*Los Angeles Times*

"You could call it Sex in the Arabian City. . . . A refreshingly realistic portrayal of an often-stereotyped group. . . . Engaging, enlightening and enjoyable." —The Associated Press

"An important book . . . it obliterates many misunderstandings about Islam and emphasizes the overwhelming role of culture in the way Saudis live their lives." —*Time*

"*Girls of Riyadh* sensitively portrays a land where marriage has cruelly been made to war against love. . . . [Alsanea] courageously highlights various social ills bedeviling her country. . . . *Girls of Riyadh* candidly and sometimes movingly illustrates the shackled lives of young, lovelorn women in Saudi Arabia." —Rayyan Al-Shawaf, *The St. Petersburg Times*

"Funny, heartfelt and universally relatable." —*Jane*

"Get on a plane to Riyadh, Saudi Arabia. Rent a house, find a job, settle in. Learn Arabic, make friends, spend years in the country. Still, you will never get as full a glimpse into the lives of young urban Saudi women as you will from reading . . . *Girls of Riyadh*. . . . The details of life on the Saudi peninsula are perfectly evoked. . . . The stories themselves are as entertaining, if not more so, than any episode of *Sex and the City*. . . . For a Western audience, the book is a first of its kind, and its value lies in introducing readers to this unfamiliar world that is surprisingly familiar." —Religionwriter.com

"A rare glimpse into ordinary life for young women in Saudi Arabia." —*San Francisco Chronicle*

"A bold new voice from Saudi Arabia spins a fascinating tale of four young women attempting to navigate the narrow straits between love, desire, fulfillment, and Islamic tradition. . . . This groundbreaking novel might be the very first that opens up their world to us—their culture, their struggles, their frustrations, their hopes, and their beliefs." —*Clutch* magazine

"Indisputably the work of a brave and intelligent young woman."
—*The Week*

"Rajaa Alsanea may be the most internationally famous Chicago author you've never heard of." —*TimeOut Chicago*

"The epistolary structure is genius; it allows the narrator to comment on the action and also provides a certain immediacy to the reader, so the characters seem to do more than just live on the page. These women could be anyone—your cousin, a friend. . . . This is a lively, fun read which also manages to be thought-provoking and worthy of the accolades it's received from those black-market readers." —*Bust*

"This is a distinctive and rare peek into a rarely revealed culture."
—*The Morning News*

"Alsanea holds her own as a writer, but her background is what sets her apart. . . . [Her] wisdom and insight into the female experience seem surreal. She captures the core, universal truths of the complications in finding and holding a life partner. . . . Astounding in [its] accuracy . . . [Alsanea] gives hope and empowerment to those of us, in every country, looking for love." —Bookreporter.com

"Rajaa Alsanea's novel . . . was officially banned in Saudi Arabia when it was published in Arabic two years ago. . . . But the book was still read, eagerly. Now, translated into English, it is easy to see why." —*The Economist*

"Intriguing." —*Milwaukee Journal Sentinel*

"In an atmosphere where every action is politicized, and where convention always trumps personal preference, human relations are reduced to envy and power play—which makes chick lit the ideal genre to discuss such problems. A friend's wedding is not just a celebration, but a political battleground. . . . A useful exposé of a social malaise." —*Reason*

ABOUT THE AUTHOR

Rajaa Alsanea grew up in Riyadh, one of six siblings in a family of doctors and dentists. She lives in Chicago but intends to return to Saudi Arabia after attaining a degree in endodontics. She is twenty-six years old, and this is her first novel.

GIRLS *of* RIYADH

Rajaa Alsanea

TRANSLATED BY
Rajaa Alsanea and Marilyn Booth

PENGUIN BOOKS

PENGUIN BOOKS

Published by the Penguin Group

Penguin Group (USA) Inc., 375 Hudson Street, New York, New York 10014, U.S.A.

Penguin Group (Canada), 90 Eglinton Avenue East, Suite 700, Toronto,
Ontario, Canada M4P 2Y3 (a division of Pearson Penguin Canada Inc.)

Penguin Books Ltd, 80 Strand, London WC2R 0RL, England

Penguin Ireland, 25 St Stephen's Green, Dublin 2, Ireland (a division of Penguin Books Ltd)

Penguin Group (Australia), 250 Camberwell Road, Camberwell,
Victoria 3124, Australia (a division of Pearson Australia Group Pty Ltd)

Penguin Books India Pvt Ltd, 11 Community Centre, Panchsheel Park, New Delhi – 110 017, India

Penguin Group (NZ), 67 Apollo Drive, Rosedale, North Shore 0632,
New Zealand (a division of Pearson New Zealand Ltd)

Penguin Books (South Africa) (Pty) Ltd, 24 Sturdee Avenue, Rosebank, Johannesburg 2196, South Africa

Penguin Books Ltd, Registered Offices: 80 Strand, London WC2R 0RL, England

First published in the United States of America by The Penguin Press,
a member of Penguin Group (USA) Inc. 2007
Published in Penguin Books 2008

1   3   5   7   9   10   8   6   4   2

Originally published in Arabic by Dar al Saqi, Beirut.

THE LIBRARY OF CONGRESS HAS CATALOGED THE HARDCOVER EDITION AS FOLLOWS:

Sani', Raja' 'Abd Allah.
[Banat al-Riyad. English]
Girls of Riyadh : a novel / Rajaa Alsanea ; translated by Rajaa Alsanea and Marilyn Booth.
p.   cm.
ISBN 978-1-59420-121-9 (hc.)
ISBN 978-0-14-311347-8 (pbk.)
I. Booth, Marilyn.   II. Title.
PJ7962.A55B3613 2007
892.7'36—dc22
2007009389

Printed in the United States of America
DESIGNED BY AMANDA DEWEY

To my most beloved;
Mom
and sister Rasha
and
to all of my friends,
the
Girls of Riyadh

AUTHOR'S NOTE

It never occurred to me, when I wrote my novel (*Banat Al-Riyadh*), that I would be releasing it in any language other than Arabic. I did not think the Western world would actually be interested. It seemed to me, and to many other Saudis, that the Western world still perceives us either romantically, as the land of the Arabian Nights and the land where bearded sheikhs sit in their tents surrounded by their beautiful harem women, or politically, as the land that gave birth to Bin Laden and other terrorists, the land where women are dressed in black from head to toe and where every house has its own oil well in the backyard! Therefore, I knew it would be very hard, maybe impossible, to change this cliché. But the success of my book in the Arab world was enough to mark me as a member of Arab intellectual society, which seemed to come with certain responsibilities. Furthermore, coming from a family that values other cultures and nations, and being the proud Saudi I am, I felt it is my duty to reveal another side of Saudi life to the Western world. The task was not easy, however.

In my Arabic version of the novel I interspersed the classical Arabic with language that reflects the mongrel Arabic of the modern world—there was Saudi dialect (several of them), and Lebanese-Arabic, English-Arabic and more. As none of that would make sense to the non-Arab reader, I had to modify the original text somewhat. I also had to add explanations that will hopefully help the Western reader better understand the gist of the text, as it was originally intended in Arabic.

In the interest of fairness, I have to make clear that the girls in the novel do not represent all girls in Riyadh, but they do represent many of them.

I hope that by the time you finish this book, you will say to yourself: Oh, yes. It is a very conservative Islamic society. The women there do live under male dominance. But they are full of hopes and plans and determination and dreams. And they fall deeply in and out of love just like women anywhere else.

And I hope you will see, too, that little by little some of these women are beginning to carve out their own way—not the Western way, but one that keeps what is good about the values of their religion and culture, while allowing for reform.

*"Verily, Allah does not change a people's condition
until they change what is in themselves."*

QUR'AN, SURAT AL-RA'D
(The Chapter of Thunder), Verse 11

GIRLS *of* RIYADH

Welcome to the Subscribers' List of

Memoirs Disclosed

To subscribe, send a blank message to:

seerehwenfadha7et__subscribe@yahoogroups.com

To cancel your subscription, send a blank message to:

seerehwenfadha7et__unsubscribe@yahoogroups.com

To contact the list manager, send a message to:

seerehwenfadha7et@yahoogroups.com

1.

To: seerehwenfadha7et@yahoogroups.com
From: "seerehwenfadha7et"
Date: February 13, 2004
Subject: I Shall Write of My Friends

Ladies and Gentlemen: You are invited to join me in one of the most explosive scandals and noisiest, wildest all-night parties around. Your personal tour guide—and that's *moi*—will reveal to you a new world, a world closer to you than you might imagine. We all live in this world but do not really experience it, seeing only what we can tolerate and ignoring the rest.

To all of you out there

Who are over the age of eighteen, and in some countries that'll mean twenty-one, though among us Saudis it means over six (and no, I don't mean sixteen) for guys and after menarche for girls.

To everyone out there

Who has got enough inner courage to read the naked truth laid out on the World Wide Web and the resolve to accept that truth, with of course the essential patience to stay with me through this insane adventure.

To all who have

Grown weary of the "Me Tarzan You Jane" brand of romance novels and have gotten beyond a black and white, good and evil view of the world.

To anyone who believes

That 1 + 1 may not necessarily be equal to two, as well as all of you out there who have lost hope that Captain Majed* will score those two goals to reach a draw in the last second of the episode. To the enraged and the outraged, the heated and the hostile, the rebellious and the bilious, and to all of you who just know that every weekend for the rest of your lives will be a total loss—not to mention the rest of the week. It's for you; it's to you that I write my e-mails. May they be the matches that set your thoughts on fire, the lighter that fuels a blaze of change.

Tonight's the night. The heroes of my story are people among you, from you and within you, for from the desert we all come and to the desert we shall all return. Just as it is with our desert plants, you'll find the sweet and the thorny here, the virtuous and the wicked. Some of my heroes are sweet and others are thorny, while a few are a bit of both at the same time. So keep the secrets you will be told, or as we say, "Shield what you may encounter!" And since I have quite boldly started writing this e-mail without consulting my girlfriends, and because every one of them lives huddled in the shadow of a man, or a wall, or a man who is a wall,** or simply stays put in the darkness, I've decided to change all the names of the people I will write about and make a few alterations to the facts, but in a way that will not compromise the honesty of the tale nor take the sting out of the truth. To be frank, I don't give a damn about the repercussions of this project of mine. As Kazantzakis put it, "I expect nothing. I fear no one. I am free." Yet a way of life has stood its ground in the face of all you'll read here; and I have to admit that I don't consider it an achievement to destroy it by means of a bunch of e-mails.

*A very popular cartoon for the 1990s generation of Saudi Arabian children. Translated from Japanese, it's a story of a boy trying to achieve his dream of becoming a soccer star.
**There is an Arabic proverb that says: "Better the shadow of a man than the shadow of a wall."

I shall write of my girlfriends,
for in each one's tale
I see my story and self prevail,
a tragedy my own life speaks.
I shall write of my girlfriends,
of inmates' lives sucked dry by jail,
and magazine pages that consume women's time,
and of the doors that fail to open.
Of desires slain in their cradles I'll write,
of the vast great cell,
black walls of travail,
of thousands, thousands of martyrs, all female,
buried stripped of their names
in the graveyard of traditions.
My female friends,
dolls swathed in gauze in a museum they lock;
coins in History's mint, never given, never spent;
fish swarming and choking in every basin and tank,
while in crystal vessels, dying butterflies flock.
Without fear
I shall write of my friends,
of the chains twisted bloody around the ankles of beauties,
of delirium and nausea, and the nighttime that entreaty rends,
and desires buried in pillows, in silence.
   —Nizar Qabbani

Right you are, Nizar, baby! Your tongue be praised, God bless you and may you rest in peace. Truth be told, though you are a man, you are indeed "the woman's poet" and if anyone doesn't like my saying so they can go drink from the sea.

My hair is now fluffed and teased, and I've painted my lips a shameless crimson red. Beside me rests a bowl of chips splashed with chili and lime. Readers: prepare yourselves. I'm ready to disclose the first scandal!

The wedding planner called out to Sadeem, who was hiding behind the curtain with her friend Gamrah. In her singsong Lebanese Arabic, Madame Sawsan informed Sadeem that the wedding music tape was still stuck in the machine and that efforts were being made to fix it.

"Please, tell Gamrah to calm down! It's nothing to worry about, no one is going to leave. It's only one A.M.! And anyway, all the *cool* brides these days start things on the late side to add a bit of suspense. Some never walk down the aisle before two or three A.M.!"

Gamrah, though, was on the verge of a nervous breakdown. She could hear the voices of her mother and her sister Hessah shrieking at the events manager from the other end of the ballroom, and the whole evening was threatening to turn out to be a sensational humiliation. Sadeem stayed at the bride's side, wiping beads of sweat from her friend's forehead before they could collide with the tears that were held back only by the quantity of kohl weighing down her eyelids.

The voice of the famous Saudi singer Muhammad Abdu finally blasted from the amplifiers, filling the enormous hall and prompting Madame Sawsan to give Sadeem the nod. Sadeem poked Gamrah.

"*Yalla,** let's go."

With a swift movement Gamrah wiped her hands along her body after reciting some verses of the Holy Qur'an to protect her from envious eyes, and raised the neckline of her dress to keep it from drooping over her small breasts. She began her descent of the marble staircase, going even more slowly than at the rehearsal with her girlfriends, adding a sixth second to the five she was supposed to count between each stair. She murmured the name of God before every step, praying that Sadeem wouldn't stumble on her train causing it to tear, or that she wouldn't trip over the floor-length hem of her dress and fall flat on her face like

*Yalla can mean "c'mon!" or "hurry up!"

in a comedy show. It was so unlike the rehearsal, where she didn't have a thousand women watching her every move and assessing every smile; where there was no annoying photographer blinding her every few seconds. With the blazing lights and all those dreadful peering eyes fixed on her, the small family wedding she'd always disdained suddenly began to seem like a heavenly dream.

Behind her, Sadeem followed her progress with utter concentration, ducking to avoid appearing in any of the photos. One never knows who might be looking at the photos from the bride's or groom's side, and like any decent girl, Sadeem wouldn't want strange men to see her in an exposing evening dress and full makeup. She adjusted the veil on Gamrah's head and gave a tiny jiggle to the train after each step Gamrah took as her radar picked up fragments of conversation at nearby tables.

"Who's *she?*"

"*Ma shaa Allah,** God willing, no envy touch her, she's so pretty!"

"The bride's sister?"

"They say she's an old friend."

"She seems a good girl—since we arrived I've seen her running around taking care of all sorts of things—it looks like she's carrying the whole wedding on her shoulders."

"She's a good deal prettier than the bride. Can you believe it, I heard that Prophet Mohammed used to send up prayers for the unlovely ones!"

"God's blessings and peace be upon him. *E wallah,*** must be true, because I swear, the ugly ones seem to be in demand these days. Not us, what bad luck."

"Is her blood pure? Her skin is so fair."

"Her father's mother was Syrian."

"Her name is Sadeem Al-Horaimli. Her mother's family is married into ours. If your son is serious, I can get you the details about her."

Ma shaa Allah is an Islamic phrase that one says in order not to jinx someone's luck.
**E Wallah* means swearing in God's name that something is true.

Sadeem had already been told that three ladies had asked about her since the wedding started. Now she heard numbers four and five with her own ears. Every time one of Gamrah's sisters came over to tell her that so-and-so had been asking questions, she murmured demurely, "May good health knock on her door."

It seemed to Sadeem as if Gamrah's marriage might indeed be "the first pearl to roll off the necklace," as Auntie Um Nuwayyir put it. Perhaps now the rest of the girls would be just as lucky. That is, if they followed the plan Auntie had concocted.

The strategy of *yaaalla yaaalla,* which means "get going, but just *baaarely,*" is the most foolproof path to a quick marriage proposal in our conservative society. The idea is to be energetic and constrained at the same time. "And after that you can be as foolish as you want," according to Um Nuwayyir's counsel. At weddings, receptions and social gatherings where ladies meet, especially the *old* ladies looking to make a match (or "capital funds and mothers-with-sons," as we girls like to call them), you must follow this strategy to the letter: "You *barely* walk, you *barely* talk, you *barely* smile, you *barely* dance, be mature and wise, you always think before you act, you measure your words carefully before you speak and you do not behave like a child." There is no end to Um Nuwayyir's instructions.

The bride took her place on the magnificently decorated platform. Her mother and the mother of the groom mounted the stairs to congratulate her on the happy marriage she had embarked on and to have their photos taken with the bride before the men came in from where they were celebrating in an adjoining room.

At this traditional Najdi wedding, where most people spoke in the dialect of the country's interior, Lamees's sophisticated west coast Hijazi accent stood out as she whispered to her friend Michelle.

"Hey! Check her out. The pharaohs are back!" The influence of Lamees's Egyptian grandmother was always readily apparent in Lamees's sharp tongue and manner.

She and Michelle studied the heavy makeup that coated the face of their friend Gamrah, especially her eyes, which had turned the color of blood from all the kohl seeping into them.

Michelle's real name is Mashael, but everyone, including her family, calls her Michelle. She answered Lamees in English.

"*Where the hell did she get that dress?*"

"Poor Gammoorah,* I wish she had gone to the dressmaker who made Sadeem's dress instead of this mess she came up with herself! Just look at Sadeem's gorgeous dress, though—anyone would think it's by Elie Saab."

"Oh, whatever. Like there's even one lady in this provincial crowd who would know the difference! Do you think anyone has any clue my dress is by Badgley Mishka? By God, her makeup is painful! Her skin is too dark for such a chalky foundation. They've made her practically blue—and look at the contrast between her face and her neck. Ewww . . . so vulgar!"

"Eleven o'clock! Eleven o'clock!"

"It's one-thirty."

"No, you idiot, I mean, turn to your left like the hands of a clock when it's eleven—you will never get it, will you—you'll never pass Gossip 101! Anyway, check out that girl—she's got 'talent,' all right!"

"Which 'talent'—front bumper or back?"

"Are you cross-eyed? Back, of course."

"Too much. They ought to take a chunk off her and give Gamrah a dose on the front, like that collagen stuff everyone is using."

"The most 'talented' of all of us is Sadeem—look at how feminine she looks with those curves. I wish I had a back bumper like hers."

"I think she really needs to ditch a few pounds and work out like you do. *Alhamdu lillah,* thank God, I never gain weight no matter how much I eat, so I'm not worried."

"What luck for you, I swear. I live in a state of permanent starvation to keep my body looking like this."

*A rephrasing of her name to make an affectionate nickname.

The bride noticed her friends sitting at the table nearby, smiling and waving their arms at her while they tried to cover up the question that lurked in their eyes: *Why isn't it me up there?* Gamrah was ecstatic, almost intoxicated with this precious moment. She had always seen herself as the least favored of any of them, but now here she was, the first of all to get married.

Waves of guests started coming up to the dais to congratulate the bride, now that the photography session was over. Sadeem, Michelle and Lamees all stepped up and hugged Gamrah while whispering something into her ear: "Gamrah, wow! *Mashaa Allah,* God's will be done! So-o-o gorgeous! The whole evening I've been praying to God to take good care of you." "Congratulations, sweetie! You look great—that gown is stunning on you!" "My God, girl, you're spectacular. A vision! Best-looking bride I've ever seen."

Gamrah's smile grew broader as she listened to her friends' praise and noted the envy half hidden in their eyes. The three of them posed for photographs with the happy bride. Sadeem and Lamees started dancing around her while the eyes of all those older women who devote themselves to arranging marriages were glued to all of their bodies. Lamees was proud to show off her distinctive height and her gym-toned body, and she made sure to dance slightly apart from Sadeem, who had expressly warned her beforehand against dancing next to her so that people wouldn't compare their bodies. Sadeem was always longing to have her curves liposuctioned so that she could be as slim as Lamees and Michelle.

Suddenly the men came shooting through the doors like arrows, the fastest arrow of all being the groom, Rashid Al-Tanbal, who headed straight for his bride on the dais. The women retreated en masse, desperately searching for whatever they or their friends had that would conceal their hair and faces—not to mention any other revealing body parts—from the eyes of those men on the march.

When the groom and his companions were just steps away, Lamees yanked up the corner of the tablecloth to cover her cleavage. Her twin sister Tamadur used a shawl that matched her dress to cover her hair and open back, while Sadeem whipped on her black embroidered *abaya** and silk veil, enveloping her body and the lower half of her face. Michelle, though, remained Michelle: she stayed exactly as she was and eyed the men one by one, paying no attention to the mutterings and truly sharp stares that she drew from some of the women.

Rashid plowed toward the stage along with Gamrah's father, her uncle and her four brothers. Each man tried to download as many female faces as he could onto his mental hard drive, while the ladies, for their part, were staring at Gamrah's uncle, in his forties, who bore an unmistakable resemblance to the handsome poet Prince Khalid Al-Faisal.

When Rashid reached his bride Gamrah, he flipped the veil back from her face as his mother had rehearsed with him, then took his place by her side, giving way for the rest of her male relatives to pass on their good wishes to her. He settled himself next to her and then the other men crowded around them to congratulate the couple on their blessed, auspicious and fortunate marriage.

The voices of the bride's friends floated upward in the ballroom's hot air. *"A thousand blessings and peace be upon you, beloved of Allaaaaah, Moham-med!"* the bride's friends chanted, and the piercing sound of women's trills filled the room. The men, except for the groom, soon left the place heading home as their part in the females' celebration was over and their own celebration—which was only a big dinner—had finished before the females' party even started. The couple, followed closely by every female relative, headed toward the food tables to cut the cake.

It was then that Gamrah's friends started chanting at the top of their voices. "We want a kiss! We want a kiss!" Rashid's mother smiled and Gamrah's mother blushed red. As for Rashid, he sent the girls a scathing

---

*An *abaya* is a long, loose black robe worn on top of clothes whenever a woman is outdoors.

stare that sliced them into silence. Gamrah cursed her friends under her breath for embarrassing her in front of him, and cursed him even more for embarrassing her in front of her friends by refusing to kiss her!

Sadeem's eyes welled with tears as she watched her childhood friend, her Gamrah, leave the ballroom with her new husband to go to the hotel where they would spend the night before heading off for a honeymoon in Italy. Immediately after the honeymoon they would leave Riyadh for the United States, where Rashid was to begin studying for a PhD.

Among the group of four girls, Gamrah Al-Qusmanji was closest to Sadeem, as they had been classmates since second grade. Mashael Al-Abdulrahman—or Michelle, as we knew her—didn't join them until the second year at middle school, after she returned with her parents and little Meshaal—or Misho, as everyone called her younger brother—from America. Her father had gone to college there, at Stanford University, where he met their mother. After college he stayed in America for a few years to work and start his family. Only a year after Michelle came back to her home country to live, she transferred to a school where all the classes were taught in English. She simply didn't have the command of Arabic that she needed in order to attend Sadeem and Gamrah's school. At her new school, she got to know Lamees Jeddawi, who became her closest friend. Lamees had grown up in the capital city of Riyadh, but, as her last name implied, her family was originally from Jeddah—a port city with a long tradition of bringing together people from many places and therefore the most liberal city in the kingdom. Gamrah's family was originally from, Qasim, a city known for its ultraconservative and strict character. Only Michelle was not from a well-known family tribe linked to a certain region.

In college, Sadeem studied business management, while Lamees went to medical school.* Michelle decided on computer science. Gamrah, the only one among them who wasn't so keen on her studies in high school,

---

*Unlike in the United States, medical school in Saudi Arabia starts right after high school and lasts for seven years.

needed to use pull from several family friends to get accepted to college as a history major, one of the easy fields to get into in college. But she got engaged a few weeks after the semester started, and she decided to withdraw in order to devote herself full-time to planning the wedding. Since she would be moving to America right after the wedding anyway so that her husband could finish graduate school there, it seemed like an especially good decision.

In her room at the Hotel Giorgione in Venice, Gamrah sat on the edge of the bed. She rubbed her thighs, legs and feet with a whitening lotion of glycerine and lemon that her mother made for her. Her mother's Golden Rule was spinning in her mind. *Don't be easy*. Refusal—it's the secret to activating a man's passion. After all, her older sister Naflah didn't give herself to her husband until the fourth night, and her sister Hessah was more or less the same. But she was setting a new record: it had been seven nights and her husband hadn't touched her. Rashid hadn't touched her even though she had been quite ready to ditch her mother's theories after the first night, when she took off her wedding dress and put on her ivory-colored nightgown (which she'd put on quite a few times before the wedding, in front of the mirror in her room, provoking the admiration of her mother, who had murmured God's name over and over to ward off envy as she gave her daughter a few suggestive winks). Her mother's delighted approval had filled Gamrah with confidence and pride, even though she knew that the expression on her mama's face was a bit overdone.

But on her wedding night she came out of the bathroom to find him . . . asleep. And although she almost could have sworn that he was faking it, a theory her mother dismissed in their last telephone conversation as "Satan's evil whisperings," she agreed to devote all of her energy to "leading him on," especially since her mother had recently announced to her on the phone that the policy of withholding had decidedly backfired in this case.

Since Gamrah's marriage to Rashid, her mother had gotten bolder about discussing "the business of men and women." In fact, before her marriage contract was signed, her mother hadn't talked about such matters at all. Afterward, though, Gamrah got immersion training in the art of seduction from the same woman who had ripped pages out of the romance novels Gamrah used to borrow from her friends at school, and who wouldn't even let Gamrah go over to her friends' houses, with the exception of Sadeem's, after Gamrah's mother had gotten to know Sadeem's aunt Badriyyah quite well through several social circles among other ladies of the neighborhood.

Gamrah's mother was a firm believer in the theory that "woman is to man as butter is to sun." But her strong convictions that girls should be utterly naïve and guys should be experienced melted away in an instant the moment the girl had that marriage contract. As for Gamrah, she started listening to her mother's anecdotes and treatises on "the enterprise of marriage" with the heightened enjoyment and sense of pride of a young man whose father offers him a cigarette to smoke in front of him for the first time.

2.

To: seerehwenfadha7et@yahoogroups.com
From: "seerehwenfadha7et"
Date: February 20, 2004
Subject: The Girls Rally Round Gamrah's Big Day, in Their Own Way

First, I have a little message for the following gentlemen: Hassan, Ahmad, Fahad and Mohammed, who made my day with their earnest e-mail inquiries.

The answer is: Uh-uh! Forget it, guys . . . no, we cannot "get to know each other."

Now that I have applied my signature bright red lipstick, I will pick up the story where I left off last week.

After Gamrah's wedding her friends lined up the petite keepsake clay jars engraved with the names of the bridal couple alongside the other souvenirs they had collected from other friends' weddings. Every last one of Gamrah's girlfriends was secretly hoping that the keepsake from her own wedding would be the next one to be added.

Well before the wedding, their little clique—the *shillah*—had made special preparations for its own intimate precelebration celebration. The idea was to put on something like the bachelorette party that, in the West, friends of the bride throw for her before the nuptials. The girls weren't interested in doing a DJ party, because these days, that was becoming as common as sand. Besides, a DJ party meant that it would have to be a positively massive dance party that might even have involved hiring a professional local *taggaga,* a female singer, the kind that once upon a time just had a drum backup but now might have a whole band. They would need to send out invitations to every one of their girlfriends and female relatives and everyone that anyone knew, while pretending to keep the bride in the dark the whole time. And, of course, the little *shillah* of friends hosting the party would be burdened with all of the expenses, which would mount up to nothing less than several thousand riyals.

But Gamrah's friends wanted to do something new. They wanted to come up with something so bold and so much fun that others after them would imitate it, and then it would become a trend, and everyone would know who had invented it.

Gamrah arrived bright red in the face—and scarlet all over her body—because she had just come from a scrubbing at the Moroccan *hammam* as well as having the hair plucked from all over her face with a thread and from her body with sticky sugar-paste *halawa.* They were all to meet at Michelle's house. The hostess greeted them wearing baggy trousers with lots of pockets and an oversized jacket—gear that artfully concealed any sign of femininity—plus a bandanna that hid her hair. To top it all off, she had on a pair of colored sunglasses that gave her the appearance of an adolescent boy who has escaped parental surveillance. Lamees wore a masculine-style flowing white *thobe* with a *shimagh* draped over her head and kept in place with a snugly fitting black *eqal.** With

*Saudi men's garments; a *thobe* is a long white loose dress, while a *shimagh* is a red and white triangular-shaped cloth worn on the head topped by an *eqal* to hold it in place. An *eqal* is a thick round, ropelike sash. Nowadays the *shimaghs* and *thobes* are designed by such famous names as Gucci, Christian Dior, Givenchy and Valentino.

her height and athletic body she really did look like a guy, and a handsome one, too. The rest of them were wearing embroidered *abayas*. But these *abayas* weren't the loose teepees that you see women wearing on the street. These were fitted at the waist and hips and they were very attractive! With the *abayas,* the girls wore black silk *lithaams* that covered everything from the bridge of their noses to the bottom of their throats, which of course only emphasized the beauty of their kohl-lined eyes, their tinted contact lenses and their outlandish eyeglasses all the more.

Michelle had an international driver's license. She took charge: she drove the BMW X5 SUV with its dark-tinted windows. She had managed to rent it through one of the car showrooms by putting the rental in the name of her family's male Ethiopian driver. Lamees took her place next to Michelle while Sadeem and Gamrah climbed into the backseats. The CD player was on full blast. The girls sang along and swayed their *abaya*-clad shoulders as if they were dancing on the seats.

Their first stop was the famous café in Tahliya Street. But when Michelle parked the vehicle, the SUV's darkened windows gave them away in an instant: since tinted car windows are only used when women who need to be concealed are inside, all the guys in the vicinity, with their keen hunter eyes and their ready instincts, knew right off that the X5 had to be a priceless catch* They jumped in their cars and surrounded the SUV on both sides. After the girls got the drinks they wanted from the drive-through, the entire parade started to move toward the big shopping mall in Al-Olayya Street, which was the girls' second stop. Meanwhile, the girls were taking down as many phone numbers as they could. They did not have to work very hard, because these numbers were generously showered upon them by the guys. The girls could memorize those with catchy sequences and repeated digits as the guys stuck out their heads through their cars' windows while driving and kept repeating

---

*An expensive car with completely tinted windows often belongs to a man who does not want his wife and daughters exposed to the eyes of young men looking for fun. Nowadays, tinting is prohibited by Saudi law for security reasons.

them for the girls to write down. The girls also copied from placards the guys had hung on the windows of their cars so that girls in neighboring cars could see the numbers clearly. The truly bold knights among them held out personal business cards, passing them through the windows to be snatched up by the girls, who were every bit as brave as the aspiring Romeos.

At the mall entrance the girls got out. Behind them appeared a rush of young men, but they all came to a stop uncertainly in front of the security guard. It was his job to keep all unmarried men from entering the mall after the call to the Isha prayer that ushered in nightfall. The weaklings fell back, but one lone fellow summoned his courage and approached Michelle. With her lovely face and delicate features, which she was quite simply incapable of concealing in her eccentric attire, Michelle had stood out from the start as a girl who was possibly bold enough to be looking for adventure. The guy asked Michelle if she would allow him to go in with them as a member of the family, and he offered her a thousand riyals for the privilege. Michelle was astonished at his nerve. But she accepted the deal without much delay, and she and her friends surged forward beside him as if he were one of their group.

Once inside the mall the young women split up into two groups, one made up of Sadeem and Gamrah, the other of Lamees, Michelle and the handsome young man.

His name was Faisal. Laughing, Lamees remarked that no guys these days had the old Najdi Bedouin names, like Obaid or Duyahhim. They all pretended they had one of those cool names like Faisal or Saud or Salman just to impress girls. He laughed along with them, swearing that it was his real name, and invited the two girls to dinner at an elegant restaurant outside the mall. Michelle turned down the invitation. Before leaving them, in fulfillment of the agreement, he gave her two five-hundred-riyal notes after writing his cell phone number on one of them and his full name on the other: Faisal Al-Batran.

Women in the mall had an annoying way of following Gamrah,

Sadeem and the rest of the girls with their eyes. It didn't matter that their face veils were in place: the girls could feel the sharp and threatening challenge of the women's inspections. They felt uncomfortably that any one of those women might as well be saying to them, *I've figured out who you are, but you don't know who I am.*

That's the way things are here in the shops and the malls: guys stare at women for their own reasons, while women stare at each other just because they are *nosy!* And they have no excuse for it. A girl can't stroll about in the malls under the protection of God without being checked out thoroughly by everyone, especially her own kind, from her *abaya* to the covering over her hair to the way she walks and the bags she carries and in which direction she looks and in front of what merchandise she stops. Is it envy? The French playwright Sacha Guitry was *so* on the mark when he said, "Women don't pretty themselves up for men: they do it to get back at other women."

The girls made their way toward the elegant Italian restaurant they had picked out for dinner. After eating, they headed for a tiny shop that sold water pipes, or what we call the *shisha*—otherwise known as the hookah or hubbly-bubbly. The girls bought enough *shishas* that they would not have to share, and each girl chose her favorite flavor of the water-pipe tobacco mixed with molasses and fragrant essences.

They spent the rest of the evening at Lamees's, inside a small tent in the house's inner courtyard where her father and his friends retired to spend their evenings two or three times a week. The men would smoke *shisha* and hold conversations ranging from politics to their wives or from their wives to politics. As usual, though, the family had gone to Jeddah, their native city, for the summer holiday. Lamees and her twin sister Tamadur had stayed behind to attend Gamrah's wedding.

But the father's *shishas* went with him wherever he traveled. Like many Hijazi men and women, he was addicted to it. So the girls set up the newly purchased *shishas* inside the tent and the maid got the coals going. The music blared and the girls danced and smoked and played cards. Even Gamrah tried smoking the *shisha,* though it's considered inappropriate among Najdi females, after Sadeem convinced her that "a girl doesn't get married every day." She liked the grape-flavored tobacco the best.

Lamees tightly fastened her spangle-edged, jingly scarf around her hips. As always, her dancing was exquisite: no one could possibly match her, especially as she shimmied to the strains of a recent version of Um Kulthum's song "One Thousand and One Arabian Nights." None of the other girls danced with her. For one thing, none of them could approach Lamees's perfection when she danced, but more importantly, they all loved to watch her. Now and then, they would come up with a funny name for a move she made. There was the "blender" move, the "juicer" move and the "follow me" move. Lamees performed these sequences over and over to popular demand. As for the third reason why nobody joined her on the dance floor, Lamees, as they all knew well, would refuse to go on dancing unless she got a good dose of loud encouragement, whistles, clapping and cheers befitting her stature as Queen of the Dance Floor.

Lamees joined Michelle that night in consuming a bottle of expensive champagne. Michelle had filched it from her father's storage cellar, which held special drinks meant strictly for important occasions. After all, didn't Gamrah's wedding deserve a bottle of Dom Pérignon? Michelle knew a lot about brandy, vodka, wine and other such things. Her father had taught her how to pour him red wine with red meats and white wine with other dishes, but she didn't drink with him except on very special and rare occasions. Since drinking alcohol is forbidden in Saudi Arabia, as it's against Islamic law, Lamees had never before tasted any of these drinks, except once at Michelle's, and then she did not find the taste of whatever it was particularly pleasant. But, hey! After all, tonight the two of them were celebrating Gamrah's wedding! So she joined in with Michelle, since they wanted to make this evening special and unique in every way they could.

When the volume of the music soared, there wasn't a girl left in the tent who wasn't on her feet dancing. It was the famous Saudi singer Abdul Majeed Abdullah's song:

Girls of Riyadh, O girls of Riyadh,
O gems of the turbaned fathers of old!
Have mercy on that victim, have mercy
On that man who lies prone on the threshold.

3.

To: seerehwenfadha7et@yahoogroups.com
From: "seerehwenfadha7et"
Date: February 27, 2004
Subject: Who Is Nuwayyir?

To all of those who abandoned whatever they were doing in order to urgently ask the brand of my bright red lipstick: It is new on the market and it is called: *Get your nose out of my business and get back to reading about things that actually matter.*

Two weeks after Gamrah's wedding, Sadeem's eldest aunt—Aunt Badriyyah—got a number of phone calls from matchmaker mothers asking for her pretty niece's hand in marriage for their sons. Ever since Sadeem's mother passed away when Sadeem was a baby, Aunt Badriyyah had tried to act as a stand-in mother figure. She had her own ways of checking out all marriage applicants thoroughly and she dropped those who, in her opinion, were unsuitable. She would only inform Sadeem's father about the short list of key applicants, she decided. After all, if it didn't work with them, the rest would still be there waiting anxiously in the wings. There was no need to tell Sadeem's father—let alone Sadeem herself—about every single man at once. Aunt Badriyyah was anxious to protect the heads of her dear niece and her esteemed brother-in-law from the danger of swelling up larger than her own—no need to encourage them to feel superior to her and her daughters.

Waleed Al-Shari, BA in communications engineering, level VII civil servant. He is the son of Abdallah Al-Shari, one of the truly big real estate magnates in the kingdom. His uncle, Abdul-elah Al-Shari, is a retired colonel and his aunt Munirah is headmistress of one of Riyadh's biggest private girls' schools.

This is what Sadeem told Michelle, Lamees and Um Nuwayyir, her next-door neighbor, when she met up with them in Um Nuwayyir's home. Um Nuwayyir is a Kuwaiti woman who works for the government as a school inspector of mathematics curricula. Her Saudi husband divorced her after fifteen years of marriage to marry another woman.

Um Nuwayyir has only one child, a son called Nuri—and there's an odd story attached to this Nuri of hers. Since the age of eleven or twelve, Nuri had been enthralled by girls' clothes, enchanted by girls' shoes, fascinated by makeup and infatuated with long hair. As things *developed,* Nuri's mother became truly alarmed, especially as Nuri seemed to get more and more carried away with creating the persona of a sweet, soft, pretty boy rather than the tough masculine young man he was supposed to turn into. Um Nuwayyir tried fiercely to steer him in other directions. She found various means of discouraging him. She tried tender motherly persuasion and she tried firm motherly thrashings, but nothing worked.

Meanwhile, Nuri's father was much sterner with him. Nuri was careful not to exhibit his soft side in front of his father, of whom he was in dire awe. The father heard things by way of the neighbors, though, and what he heard put him into a fury. Bursting into Nuri's room one day, he began to pummel and kick his son. The boy suffered fractures in the rib cage and a broken nose and arm. Following this incident, the father left the household to move in entirely with his second wife, permanently distancing himself from this house and this faggot boy who was such a freak of nature.

After this confrontation, Um Nuwayyir surrendered to the will of God. It was a trial visited upon her by her Lord, she decreed in her own head, and she must bear it with patience. She and Nuri avoided mentioning the subject and stirring up fresh trouble. So it was that Nuri went on just as he had, and people began to call her, instead of "Mother of Nuri," "Mother of Nuwayyir," i.e., the girlie version of the name. That's how she became Um Nuwayyir rather than Um Nuri, and she stayed Um Nuwayyir even after moving to the house next to Sadeem's, four years before the date on which Waleed presented himself as a suitable match for Sadeem, and after Nuri rejected his mother's suggestion that they move to Kuwait.

In the beginning, Um Nuwayyir was truly shaken by society's shallow view of her tragedy, but as time passed, she grew accustomed to the way things were and accepted her trying circumstances with such patience and acceptance that she even started introducing herself to new acquaintances deliberately as Um Nuwayyir. It was her way of affirming her strength and showing how little she thought of society's unfair and oppressive attitudes toward her.

Um Nuri—or Um Nuwayyir—was thirty-nine. Sadeem often visited her or arranged to meet her friends at Um Nuwayyir's house. Despite, or perhaps because of, her grief, Um Nuwayyir was an eternal fount of jokes and, if she chose, she could use her humor and insight to cut a person to pieces. But she was one of the sweetest and most truly *good* women Sadeem had ever met in her life. Sadeem's mother had died when Sadeem was just three years old, and she was an only daughter, and all of this brought her closer to Um Nuwayyir, whom she came to consider as much more than a neighbor and older friend. Truth told, Sadeem really saw Um Nuwayyir as a mother.

How very often Um Nuwayyir was the preserver of the girls' secrets! She was always right there with them when they were thinking through some issue or other, and she was always generous about suggesting a solution when one of them set out a problem for the clique to ponder. For her, it was a comfort to have them around, not to mention a diversion and source of entertainment, and her home became the perfect setting for trying out the freedoms to which they had but little access in any of their own homes.

Um Nuwayyir's place was the safe haven par excellence for sweethearts. For example, the first time Michelle called Faisal after he "numbered" her at the mall, she told him to pick her up from Um Nuwayyir's place after she gave him the directions. She said she had a couple of hours free and suggested that they go out for coffee or ice cream somewhere.

Michelle did not want to give Faisal any advance notice of her plans. She called him only a few minutes before he had to pick her up. That way, she figured, he would not actually be able to prepare for the date and then she could see him as he really was. When she came out of the house to climb into his car, she was stunned to find how much more handsome he was in jeans and a T-shirt and an unruly, unshaven beard than he had looked in the mall in his classy long white *thobe* and the Valentino *shimagh* ringing his head. She couldn't help noticing that his T-shirt showed off his broad chest muscles and biceps in a very flattering way.

Faisal paid for two cups of iced coffee and cruised around the streets of Riyadh with her in his Porsche. He took her to his office at his father's company and launched into an explanation of some of his responsibilities at the business. Then they dropped by the university, where he was studying English literature. He circled around the parking lot for a few minutes before a campus patrolman informed him that he was not allowed to drive around the university grounds at this hour of the night. After two hours or so, Faisal returned Michelle to Um Nuwayyir's. Her head was spinning. He had simply, and surprisingly, swept her off her feet.

4.

To: seerehwenfadha7et@yahoogroups.com
From: "seerehwenfadha7et"
Date: March 5, 2004
Subject: What Did That *Jerk* Do to Gamrah on That Night?

> *This culture we claim—*
> *bursting bubbles of soap, of slime*
> *We live on, by the logic of key and lock*
> *We swathe our women in cotton shrouds*
> *We possess them like the carpets beneath us,*
> *like the cows in fenced fields,*
> *to flock home at night's end,*
> *for our due, bulls and steeds unpenned.*
>   —Nizar Qabbani

Sitting in my own silent room, I can practically hear the blasts of condemnation and profanity coming from Saudi and Arab men among my readers when they see this verse posted. I wish you men could understand it as I believe Nizar Qabbani intended it to be understood . . . Oh, Nizar, in love there's been no one before you and there will never be anyone after you, even if your compassion toward women isn't due to a mutation in one of your male chromosomes but rather to the suicidal end of your poor sister's tragic love story. So it seems, I'm sorry to say, that no woman among us will find her own Nizar until after she has finished off one of his sisters, so that the tale of beautiful love will have to be titled "Gone to Prison" rather than "Gone with the Wind."

Heart of mine, don't grieve.

When the honeymoon was over, Gamrah and her husband headed for Chicago where he was working for his PhD in electrical engineering, after getting his BA in Los Angeles and his master's in Indianapolis.

Gamrah began her new life in absolute fear and trepidation. She felt like she died of terror every time she walked into the elevator that took her up to the apartment they shared on the fortieth floor of the Presidential Towers. She felt the pressure splitting her head open and blocking her ears as the elevator shot upward through the floors of the skyscraper. She got dizzy every time she tried to look out of a window in the apartment. So very far down, everything appeared tiny and fragile. She stared down at the city streets, which looked to her exactly like the streets in the Lego sets she played with when she was little, with their minuscule cars no larger than matchboxes. Indeed, from this height the cars looked like ants in rows: they were so very small and so neatly and quietly arranged in long and slow-moving lines.

Gamrah was afraid of the drunken beggars who filled the streets and shook their paper cups in her face, demanding money. The stories of thefts and murders that she always seemed to be hearing terrified her. Every story she heard had something to do with this dangerous city! She was just as afraid of the huge black security guard at their building, who ignored her whenever she tried to get his attention with her poor English hoping he would help her commandeer a taxi.

From the moment of his arrival, Rashid had been completely immersed in the university and his research. He left the apartment at seven o'clock in the morning, returning at eight or nine and sometimes as late as ten in the evening. On the weekends, he seemed determined to occupy himself with anything he could find to take him away from her; he would sit for hours staring at the computer or watching TV. He often fell asleep on the sofa while watching a boring baseball game or the news on CNN. If he did go in to their bedroom to sleep, he kept on the long white underwear that Saudi men always put on underneath their *thobes*—we call them "Sunni underpants" (I have no idea why)—and T-shirt. He would collapse onto the bed as if he were a very old man depleted of all his energy, not a brand-new husband.

Gamrah had dreamed of much more; of caresses and love and tenderness and emotion like the feelings that stirred her heart when she read romance novels or watched romantic movies. And now here she was, facing a husband who clearly felt no attraction toward her and indeed had not touched her since that ill-fated night in Rome.

At that time, after dinner in the elegant hotel restaurant, Gamrah had made an irrevocable decision that this would be her true wedding night, something for which she had waited too long. As long as her husband was so bashful, she would have to help him out, smooth the way for him just as her mother had advised her. They went up to their room and she began to flirt with him shyly. After a few moments of innocent seduction, he took things into his own hands. She gave herself up to it despite the enormous confusion and anxiety she felt. She closed her eyes, anticipating what was about to happen. And then he surprised her with an act that was never on her list of sexual expectations. Her response, which was shocking to both of them, was to slap him hard on the face then and there! Their eyes met in a stunned moment. Her eyes were filled with fear and bewilderment, while his were full of an anger the likes of which she had never seen. He moved away from her quickly, dressed hurriedly and left the room amid her tears and apologies.

Gamrah did not so much as see her husband until the evening of the next day, when he sullenly accompanied her to the airport in time to catch the airplane to Washington, followed by another to Chicago.

5.

To: seerehwenfadha7et@yahoogroups.com
From: "seerehwenfadha7et"
Date: March 12, 2004
Subject: Waleed and Sadeem: A Typical Love Story from Contemporary
Saudi Life

Men have written to me saying: Who authorized you to speak for the girls of Najd?! You are nothing but a malevolent and rancorous woman deliberately attempting to sully the image of women in Saudi society.

And to them I say: We are only at the beginning, sweethearts. If you are mounting a war against me in the fifth e-mail, then imagine what you will be saying about me after you have read the many e-mails to come! You're in for a ride. May goodness and prosperity come to you!

Sadeem and her father walked into the elaborate formal reception room of their house to meet Waleed Al-Shari. It was the occasion of the *shoufa*, that one lawful "viewing" of the potential bride according to Islamic law. Sadeem was so nervous that her legs nearly buckled underneath her as she walked. Gamrah had told her of her own mother's warning to not under any circumstances offer to shake hands with the groom at this meeting, so Sadeem refrained from extending her hand.

Waleed stood up respectfully to greet them, and sat down again after she and her father were seated. Her father immediately started asking questions on a seemingly random variety of topics and then, a few minutes later, left the room to allow the two of them to talk freely.

Sadeem could tell right away that Waleed was taken with her pretty looks; the way he stared at her made that clear enough. Even though she had barely lifted her head to look at him when she first walked in, she had seen him studying her figure, which nearly made her trip over her own feet. But as they talked, Sadeem gradually gained control of her nervousness and, with his help, conquered her shyness. He asked her about her studies, her major at the university, her future plans and what she liked to do in her free time—all on his way to arriving at that one question every one of us girls fears and considers rude to be asked in a *shoufa*: Do you know how to cook?

"What about you?" he said. "Don't you want to ask me anything? Do you have anything that you want to tell me?"

She thought for a few minutes, and finally she said, "Uh . . . I want to tell you that I have bad eyesight."

He laughed at her confession and she laughed, too. After a moment, he said to her, a little provocatively, "By the way, Sadeem, you know, my job requires that I travel overseas a lot."

This time she answered him without a pause, raising one of her eyebrows flirtatiously. "Not a problem. I love to travel!"

He told her that he found her mischievousness and quick wit delightful, and she lowered her head, blushing fiercely and cursing her inability to control her runaway mouth, which might turn out to be the cause of a runaway groom. Seconds later, her father unwittingly came to the rescue by walking through the doorway. She excused herself hurriedly and made straight for the door, giving Waleed a big smile, which he returned with an even bigger one. She left the room with butterflies in her stomach.

She had found Waleed handsome, even if he wasn't really her favorite type. She preferred darker skin; his complexion was fair with a pinkish hue. His shadowy mustache and goatee and those glasses with the thin silver frames added a lot of charm to his face, though, she thought.

Once she was out of the room, Waleed asked her father's permission to phone her so he could get to know her better before it was announced that they were officially engaged. Her father agreed and gave him Sadeem's cell phone number.

Waleed called late that night, and after allowing the phone to ring a decently long time, she answered. He told her how much he liked her. He would speak a little and then go quiet, as if he expected her to comment on what he was saying. She told him that she had been happy to meet him, but said no more. He told her that he *really* liked her, that in fact he had been bewitched by her and that he found it unbearable to wait until Eid Al-Fitr, after which they could sign the marriage contract.

After that, Waleed called her dozens of times a day—he called the minute he woke up in the morning, before going to work, at work, after work and finally for a long conversation before going to sleep that would stretch on sometimes until the sun was peeping over the horizon. He even woke her up in the middle of the night to have her listen to a song he had dedicated to her on the radio. And every day he would ask that she pick out at the store a pair of glasses for him, or a watch, or cologne—he would immediately buy whatever she dictated, he said, so that everything he wore would be completely to her liking.

The other girls began to envy Sadeem, especially Gamrah, who would become overwhelmed with self-pity whenever Sadeem described to her on the telephone how fond she was of Waleed and how he adored her in return. Gamrah started making up stories about her blissful life with Rashid—how loving he was toward her, how many gifts he brought her.

Waleed and Sadeem signed the marriage contract in a small ceremony. Sadeem's aunt wept uncontrollably as she thought of her sister— Sadeem's mother—who had never gotten the chance to see her daughter married. She also cried secretly for her son, Tariq, whom she had always hoped would be the one to marry Sadeem.

During the official proceedings Sadeem pressed her fingerprint onto the page in the enormous registry book after her protest about not being allowed to sign her name was dismissed. "My girl," said her aunt, "just stamp it with your fingerprint and call it a day. The sheikh says fingerprint, not signature. The men are the only ones who sign their names."

After the signing ceremony, her father threw a huge banquet for the two families. On the evening of the next day, Waleed came over to see his bride, whom he had not met in person since that one legally permitted viewing. On this visit, Waleed presented her with the customary gift for the engagement period nowadays: a cell phone, one of the very latest models on the market.

In the months to follow, during the *milkah* period, the traditional time between the official signing of the documents and the actual wedding ceremony, Waleed's visits to Sadeem grew more and more frequent. Most visits her father knew about, but there were a few little encounters that escaped his attention. During the week, Waleed usually dropped by after the evening prayers, and usually stayed until two o'clock in the morning. On weekends he rarely left before dawn.

Every few weeks Waleed took her out for dinner in a fancy restaurant, and on other evenings he would bring her food or sweets that she loved. They spent their time talking and laughing, watching a film that one of them had borrowed from a friend. Then things began to progress, and they developed far enough that she experienced her first kiss.

Waleed had been accustomed to kissing her cheeks when saying hello and good-bye to her. But one evening his parting kiss was decidedly hotter than usual. Maybe the tragic end of the movie they had watched together (*Armageddon*) played a role in creating the right mood for him to plant that long, needy kiss on her virgin lips.

Sadeem started preparing for the wedding, browsing around in the shops with Um Nuwayyir or Michelle or Lamees. Sometimes Waleed would go with her, especially if she was planning to buy nightgowns.

The wedding celebration was set to occur over the summer vacation, a week or two after Sadeem's final exams, as Sadeem had requested. She was afraid to get married during Eid Al-Adha break, worried that it would interfere with her ability to study for her exams—Sadeem was always a top student, vigilant about getting good grades. But her decision upset and distressed Waleed, who was anxious to get married as soon as possible. Sadeem decided to make it up to him.

One evening she put on the black lace nightgown he had bought for her but which at the time she had refused to try on in his presence. She invited him to come over for the evening without informing her father, who was out camping with friends in the desert.

The red petals she strewed across the sofa, the candles placed here and there, the soft music wafting from the well-hidden music system—none of it impressed Waleed as much as the black nightgown that revealed more of her body than it concealed. Since Sadeem had vowed to make her beloved Waleed happy that night, and since she wanted to erase his disappointment over her insistence on delaying the wedding, she allowed him to go further with her than ever before. She did not try to stop him—as she had gotten used to doing—when he attempted to cross the line that she had drawn, for herself and for him, in the early days after the signing of the contract. She was convinced that he wouldn't be satisfied unless she offered him a little more of her "femininity," and she was willing to do anything to please him, the love of her life, even if it meant exceeding the limits she had spent her lifetime guarding.

As usual, Waleed left after the dawn call to prayer, but this time Sadeem thought he seemed distressed and troubled. She figured he must be feeling as nervous as she was after what had happened. She waited anxiously for his usual phone call once he got home, since she especially needed to hear his tender voice after such a night, but he didn't call. Sadeem didn't allow herself to call him and waited until the next day, but he didn't call then, either. As difficult as it was for her, she decided to give him a few days to calm down before calling him to ask what was wrong.

Three days passed without a word from Waleed. Sadeem decided to drop her resolve and called, only to find that his cell phone was turned off. She kept calling through the entire week, at different times of the day and night, desperate to reach him. But his cell phone was always switched off and the private line in his room was always busy. What was going on? Had something awful happened to him? Or was he still angry at her, *this* angry even after all of her efforts to please him? What about everything she had given him on that night? Had he gone insane?

Had she been wrong to give herself to Waleed before the wedding celebration? Did it make any sense at all to believe that *that* was the cause of him avoiding her? Why, though? Wasn't he her legal husband, and hadn't he been her legal husband ever since they signed the contract? Or did getting married mean the ballroom, the guests, the live singer and the dinner? And what she had done—did it somehow deserve *punishment* from him? Hadn't he been the one who initiated it? Why had he encouraged her to do the wrong thing and then afterward abandoned her? And anyway, was it wrong, was it a sin, in the first place? Had he been testing her? And if she had failed the test, did that mean that she was not worthy of him? He must have thought she was one of those girls who were easy! But what kind of stupidity was this? Wasn't she his wife, his lawful partner? Hadn't she on that day placed her mark in that big register next to his signature? Hadn't there been acceptance, consent and commitment, witnesses and an announcement to the world? No one had ever cautioned her about this! Would Waleed make her pay for what she did not even know? If her mother had been alive, she would have warned her and directed her, and then none of this would have happened! And besides, she had heard a lot of stories about young women who had done what she did, and maybe more, after signing the contract and before the wedding party! She even knew of cases where the brides had given birth to full-term babies only seven months after the wedding. Among the people who were aware of such events, only a very few seemed to care. So where was the error? Where was the sin?

Who would draw for her the fine line between what was proper behavior and what wasn't? And, she wondered, was that line that their religion defined the same as the one in the mind of a young man from conservative Najd? Waleed had criticized her every time she put a stop to anything, saying that she was his wife according to the religion of God and His prophet. Who was there to explain to her the psychological makeup of the young Saudi man so that she could understand what went on in his mind? Had Waleed now come to believe that she was a young woman of "experience"? Did he actually *prefer* it when she told him to stop? She hadn't done anything more than go along with him, the way she saw things done on TV and heard from her married girlfriends. He had done the rest! So why was she at fault for following his lead and instinctively knowing how to conduct herself? It wasn't something that required knowledge of chemistry and physics to figure out! What was it that had taken possession of Waleed, to make him so irrational?

She tried to call his mother but was told that she was sleeping. She left her name with the maid and asked her to inform her mistress that she had called, and then she waited expectantly for a call from Um Waleed that never came. Should she tell her father what had happened on that bitter night? How would she tell him? What would she say? If she said nothing, though, was she going to say nothing all the way to the wedding day? What would people say on that day? That the groom jilted her? No, no! Waleed couldn't possibly be as horrible as this. He must be lying in a coma somewhere in some hospital. To think of him lying in a hospital bed was a thousand times more bearable than to think that he could be deserting her in this way!

Sadeem was afloat in a state of bewilderment, waiting for a call or visit from Waleed, dreaming that he would come to her on his knees begging for forgiveness. But he didn't visit and he didn't call. Her father asked her what was wrong, but she had no answer for him. An answer did come from Waleed three weeks later, though: divorce papers! Her father tried hard to find out from Sadeem what lay behind the horrible surprise, but she collapsed in his arms and exploded into tears without confessing. In anger, he went to Waleed's father, who denied knowing anything and said he was as surprised as Sadeem's father was. All Waleed had said to his father was that he had discovered he was not comfortable with his bride and he preferred to break the contract now before the wedding was consummated.

Sadeem kept her secret from everyone. She licked her wounds in silence until the second shock arrived: in her first year at the university, she had failed more than half of her courses.

6.

To: seerehwenfadha7et@yahoogroups.com
From: "seerehwenfadha7et"
Date: March 19, 2004
Subject: Lamees, the One and Only!

Many e-mails have come my way that ask me to reveal my true identity. Am I one of the four girls I am writing about in these e-mails? So far, most of the guesses have veered between Gamrah and Sadeem. Only one guy thinks I'm likely to be Michelle, but then he said he wasn't sure since Michelle's English is better than mine!

What really got me howling was an e-mail from Haitham, from *Al-Madina*, City of Light, in which he slams me for my extreme partiality toward the "Bedouin" girls of Riyadh and my neglect of Lamees, his heart's darling. You people are starting to act as if you know my four friends better than I do! Don't let it bother you, dear Haitham. My e-mail today will concern Lamees and only Lamees.

Though Lamees and Tamadur looked very much alike, enormous differences in character and in their thoughts and ideas separated the twin sisters. True, they had attended the same classes in elementary and middle school, and even as far as high school and university, where they both studied at the College of Medicine. But Tamadur alone drew the admiration of professors for her intense seriousness and hyperdisciplined personality. Lamees, on the other hand, was the cool A+ student who was also the favorite of her classmates because of her wit and her friendliness to everyone. At the same time, she also managed to maintain her good grades. Lamees had more courage—and also more sheer nerve—than Tamadur, who always described her sister as careless, daredevilish, and rash, not to mention flighty and a bit flirtatious.

Their father, Dr. Asim Hijazi, was a former dean of the College of Pharmacology at the university and their mother, Dr. Fatin Khalil, had been a deputy administrator in the same department. Dr. Asim and Dr. Fatin were the keys to their daughters' success and their distinctive academic superiority. Ever since the twins' birth, the parents had been as careful as could be to parcel out their roles and attention so that the two little girls would get all the consideration and care they needed. As Tamadur and Lamees entered nursery, and then kindergarten, and then real school, the parents' attentiveness grew rather than dwindled. So did their aspirations for their daughters' ongoing—and accelerating—academic distinction.

The couple had only these twins, and moreover had had them only after enduring much suffering and medical attention over a span of fourteen years, after which they had been given, by God's mercy, these two lovely baby girls. They did not try for any more children, since by then the mother's age was somewhat advanced and any attempts to have another child might be bad for her health and that of the unborn baby.

One of the more infamous episodes of Lamees's high school career occurred in her first year. She, Michelle and two of their other classmates executed a massive and perfectly planned video exchange. On the appointed day, each girl brought four films to school. The idea was that at the end of the school day, they would parcel out the sixteen films among themselves, but bad luck had it in for them. No sooner had they arrived at school than the girls heard about the administration's intention to search all of the classrooms and everyone's schoolbags that day, looking for prohibited items. The list of contraband items was long and included photo albums, diaries, perfume bottles, romantic novels, music cassettes and videotapes.

Lamees didn't know whether someone had ratted on them or whether it was merely the bad luck that always seemed to chase her. When the news got around, the four girls were thrown into utter chaos, aghast at this unexpected development. And the true disaster was that this wasn't a question of one or two tapes; it was a matter of *sixteen*!—found with four of the school's leading students! What a total scandal—and the possibility hadn't crossed anyone's mind!

Lamees gathered up the videos from her classmates, stuck them inside a large paper bag, and asked them all to act normal. She assured them that everything would turn out just fine and that she would handle the whole mess and take care of everything.

During recess, she carried the bulging paper bag into the bathroom to search for a hiding place, but it was a *big* bag and she couldn't find a good place to stash it. She worried that any school employee might stumble on it and steal it or take it to the authorities. If that happened, her problem wouldn't just be a school scandal but—and maybe this was ten times worse—she would have a real issue on her hands with her classmates, none of whom would be particularly happy to have her own tapes seized!

Next, Lamees considered stuffing the bag into the classroom cupboard. But the spot was pretty open to view, not to mention being an obvious place to look. Lamees began to feel desperate. The whole thing was like a dangerous game of hide-and-seek played at a time and in a place that simply were not suitable for playing games at all.

But just then the perfect solution popped into her head. Brilliant! She knocked on the door to the teachers' lounge and asked to see her favorite teacher, Ms. Hana, who taught chemistry. Ms. Hana appeared in the doorway, full of welcomes for this surprise visit, and boldly Lamees explained her difficult situation. The teacher's welcoming expression disappeared.

"*Shu badik?*" Ms. Hana wailed. "So what do you want *me* to do, Lamees? I have my position to think of! It's impossible! I can't help you with this!"

"If the principal finds out, I'm *screwed!*" Lamees wailed back.

"Are you crazy? Bringing films to school. Sixteen of them at once? Shame on you."

After a great deal more resistance, the teacher took the enormous bag from Lamees, who had not stopped begging for her salvation for a second. She promised Lamees that she would do whatever she could to snatch her good name from the jaws of disaster.

About halfway through the day, some administrators swooped down on Lamees's class and began to search through all of the students' schoolbags. They poked into the desk drawers and the cabinet, searching high and low for any prohibited items. Some students hid the music cassettes that they were carrying, or a bottle of perfume, a small photo album or pager (that was in 1996; cell phones weren't popular yet) in the big pockets of their school uniforms, and stood with their backs plastered to the classroom wall. The eyes of Lamees's friends followed the inspectresses in terror, in anticipation of their finding their films in Lamees's bag.

In the last class hour, one of the office girls came into Lamees's class to tell her that the principal was asking to see her. Lamees lowered her head. *So, Ms. Hana,* she thought, *is this what it has all come to? You go and inform on me, just like that? You chickened! A grown-up teacher is more afraid of the principal than I am!*

Lamees strode into the principal's office fearlessly. The damage was done and feeling afraid was not going to help her. But she did feel mortified. This was not the first time she had been summoned to the principal's office for bad behavior.

"Sooo, Lamees, what are we going to do with you? It isn't enough, what you did last week, when you wouldn't tell me which girl it was who put the red ink on the teacher's chair in the class?"

Lamees hung her head and smiled in spite of herself when she recalled how their classmate Awrad had dripped a few drops from her red fountain pen refill onto the teacher's chair between classes. The teacher came in and immediately panicked when she caught sight of the red splotches on the leather seat of her chair. She froze in place for several seconds as the students tried to control their laughter. "Who had the class before this one, girls?" she finally ventured.

They answered in one voice. "Ms. Ni'mat, ma'am."

She shot out of the room to go in search of her friend Ms. Ni'mat whom the girls all despised. The teacher ran to tell Ms. Ni'mat about the "blood" drops on her beige skirt. It must have been her "time of the month"! When she got back, proud of the favor she did to save her friend from walking around the school with that *embarrassing* stain on her skirt, the girls' stomachs were aching from so much laughing.

That day, dragged before the principal, Lamees had responded to her angrily. "Ms. Elham, I told you, I can't inform on my friends."

"This is called a negative attitude, Lamees. You have to cooperate with us if you are going to keep up your grades. Why aren't you like your sister Tamadur?"

After this cruel threat, and the usual provocative remark about her sister, Lamees had to tell her mother about the incident. Dr. Fatin came to school to meet with the principal. Lamees's mother cautioned the principal in no uncertain terms against speaking to her daughter in such a way ever again. As long as Lamees herself had not been behind the prank, they had no right to make her divulge the secrets of her friends. It would be more appropriate for them to search for the real culprit on their own, instead of trying to force Lamees to be their spy, and lose her self-respect and her classmates' great affection for her.

It was true that the teachers were always asking her why she was not more like her sister Tamadur, but, in compensation, her friends would ask her why Tamadur wasn't more like her!

Lamees had been sure that the principal would be easier on her this time around, especially since it had only been a few days since her mother's last visit. Dr. Fatin had some prestige and weight to throw around at that school, since for the past five years she had been president of the Mothers' Association—a Saudi version of the PTA. She had worked hard to further the school's charitable activities, in addition to the fact that her daughters were among the school's top pupils and were very often selected to represent it in regional academic competitions.

"As you can see, a certain paper bag has reached me," the principal said to Lamees, sitting in her office. "However, I promised Ms. Hana that I would not punish you, and I am sticking to my promise. All I will do is take the films with me today, and I'll return them to you after I've watched all of them."

"Watched all of them? Why?"

"To make sure there isn't any of *that* sort of film among them." She winked.

How rude of her! What sort of film was she insinuating? Each tape had the name of the movie written on it. They were the latest American movies and she was sure that Ms. Elham had heard about each one of them. There were *Braveheart, The Nutty Professor* and a few others that the girls' brothers got from Dubai or Bahrain or from American compounds in Riyadh where they sell noncensored movies. She wasn't carrying sex tapes! Maybe Ms. Elham just wanted to watch the movies for fun! But why didn't she just ask to borrow them in a direct way instead? In any case, Lamees decided that this horrid principal was not going to get the pleasure of watching *her* films, after all of the misery she inflicted on Lamees every day.

"I'm so sorry. The films aren't mine. If my friends knew the films had been taken they would skin me alive, as some of them belong to their brothers."

"And just who are these friends of yours?"

My God, Lamees thought. *Doesn't this woman ever stop asking these kinds of questions?*

"As you know, ma'am, I can't tell you that."

"Your problem, Lamees, is that you think you're the godfather of your own little *mafia*, willing to take the blame for everything wrong they do. Either you tell me the names of the girls who are with you or I will confiscate the movies."

Lamees considered the principal carefully. "If I tell you their names, can you guarantee that my friends won't find out? They will never know that I told on them? And do you promise that you won't punish them?"

"Yes, Lamees. I promise."

Lamees divulged the names of her partners in crime, took back the films and after school distributed them to the four of them to watch over the weekend. Where was her hiding place, they wanted to know, and how had she managed to hide this enormous bag? But Lamees just replied with a confident smile and her usual line: "Hey, I'm Lamees! The one and only."

7.

To: seerehwenfadha7et@yahoogroups.com
From: "seerehwenfadha7et"
Date: March 26, 2004
Subject: The Legends of Street No. 5

Many people have accused me of imitating the way certain writers write, though they say I put all of them together in one big pot and end up writing in an eclectic and strange way. Frankly, this is a great honor as far as I'm concerned, as long as they truly believe I am imitating writers like those whom they mention! Even though, I swear, in truth I am too insignificant to imitate them.

O ur Saudi society resembles a fruit cocktail of social classes in which no class mixes with another unless absolutely necessary, and then only with the help of a blender! The "velvet" Riyadh upper class was, to the four girls, the whole world, but it comprised only a tiny fraction of the university world's enormous diversity.

When the girls entered the university, they got to know for the first time girls who had come from faraway areas about which they had heard very little. If you counted up all of the girls who came from beyond greater Riyadh, they would make up more than half of the entering class of sixty young women. The closer she got to those girls, the more admiration Lamees felt for them. They were energetic, independent and strong. Graduates of public government schools, these girls from the kingdom's interior had not had a quarter of the resources and support she and her three friends had had in their posh private schools. Yet they had excelled and obtained the highest examination marks, and if it were not for the fact that most of them were weak in English, no one could have told them apart from her friends, except perhaps by the simplicity of their clothing. None of them had ever heard of the famous brands that everyone in the little four-person *shillah* exclusively bought.

Michelle was surprised and upset one time when she heard one of the students who was walking close behind her and Lamees vigorously start asking forgiveness from God when she happened to hear Lamees's description of the sexy dress she was going to wear that evening to her cousin's wedding! And Sadeem told her that one of their classmates was always saying that she was on the lookout for a bride for her husband, whom she had married just one year before, so that she could present him with the bride herself! The reason she gave was that she wanted to find some time in which she could clean the house and dye her high-lighted hair roots and beautify her hands with henna designs and adorn herself for him, and care for their child and the children still to come. She'd be able to do all of that, she said, during the times her husband was with his other wife!

Among the four girls, Michelle was the only one who could not stand this type of girl. She wasn't interested in entering into deep discussion and debate with any of them, and she wasn't at all happy at Lamees's obvious enthusiasm for associating with them. She privately accused Lamees of playing the Alicia Silverstone character in the movie *Clueless,* which had been everyone's favorite film when they were teenagers.

Lamees, she said, was taking the least sophisticated girls on a voyage of beautification and cultivation—giving them complete makeovers—only to make them aware of Lamees's superiority.

What made Michelle more resentful was that Sadeem shared Lamees's interest and easy rapport with those girls. With all of their simplicity, the girls were utterly polite and very delicate and, in a way, refined. Their innocent goodness attracted everyone to them, in addition to their sense of humor, a trait that had been all but obliterated in the refined circles of society.

Is there an inverse relationship between one's social and economic status, on the one hand, and good humor and a merry personality, on the other? In the way that some people believe in the existence of an invariable relationship between being fat and being funny? Personally, I believe in such things. Being disagreeable, dull, constitutionally insufferable or truly odious—these are widespread diseases among the rich. Look at the degree of dullness among blond females, especially upper-class blondies, and you'll know exactly what I mean!

Lamees began to sense Michelle's instant jealousy whenever Lamees showed signs of getting close to any other girl at the university. In the first term of their first year, Lamees and Sadeem would meet daily on the sidewalk of Street No. 5, or "the Champs," as they called it, after the Champs-Élysées in Paris, because it was the street that all girls in the university spent their free time between classes walking down. It had been the two girls' dream to see the Champs of Olaisha, after all that they had heard about it. And now here it was, nothing more than a few old wooden benches placed in front of Gate No. 5. The Olaisha Campus, one of King Saud University campuses, consisted of just a few buildings on the point of collapse. It was initially built in 1957 and was strictly for male students at that time. Later on, the males were moved to a huge new campus, leaving Olaisha for females. Inside the Olaisha Campus, the streets were layered with the remnants of dried dates that had fallen from the palms that lined the streets. The place was so neglected that even the clusters of hanging dates had despaired of seeing anyone come to gather them. Even after dropping to the ground, they were ignored year after year; no one came to pick them up.

Michelle, who had come from her college in the Malaz Campus one morning expressly to explore the Champs of Olaisha, was so disappointed that she loudly bewailed the fate that had decreed she attend a university in Saudi rather than in America. It was all the fault of her aunts. Her father's nosy sisters had really gone out of their way in this case to stuff her open-minded father's head with retrograde ideas. They warned him of the likely consequences of letting her go abroad all by herself to study. Girls who traveled out of the kingdom to study, the aunties argued, found lots of unflattering talk swirling around them when they returned. And then they couldn't find anyone who would marry them. The greatest tragedy of it all was that her highly civilized father was persuaded by these ridiculous, stupid arguments!

The sidewalk of Street No. 5 had its secrets, many of them having to do with legendary students. Many stories were told, some of them true and some of them highly embroidered.

One of the famous tales of the Street No. 5 sidewalk, transmitted like wildfire among university students within Olaisha Campus, was the story of Arwa. She was a student known for her lovely features and set apart by her extremely short hair and her masculine stride. Everyone sought Arwa out, mainly because everyone was so afraid of her. One of the girls swore that she had seen Arwa one day sitting on the Street No. 5 sidewalk with the white hem of a man's long underpants showing from beneath her long black skirt. Another student was sure that a friend of hers had seen Arwa slipping her hand around the waist of another girl in a most dubious manner. Sadeem mentioned that she had nearly died of fright when Arwa happened to walk by her while she was gossiping about her. She had never met Arwa before, so she didn't realize what a fix she'd gotten herself into until another girl mentioned that the girl leaning on the wall with her gaze fixed on Sadeem and a mysterious smile on her lips was none other than Arwa! "Do you think she heard me, girls? If she heard, what will she do to me now?" Sadeem asked her friends, sweat beading on her forehead. Her friends cautioned her against walking alone on the campus grounds from then on, for it was clear that she had been added—*seriously* added—to Arwa's blacklist.

"May God protect you, Saddoomah, dear! Stay away from Building No. 4 which is the oldest and farthest away. They say that Arwa stalks the girls who go there—every one of them!—because the place is so out-of-the-way and deserted that even if a girl were to scream or smash everything to pieces out there, no one would ever hear or know."

Arwa the lesbo! Good God! Could it be true that she really did graduate from Olaisha? I haven't heard anything about her for quite a long time. Arwa has become a legend, like all the other myths of this ancient and venerable campus.

After that first term, Lamees and Tamadur moved to the Science Department at the women's campus in Malaz, where Michelle was already studying computer science. That would last only one term, after which they would move to the College of Medicine for Women, also in Milaz, for two years; after which they would move—their final move—to the King Khalid University Hospital to complete their training. This end station on the road through the educational system was what made them the envy of the other girls. For studying in the very same hospital were the guys coming from their own College of Medicine, as well as the Colleges of Dentistry, Pharmacy and Applied Medical Sciences.

The thought of finally mixing with the the opposite sex was a grand dream for many, many students—guys and girls alike. Some joined these colleges primarily for that reason, even if the mixing that they anticipated so eagerly was heavily restricted. Male doctors taught female medical students and male students were allowed to examine female patients, but it was not allowed for male and female students to share a classroom or a lounge. Contact with the opposite sex would never go beyond some coincidental and transient encounter in the breaks between lectures or at prayer times (facilitated by the fact that the male students tended to pray in the prayer area close to where the female students habitually were), or quick glimpses and stolen glances while walking about the hospital or riding the elevators. Still, it was better than nothing.

8.

To: seerehwenfadha7et@yahoogroups.com
From: "seerehwenfadha7et"
Date: April 3, 2004
Subject: On Those Who Do Not Marvel at the Marvelous

First, I offer all of you my apologies for my unintended tardiness in sending out this e-mail. I had a nasty flu that prevented me from writing yesterday, which was Friday, so you are getting my e-mail on a Saturday instead. Easy on me, Abdullah, because I gave you back your grim Friday afternoon,* after you had grown used to my e-mails lightening Friday's tedium for you. And, pardon me, Ghada (and by the way I thank you, for being the first girl to e-mail me since this scandal-sheet series began), for not providing you with any material you could talk about all day at the bank this Saturday. And forgive me, Ra'id, you funny guy you, for having messed up your weekly schedule, making you doubt what day it was and what date as well, so you almost didn't go to work on Saturday morning and your life was a mess and it was ALL because of my late e-mail!

I have brushed on my bright red rouge, and there is a big plate of pick-

*The weekend in Saudi Arabia is Thursday and Friday.

led cucumbers next to me. This time around, I really need some munchies with bite, to keep me reminded of the sharp flavor of what I am about to write in this e-mail.

Gamrah accustomed herself to her new life. It had become clear to her that Rashid's behavior toward her was not just a matter of feeling shy or embarrassed with the wife who had suddenly assailed his life. It was something more. Gamrah did not have it in her to actually give a name to his doings—not, anyway, the name that echoed in her head, even if a certain string of words kept on seeping out from her mind in spite of herself, and then creeping into her troubled heart: *My husband, whom I love, hates me. He wants to throw me out.*

Just a few weeks after their arrival in Chicago—and after Rashid's grumbling about her laziness and how she never left the apartment had grown louder—Gamrah got used to going out by herself to shop for household goods at the end of every week. Rashid himself was not prepared to teach her to drive, but he had no confidence that she could understand and be understood by a foreign teacher with her poor, broken English. So he turned for help to the wife of one of his Arab friends who had offered to teach Gamrah how to drive, for a fee. After Gamrah failed the driving test three times in a row, however, Rashid put a stop to the driving lessons and ordered her to learn how to use public transportation to do what she had to do.

Whenever she went out, Gamrah wore a long overcoat with a *hijab*.* Even her clothes became a source of irritation to her husband after a while: "Why don't you wear ordinary clothes like the other women here? It's as if you are trying to embarrass me in front of my friends with the things you wear! And then you wonder why I don't take you out with me!"

---

*In Islam, a *hijab* is any kind of head covering that conceals the hair and neck of a woman.

Neither Gamrah nor her mother could really understand why he was so annoyed. What was the source of the constant irritation and tension that seemed to have overcome Rashid? Yet, in spite of her distress and misery, Gamrah was prepared to do anything to make the marriage work. Or at least to keep it going.

On one of the rare days when they were both at home, Gamrah kept after her husband to take her to a movie, and he finally relented. After they arrived at the theater and he found two seats for them, she surprised him by taking off her coat and *hijab* before sitting down. She gave him a shy smile, trying to read his thoughts at that crucial moment. He studied her with a sidelong stare, and after just a few seconds, he said, "Taking them off isn't making you look any better. So just put them on again."

Before the wedding, her delight about the engagement, and about the groom, who was such a good catch—so totally elegant—and all of the bridal finery from Lebanon with a dowry that no girl in the family had been able to top—all of this was too much to allow any doubts to creep up on Gamrah. But now there were plenty of doubts and even more questions.

So why would he marry me if he didn't want me? Gamrah asked herself time and time again. She asked her mother whether she had heard anything from Rashid's family to suggest that he had been forced to marry her. But did it make sense that a *man*—and he was every inch a man, whatever else he turned out to be—would be forced to marry a woman he didn't want, no matter how compelling the reasons?

Before the wedding, Gamrah had seen Rashid only once, and that was on the day of the *shoufa*, the day set for the bridegroom's lawful viewing of the bride-to-be. The traditions of her family did not permit the man seeking the engagement to see the bride again before the contract signing. Moreover, in this case there was no more than a two-week gap between the signing and the marriage celebration itself, and Gamrah's and Rashid's mothers agreed between themselves that Rashid would not see his bride during that time, so that she would have no interruptions as she prepared for her wedding. It was all completely logical in Gamrah's eyes, except she did find it a little odd that Rashid had not asked her father's permission to talk to her on the phone so that he could get to know her better like all men do these days.

Gamrah had heard that most young men these days insisted on getting acquainted with their fiancées by telephone before the contract-signing, but her family's particularly conservative practices didn't allow for that. As far as they were concerned, marriage was—as they always said—like the watermelon on the knife, you never knew what you were going to get. Her older sister Naflah's watermelon had turned out to be one of those extra-sweet ones, while her own watermelon and her sister Hessah's were more like dried-out, empty gourds.

Gamrah kept cataloging instances of Rashid's difficult personality and they began to grow and mass like a snowball rolling down a mountain, swelling to more and more gigantic proportions. Gamrah kept up her investigation, turning over in her mind every little detail, trying to unearth the real reason why he was hostile to her—even, it seemed clear, repulsed by her. What, Gamrah puzzled, was the truth behind his contempt? What was it that had driven him, through all of these months, to positively insist that she take birth-control pills, even though she was dying to have a baby with him?

Real, serious doubts began to sink into Gamrah's heart and soul after she had been married for a few months. The way Rashid treated her was not a whole lot different from the way her father treated her mother. But it was different from the way Mohammed treated her sister Naflah, and even from the way Khalid was with Hessah, at least when they had first been married. And it was thoroughly unlike the way their Emirati neighbor behaved toward his wife, whom he had married just six months before Rashid and Gamrah's wedding.

Although her husband was rough and rude to her sometimes, Gamrah loved him. She was even devoted to him, in spite of everything, for he was the first man she had ever spent time with outside of the company of her brothers, father and uncles. He was the first man who had come forward to ask for her hand, and by doing so he had made her feel as though there were someone in this world who knew—maybe even appreciated—that she was alive. Gamrah did not know if she had come to love Rashid because he was worthy of being loved, or if she simply felt it was her duty as his wife to love him. Now, though, the doubts that began to overtake her were troubling her sleep and darkening her days.

One day as she was shopping in the Al-Khayyam Arab Grocery on Kedzie Avenue, she heard the owner singing along with the famous Egyptian singer Um Kulthum. He was obviously enjoying himself and was completely immersed in a trance brought on by the music. Gamrah listened to the melancholy tune and the words that pressed hard against a wound that sat deep inside of her. Her eyes filled with tears as the idea hit her: *Can Rashid possibly be in love with someone else?*

When Gamrah visited Riyadh during the New Year's break, Rashid did not go with her. She spent nearly two months with her family, hoping that Rashid would ask her to come back once he had had enough of being alone. But he never did ask her to return. In fact, her feelings told her that he was hoping she would stay in Riyadh and never come back. How many hundreds of times each day he stabbed her to death with his icy coldness! She had tried everything to win him over, but it was no use. Rashid was the epitome of the Leo man, in his innate stubbornness and his elusiveness.

Lamees had always served as astrological consultant for their little *shillah*. From Beirut she would bring books on the signs of the zodiac. For each of the girls, Lamees would read out the personality traits for her sign and the degrees of compatibility between that sign and all the others. It was a given that the girls would consult with Lamees before launching into any relationship of any sort, and so during the engagement Gamrah had gotten in touch to ask her how much compatibility there was between her sign, Gemini, and Rashid's, Leo. Sadeem, too, went to Lamees for advice when Waleed the Aries guy asked for her hand. Even Michelle, who had never shown much enthusiasm for such things, contacted Lamees as soon as she discovered that Faisal was a Cancer. She wanted to hear from the experts how successful their relationship would be.

Before Gamrah got married and went to Chicago, Lamees gave her a photocopy of one of her priceless zodiac manuals. Gamrah would reread it regularly, underlining whatever applied to her:

The Gemini female is attractive and alluring and her beauty turns people's heads. Energetic and lively, she lets her small reservoir of patience rule even in matters of love. She is the truest type of the capricious whimsical fancy-free woman who won't settle on anything, or on any one person. She's an emotional one—indeed, her emotions blaze if she meets the right man who is capable of satisfying her heart, mind and body all together. In spite of herself, the Gemini woman is a complex person. She is high-strung and has many fears. But she is always stimulating and entertaining, and those who know her don't know what it means to be bored . . .

The Leo male is a practical guy, clever and careful with his money, who doesn't like to waste his time with unprofitable games. He is nervous and quick to react, egotistical and stubborn and he roars when angry. When Leo loves, he is jealous and possessive of his beloved. Expect him to be dominating in his love, but he is also exuberant and impetuous, like a volcano pouring forth the lava of passion. The woman he loves must close her eyes; she must not be upset when he interferes in her personal business and she must not magnify things out of proportion. The Leo man does not hesitate to show his violent side if the slightest doubt assails him about her obedience and loyalty to him . . .

The worst sentence of all that Gamrah read before her marriage spelled out the degree of compatibility between a Gemini woman and a Leo man: "No more than fifteen percent!"

It's difficult to find agreement and harmony between the Gemini woman and the Leo man. They can work together for a fixed period of

time, for the sake of achieving a practical success. As for emotional relationships, however, they are likely to be lukewarm at best, to stagnate,
resulting in mutual dislike and liable to end in undeniable failure.

Before her marriage, reading these lines Gamrah would mutter,
"These things are a bunch of lies, even if some of them turn out to be
true." But now she read the same lines with more conviction as she
remembered their North African cook in Riyadh, who used to read the
inside of the coffee cup for her, finding meaning in the patterns of the
thick and black Turkish coffee grounds. The cook also read her palm and
said it was as clear as day that her marriage to Rashid would be one of
the most successful marriages the family had ever known and that she
would be blessed with many children. She even described them to her as
if she could see their features in the splotches of coffee across the hollow
of the cup or inside the folds of her palms.

She thought about the Ouija board, which she had played as a teenager with her three friends after Michelle brought it back from one of
her trips to America. The board told her that she would marry a young
man whose name began with the letter *R,* and that she would travel
abroad with him. She would have three sons and two daughters. The little
glass piece, which she touched lightly with her fingers, moved over the
letter-filled game board in the darkness of the room that night, guiding
her to the names of her children, one by one.

Gamrah tried to rid herself of the wicked thoughts that were growing like a tumor inside her head. To calm herself, she called her mother
in Riyadh and asked her how to prepare *jireesh,* a traditional Saudi dish.
She stayed on the phone the whole time it took to cook, listening to the
latest news of her relatives and her neighbors. There were a few new stories about Naflah's clever naughty little boys, and the usual commentary
about Hessah's patience with her husband Khalid.

9.

To: seerehwenfadha7et@yahoogroups.com
From: "seerehwenfadha7et"
Date: April 9, 2004
Subject: Treasure in a Poem

A lot of angry e-mails came my way last week. Some were angry at Rashid for his cruelty. Others were angry at Gamrah for being so passive. And the rest—and that was most of them—were angry at me for talking about the sun signs and the Ouija board and reading coffee cups which not so many believe in.

Okay. I accept your anger. And I also don't. As you can see, and as you will see, I am an ordinary girl (Okay maybe a little nutty, just a little!). I don't analyze every move I make, and I don't worry about every act possibly being taboo and against social or religious laws. All I *can* say is that I do not claim to be perfect (as some people do).

My friends are standard examples, and they are pretty good ones, of who we all are. Some might purposely ignore what their stories show us about ourselves, while others are just blind to it. I am forever hearing people say to me: "You will not reform the world and you will not change people." They have a point, a very good point, but what I WON'T do is to give up the attempt, like everyone else does. *There* is the difference between me and other people. As the hadith,* the words of Prophet Mohammed, peace be upon him, says, "Deeds are measured by the intentions behind them." May God consider my writings as good deeds, as I only have good intentions. Let me say it again in case someone didn't get it the first time around: "I do not claim perfection!" I confess to my ignorance and flaws, but "Every child of Adam commits errors, and the best of those who commit errors are those who repent." I work hard to correct my errors and to cultivate myself. If only those who find fault with me would turn around and straighten themselves out before they start agitating to straighten me out.

May all repent for their sins after reading about them on the Internet. May all discover some hidden tumors and extract them after having been shown some ugly examples under a microscope. I see nothing wrong in setting down my friends' problems in my e-mails so that others will benefit—others who have not had the opportunity to learn in the school of life, the school that my friends entered from the widest of gates—the gate of *Love*. The true and shameful wrong, the way I see things, would be for any of us to stand in each other's way, disparaging each other, even though we all admit the unity of our goal, which is reforming our society and making every one of us a better person.

O n Valentine's Day, Michelle put on a red shirt and carried a matching handbag. A large number of the other female students did the same, enough of them so that the whole campus looked bright red, by means of clothes and flowers and stuffed animals. In those days, the holiday was still a really new fad and the guys liked it; they cruised the streets stopping every girl they saw to give her a red rose with their phone numbers wrapped around the stem. The girls liked it, too, since now they had finally found someone to give them red roses the way they always saw it done in films. That was before the Religious Police

---

*The hadith are collections of the sayings of the Prophet Mohammed.

banned anything that might remotely suggest a celebration of the holiday of love, Saint Valentine's Day, as in Islam there are only two holidays, or Eids: one is Eid Al-Fitr, the day following the month of Ramadan, and the other one is Eid Al-Adha, after the days of pilgrimage to Mecca. Saudis started celebrating Valentine's Day in the late nineties after they heard about it through satellite TV channels broadcast from Lebanon and Egypt. It was before punishments and fines were instituted for owners of flower shops who gave out red roses to their VIP customers by the most intricate and convoluted ways as if they were smuggled goods. Although celebrating this holiday in Saudi Arabia was prohibited, the celebration of Mother's or Father's Day was not, even though the principle behind both ideas is one and the same. Love was treated like an unwelcome visitor in our region.

Faisal's chauffeur was waiting for Michelle at the university entrance to give her Faisal's Valentine's Day gift. It was an enormous basket filled with dried red roses and red heart-shaped candles. Nestled in the middle sat a little black bear holding a crimson velvet heart. When you pressed on the heart, the tune of Barry Manilow's song "Can't Smile Without You" came floating out.

Michelle sauntered toward the lecture hall, feeling really special. She looked benevolently down at her girlfriends, whose hearts were slowly disintegrating from total jealousy as she read to them the poem Faisal had written on the card accompanying the gift. They were so jealous, in fact, that quite a few of them brought in dolls or stuffed bears and flowers the next day, just to prove that they had been surprised with gifts like hers after returning home from school.

On that day, many girls cried for a lost love or mourned for an old crush. Many gifts were confiscated and the girls who had worn red clothes or accessories had to make pledges that they not repeat their behavior next year. In the years that followed, clothes were subject to inspection even before the girls were inside the campus gates where they could take off their wraps. That way, the inspectresses could return the culprit to her chauffeur, who still would be waiting there, to be taken immediately home if there was the slightest sign of the *Crime of Red* on her person, even if it was a mere hair tie.

But Faisal's gift to Michelle did not end with his romantic poem. On her way home, as she was tossing the soft black bear from hand to hand and breathing in Faisal's elegant Bulgari scent, which he had sprinkled over the bear, she suddenly caught sight of a pair of heart-shaped diamond earrings that Faisal had hung in the bear's cute little ears for his cute little Michelle to hang in hers.

10.

To: seerehwenfadha7et@yahoogroups.com

From: "seerehwenfadha7et"

Date: April 16, 2004

Subject: When Grief Becomes Pleasure

He said to her one day, All a man wants from a woman is that she understand him. And so the woman snapped loudly into his ear, And all a woman wants from a man is that he love her.
   —Socrates

Among the many criticisms that have begun flooding into my inbox are a large number slamming me for quoting lines by the late poet Nizar Qabbani and—way back in my first e-mail—asking God's mercy on him. I quote Qabbani for a simple reason: There isn't anything out there today that could compare. I've never read any modern poetry that has the simplicity and the clear eloquence of his. I have never felt even slightly moved or influenced by those modernist poets who compose a *qasida* of thirty lines in which they talk about nothing! I do not get any pleasure from reading about *the festering pus on the forehead issuing from behind the haunch of eternal grief.* I am in sync only with Nizar's essential lines, lines that not a single one of those new poets (with all due respect to them) has been able to compose, despite their simplicity.

After Sadeem flunked out of school, which came as a huge surprise to everyone since she was known for her academic excellence, her father proposed that the two of them travel to London for some fun. Sadeem asked him, though, to let her go alone and stay in their flat in South Kensington. She wanted to spend a stretch of time by herself, she said. After some hesitation, her dad agreed, and he furnished her with some telephone numbers and addresses of friends of his who, accompanied by their families, were spending the summer in England. She could contact them if she wanted a little break from herself. He urged her to occupy her free time by signing up for a computer or economics course of some kind so that she could benefit from her time away once she returned to her college in Riyadh.

Sadeem packed away her wound along with her clothes and carried it all from the Dust Capital of the World to the Fog Capital of the World. London was not new to her. In fact, spending the last month of summer there had become a familiar yearly ritual. London this time around was different, though. This time, London was a huge sanatorium where Sadeem had decided to take refuge to overcome the mental maladies overwhelming her after her experience with Waleed.

Before they began the descent at Heathrow airport, Sadeem headed for the airplane bathroom. She took off her *abaya* and head covering to reveal a well-proportioned body encased in tight jeans and a T-shirt, and a smooth face adorned with light pink blush, a little mascara and a swipe of lip gloss.

Coming from Riyadh's heat, Sadeem had always enjoyed walking beneath London's summer rains, but on this trip, all that poured over her was misery. London was nothing but gloom, she decided; the city was as dark and cloudy as her mood. The silent apartment and her empty pillow added to her unhappiness, leading her to shed more tears than she had known it was possible to produce.

Sadeem spent a lot of time crying. She wept tears that burned her eyes, for the wrong, the darkness that had enveloped her, that had shrouded her defamed femininity. She cried and cried, mourning her first love, buried alive in its infancy before she could even find pleasure in it. She cried and she prayed, she prayed and prayed, in hopes that God would set guidance before her in her plight, for she had no mother to comfort and reassure her, no sister to stand by her side in this trial. She still did not know whether to tell her father what had happened between her and Waleed on the last night they had been together. Or whether she should carry the secret to her grave.

All that she had the power to do was seek God's forgiveness and send one prayer after another into the air, imploring that the despicable Waleed would not scandalize her by revealing why he had divorced her; that, having dumped her, he would not say anything that would drag her name through the mud. "Allah, shield me! Keep his evil from me! Allah, I have no one but You to come to, and You are the most knowledgeable of my condition."

It was during this difficult time that Sadeem became addicted to songs of grief, pain and parting. During those weeks in London, she listened to more sad songs than she had ever listened to in her entire life before. She would feel transported, even elated, whenever she listened to one of the classic love songs by famous Arabic singers that were full of romance and melancholia.

These songs would drench her in sadness and envelop her like a warm, clean bed. As the days passed, she no longer listened to such songs to give herself comfort, but rather to keep herself immersed in the intoxication of grief that she had discovered after the failure of her first love. This was an experience she had in common with most lovers who have suffered loss or betrayal; a masochistic ordeal where pain becomes pleasurable. The trauma leads us to create a tent of wise thoughts in which we sit to philosophize about our life that is passing by outside. We are transformed into tender, hypersensitive beings and the teeniest thought can make us weep. Our damaged hearts dread the next emotional break, so they stay inside their lonely tents of wisdom, avoiding ever falling in love again. One day another Bedouin comes along. He shows up to mend the tent's tendons . . . When this other man passes by, we invite him in for a thimbleful of coffee and keep him there, only for a little while to warm up our sad solitude, but unfortunately, this other man always ends up staying—for too long, and before we know it our tent of wisdom falls down around us both! And then we are no smarter than we were before.

After two weeks of solitary confinement in the apartment, Sadeem decided to eat her main meal of the day out, as long as she could find a restaurant not inhabited by streams of tourists from the Gulf. The last thing she wanted, when she was in this state, was to meet a young Saudi man who would try to chat her up.

She didn't feel any better in the restaurant than she had inside the four walls of the apartment. The atmosphere inside the Hush Restaurant was, as its name might suggest, quiet and romantic. Sadeem thought she came across as the victim of some contagious disease whose family had abandoned her. There she was, eating her meal in solitude, while couples all around her were talking and whispering in the glow of the candlelight. Sadeem couldn't help but recall her poetic dinners with Waleed and the way they had planned for their honeymoon. He had promised to take her to the island of Bali. She had asked that they spend several days in London before returning to Riyadh after the honeymoon was over. For so long she had dreamed of someday going with her husband, whoever he might be, to the places she had been going to alone for years.

She had had it all planned. She would take him to visit the Victoria and Albert, the Tate, and Madame Tussaud's. Even though art did not appeal to Waleed the way it did to her, she had figured she would change all of that after their marriage, just as she would force him to stop smoking, a habit that annoyed her greatly. They would drink shoga apple and eat sushi at Itsu on Draycott Avenue. They would slowly drown themselves in Belgian chocolate crepes at the shop near her flat. She would take him to shows at Ishbilia, the Lebanese restaurant, and—of course!—she would not forget to take him on a sea cruise to Brighton. At the end of their time in London she would take him shopping in Sloane Street. She would get him to buy her the latest fashions in clothes and accessories, just as Gamrah's mother had advised her to do, instead of buying them in Riyadh in advance of the wedding with her dowry.

How very painful these memories were now! Her fancy wedding dress and gorgeous wedding veil (which had been shipped custom-made from Paris) were still lurking in her wardrobe in Riyadh, sticking out their tongues at her in derision every time she opened the closet door. She could not get rid of them. It was as if something inside of her were still waiting for Waleed's return. But he would not return. And her wedding dress and veil were ugly and ever-present witnesses to her beloved's low-minded and despicable nature.

Her destination the next morning was an Arabic bookshop. She bought two novels by Turki Al-Hamad, *Al-Adama* and *Al-Shemaisi,* after seeing a man from the Gulf who looked to be in his forties requesting them from the clerk. She also bought *Sheqat Al Horreya,* or *Freedom's Nest,* by Ghazi Al-Qusaibi, which she had seen as a TV series on some satellite channel a few years before and liked very much. She took a bus back home to find a voice message from her father. He told her that he had arranged things so that she would have a summer internship in one of the London banks that he dealt with regularly. It would begin in a week's time.

She liked the idea. Summer work, added independence, and some self-improvement. Beyond the books she had just bought and—now—working at the bank, she had no other plans for the summer. Well, she did have one: to study psychology under the guiding hand of Sigmund Freud, aided by the books she had brought with her, so that she could better analyze Waleed's personality and arrive at a clear understanding of those factors that had pushed him to no-fault divorce. Meaning, no fault of hers.

Reading the books she had just bought was a pleasure, but it depressed her that she had no idea what she ought to read next. She wished she had a list of must-reads for the cultured and intelligent person.

In the novels of Al-Qusaibi and Al-Hamad, she found a lot of political allusions that reminded her of the novels of the Egyptian writers she had been addicted to as a teenager. She recalled suddenly the demonstration she and her classmates had been prohibited from participating in, in those days, when all of the Arab nations were protesting to show support for the Palestinian Intifada and the Al-Aqsa Mosque uprising. She remembered how a lot of countries started boycotting American and English products a while back, but only a few of her friends in Saudi participated and even the ones who did didn't stick with it for more than a few weeks. Had politics been within reach of everyone once upon a time, but were now accessible only to generals and rulers?

Why had none of her relatives, male or female, gotten involved in a political cause, supporting it with their very souls as had been the case when Ghazi and Turki were young? Why was it that young people these days had no interest in foreign politics unless it was the scandalous behavior of Bill Clinton and Monica Lewinsky? Or, in domestic politics, only the flagrant corruption at the Saudi Telecom Company? It wasn't just her, Sadeem—all of her classmates and everyone at their age were on the margins when it came to political life. They had no role, no importance. If only she understood politics! If only she had a particular cause to defend or one to oppose! Then she would have something to keep her occupied and to turn her away from thinking about Waleed the bast . . . !

11.

To: seerehwenfadha7et@yahoogroups.com
From: "seerehwenfadha7et"
Date: April 23, 2004
Subject: Um Nuwayyir's Classification of Human Populations

There is no God but Allah, the Mighty and the Clement One. There is no God but Allah, Lord of the Great Throne. There is no God but Allah, Lord of the Heavens and Lord of the Earth and Lord of the Throne most gracious. Everliving, Everlasting, there is no God but You; and in Your mercy we seek succor.
   —Prayer to release worry, trouble and grief

Over the past two weeks, I have read what has been said about me in some of the famous Saudi Internet forums. Some of the talk was as soft as the granules in my daily facial soap but some of it was as rough as the black stone I use on my perennially problem knees. As I followed these discussions swirling like a sandstorm around *me*, I felt as though I were watching a bullfight—that is, two bulls fighting. Can any of you out there believe that someone would call for my blood? Well, fine, that's enough to deal with, but then there is the one who claims to be my sister, which is a whole other deal! She claims to have observed that, every Friday, starting early in the morning, her sister secludes herself in her room, in front of her computer screen. One time when this sister of hers was out of the way, the "sister" who is writing says she searched through her sister's files for evidence that would confirm her suspicions. And, listen to this! She stumbled across all thirty e-mails. And she is ready to sell them to the highest bidder!

After reading *Introductory Lectures on Psychoanalysis, Essentials of Psychoanalysis, Three Essays on the Theory of Sexuality, On Narcissism* and *Totem and Taboo,* Sadeem gradually realized that Freud, with all his totems, tomatoes, cucumbers and green salad vegetables, was not going to be much help in solving her problem! Sigmund was not about to yield an explanation of why Waleed had left her.

Sadeem had stumbled across two of Freud's works, translated, in the Jarir Bookstore in Riyadh. The rest she had asked a university friend to bring her from Lebanon before her own departure for London.

She did not find Sigmund Freud's thought nearly as convincing—at least, not in explaining Waleed's behavior—as she had found Um Nuwayyir's classification of human groups. In a happier time, with Sadeem as her audience, Um Nuwayyir had explained her own analysis of men and women in the Gulf states. It was a complicated system of groups and subgroups that covered just about every personality type, and Sadeem had taken notes so she could remember it all.

Um Nuwayyir classified people of the Gulf and Arabs in general based on a number of factors, including strength of personality, self-confidence, good looks and so forth. These general categories applied to both men and women and were then further subdivided.

For example, "strength of personality" is subdivided into two groups: the strong and the weak. In general the strong usually show a lot of motivation for economic self-improvement. These people watch the examples of success they see around them and seize their opportunity to benefit. The weak, led-by-the-nose types lack initiative and only get off their butts when their family or their entire environment gets an upward kick. But these groups are also subdivided as follows:

1. The Strong
A. The logical type who respects the views of everyone he (or she) encounters even when he has a different point of view.
B. The person who has to have his own way and doesn't care about the views of others.

2. The Weak
A. The person whose family can easily bend him (or her) one way or the other. This person is incapable of acting independently because, as Um Nuwayyir points out, "Without his family he isn't worth a penny."
B. The person who is easily swayed by his friends and can't stop swaying. This case is even worse than the first one because this person is convinced that his family is against him and only trusts his friends, who, in general, are likely to be in even worse shape than he is.

Um Nuwayyir worked out the same kind of analysis under the heading of "self confidence." Here also there are two main groups, the secure and the insecure, and, of course, each group is divided by Um Nuwayyir into subgroups as follows:

1. The Secure
A. The sensible type. People belonging to this group are at peace with themselves, displaying a clear degree of confidence that makes everyone respect them and even hold them in awe. But at the same

time, they maintain the love and affection of others due to their modesty and genuine accomplishment.

B. The Overconfident

This includes people who really don't have anything to be proud of. They have an excess of self-confidence, though they lack any reason for it; no great achievements or outstanding personality or even appealing looks. This type is abominable and, unfortunately, more common than the first one. But both A and B together are less common than the second main group:

2. The Insecure

A. Those who claim to be secure. They affect a self-confident pose that isn't matched by any sincere belief on their part. They take every word said to them with extraordinary sensitivity and reply with great aggressiveness, shielding their failures with their loud personalities. They make mountains out of molehills, or, as we say, "a dome out of a seed."

B. Those who are really insecure. People in this group don't act or claim to be something they're not. It's apparent from the first that they are pitiful and they make you feel sorry for them. Sometimes they have an obvious physical problem that lowers their self-esteem, like obesity, short height or even a big nose. Or it could be a social problem like poverty or even a mental one like stupidity. Or sometimes it could be a hidden problem that no one else is aware of, like a broken heart from a lost love that never healed.

Sadeem's favorite classification was that of "religious types before and after marriage," and this was the only one that strictly separated men and women. There were three categories: The extremely religious type, the rational moderate religious type and the wild type, who mostly ignored the strictures of their religion. The men and women are mirror images of each other. Let's look at the men first:

1. *The Extremely Religious Type*

A. He was once wild but he turns religious.

B. He fears wildness so he becomes religious.

Both fear they will degenerate morally after marriage, so they often end up in polygamous marriages, preferring their wives to be at least as zealous as they are.

2. *The Moderate Type*

A. A strictly religious man who differs from the first group in the way he treats women: tenderly and without interference. This type can marry a relatively liberal woman as long as he is confident of her love and certain of her morals.

B. The seculars. This man believes that Islam is built on five and no more than five basic and compulsory beliefs. He only attends the assigned five prayers and fasts only during Ramadan. After he has gone on the Pilgrimage to Mecca, he feels he has done his part, as long as he has also adhered to the declaration of the faith and given alms to the poor. This kind of man does not marry a woman unless she is on the same level of liberation as he is. He wouldn't marry someone who wears *hijab,* for example, and would insist that his wife be pretty, open-minded and stylish so that he could proudly show her off in front of his friends, who share his point of view.

3. *The Wild or Escapee Type*

A. Gradual escapee. Someone in this group may have grown up in a very strict religious atmosphere and "escaped" in a religious and moral sense. His escape is a gradual one, happening whenever he gets a chance to be away from the authority of his community. This type might pretend to belong to the first group to prevent any social embarrassment.

B. Liberal upbringing. This type has been brought up in an extremely liberal home to the point of atheism in his religious beliefs and the absence of any kind of bulwark against "bad behavior." And as we all say in these parts: "He who grows up doing something, grows old doing it." The problem you find in this type of man is pathological suspicion. Unfortunately, and due to his experiences with some cheap girls, whom we will be discussing later, he believes that every girl is guilty until proven innocent. This is why a man in the "wild" category always prefers to marry an inexperienced girl; she will always view things from his corrupted point of view. Sometimes a man of this type marries a girl who is a flirt but knows how to play the game. She knows perfectly well what her husband is really like and she knows how to manipulate and pretend so that her actions won't end up being misinterpreted. This is exactly what happened to Sadeem, who didn't realize who Waleed really was until it was too late and after he had made up his mind that she was "bad."

Now we come to the matching categories for women.

1. The Extremely Religious ("Bowing to the Faith") Type

A. The sheltered one. Brought up in a strict religious family, a woman of this type has never been exposed to any conflicting outside forces. If she's very lucky, she will marry someone equally religious. As long as both are able to accept and be happy with what fate has brought them, they can live "happily ever after" in a peaceful and secure life. But if she ends up marrying a man more liberal than she is, she will be miserable because she will never understand how to please him, since she has no knowledge of his way of life.

B. Sheltered, but with fantasies. This woman also has grown up in a sheltered setting, except that fantasies of bursting out into something new, into some kind of liberation, have always pursued her. She is also pure, not because of ignorance of the world "out there," but because of her own will, her self-discipline or the surveillance of her family.

2. The Moderate Type

A. Fashion victim. This woman changes her behavior according to the current fashion. If the trend during a certain time is to act all spiritual, attend religious gatherings and wear the *hijab* outside the kingdom, she will do it and "go with the flow." But if the trend is to dump your *hijab* once you get outside the country, and when you are inside to spend a lot of time in the malls wearing a tight-fitted *abaya* that shows off the features of a woman's body, then she will go with that flow, too. These trends are usually under the control of men's preferences during their search for suitable wives, or mothers who are hunting for future daughters-in-law.

B. Not religious, but not liberated, either. This woman is less strict than the extremely religious woman but more observant than the more liberal one. A woman from this group tends to resist sinning because of her morals and principles rather than her actual religious belief. She often has a strong personality, so she might mistakenly be listed as a liberal because she doesn't submit to all the rules of the more zealous groups.

3. The Wild Type (or "Escapee")

A. Wild before marriage. This woman normally reforms after marriage. She might turn into a very committed woman (or at least one of moderate commitment). That depends on her husband. If she marries someone who isn't right for her, she remains in the wild category even after her marriage.

B. Wild after marriage. This woman is usually a member of one of the sheltered groups, but she goes "bad" after marriage because she can't acclimatize to the demands of a liberated husband, or because of a rocky marriage or an unfaithful husband.

These were some of the complicated sets of categories that Sadeem took down while Um Nuwayyir dictated. Even months after writing it all down, Sadeem was still trying to absorb everything. The soundness of the whole complicated scheme became clearer and clearer with the passing of every day that Sadeem lived in the school of life. After all, that was the school where Um Nuwayyir had gotten her information and formulated her theory.

Sadeem's thoughts about Um Nuwayyir reminded her of the evening gatherings at home with her three friends. She could almost taste the Kuwaiti desserts—the syrupy sweetness of the *zalabya* and the smooth powdered *darabeel*—that Um Nuwayyir used to ply them with, together with hot tea. Her memories flew her home to Riyadh, all the way to the metallic gate with its gilt-edged bars, where she had so often stood after the evening prayer time waiting for Waleed to arrive. She saw in her mind's eye the swing by the swimming pool where she had spent evenings with his arm around her; the formal living room where guests were received, and where she had seen him for the first time; the television in the family living room where together they had watched all of those films; and the room that witnessed the birth of their love as well as its death. Had her love for Waleed truly died?

She got up to turn on the cassette player. She picked up a tape from among the many that were scattered across the floor. She pushed it into the machine, crept back to her bed and rolled into a ball like a fetus in its mother's womb. She listened woefully to Abdul Haleem's* mournful voice:

Rid yourself of woe and tears
Instead of crying years and years

*A famous Egyptian singer from the 1960s.

Oh you who've wept the traitor man
Weep on today, if you well can.
But watch that no one sees tears fall
For such will please the traitors all.

Sadeem cried and cried, and cried, alone in her London flat, wishing and hoping to rid herself of woes and tears, instead of crying years and years. Instead of crying spring and fall, bringing joy to traitors all.

12.

To: seerehwenfadha7et@yahoogroups.com

From: "seerehwenfadha7et"

Date: April 30, 2004

Subject: A Life That . . . "Could Be Worse"

I asked Aisha "Prophet Mohammed's wife," What did the Prophet— peace be upon him—do in his home? She said, He was occupied in the vocation and service of his family . . .

—The hadith collection of Al-Bukhari, verse 676

Frankly, I did not anticipate all of this flurry, all of this back-and-forth, around my modest little e-mails!

A number of you ask how I conceived of this project.

It all started in my mind about five years ago in 1999, that is, around the time when the story of my friends, as I am writing it to you and for you now, started. I didn't do anything to turn this idea into a reality until very recently, however. What got me going was that I saw my brain's capacity to hold anything reaching DISK FULL. The time had come to squeeze out the sponge of my mind and my heart, to really wring out that sponge so that I could absorb something new.

The marital relationship between Rashid and Gamrah was not exactly the cinematic ideal. However, it wasn't so utterly miserable, either. Preoccupied with his studies, Rashid left the responsibility for taking care of things at home to Gamrah after he realized how completely unenthusiastic she was about enrolling at the university. Even though it was difficult in the beginning to shoulder all of the household-related tasks, gradually Gamrah learned how to depend on herself. She began to find the courage to ask people on the street where an address was, or to ask salespeople in shops how much this or that cost.

She didn't actually see Rashid very much, but she got the money she needed whenever she asked for it, and most of the time without even asking. Even her own private needs—those "miscellaneous" needs—he gave her enough cash to meet, from time to time, anyway.

Gamrah wasn't able to compare what Rashid was giving her with what other men would offer their wives. What she did obtain, though, seemed satisfactory enough. The only needs she wasn't attending to were her emotional ones, and if that was all that was left out, she figured that she ought to consider herself a lot luckier than many women of her age and circumstances.

Once she had lived with Rashid for a while, Gamrah began to see his good side revealed, even though this goodness never emerged openly in his dealings with her. She could glimpse it in his treatment of others: his mother, his sisters, people out there in the street, and children. Rashid would become a happy little child himself in the presence of children. He would play with them fondly and very gently.

She became convinced that with time, Rashid would come to love her. After all, at the very start of their married life, he had always been remote and even a little rough with her, but as time passed he seemed more accepting of her and less severe, although he still sometimes blew up at her for reasons that seemed to Gamrah trivial. But aren't all men from Najd like that? If she thought about her father or brothers or uncles and their sons, she did not think that her husband was any different. This was his nature—and that was what gave her patience with him.

What bothered her most in Rashid was that he never sought her advice or consulted with her about anything having to do with their home. When he decided to put in a receiver for cable TV channels, he chose the bundle that included his favorites, without considering the fact that HBO, which ran her very favorite show, *Sex and the City,* wasn't among them. Gamrah followed that show avidly, even though she could only understand a little of what the characters were saying to each other. So what Rashid did, not taking her into account, as if she didn't even exist, really angered her, especially when he made it clear that her irritation didn't give him a moment's pause. He might as well have said that she had nothing to do with any of the important and basic household decisions, as though this were his apartment alone!

It went on like that. Every day, he would get her worked up about things of this sort. And yet she would be in for a terrible time if she were to forget in the evening to prepare his clothes or to iron them first thing in the morning before he was even awake. Furthermore, she had no right to ask him for help in tidying up or preparing meals or washing dishes, even though he had been accustomed to living the bachelor life all those years of studying in America. As for her, in her family's home in Riyadh there had always been servants around to do her bidding, furnishing whatever she and her siblings might request from moment to moment.

Rashid spent long hours at the university. When Gamrah would ask him why he was always so late getting home, he would simply inform her that he was carrying out research on the Internet using the easy-access computers in the university library.

In their early months in Chicago, Gamrah spent her time in front of the television or reading the romance novels she had brought with her from Riyadh, which Sadeem had introduced her to when they were in middle school.

Rashid had a computer in the apartment which he did not use. He allowed her to use it if she wanted to, but it was not connected to the Internet. Gamrah spent months learning how to use it. Rashid would help her sometimes, but she tried to rely on herself as much as possible. She noticed how quickly Rashid would insist on helping her as soon as he realized her determination to teach herself. The fact that she didn't come to him for every single little thing—or every single big thing, either—as she had done at the beginning of their marriage seemed to make him more receptive. Do men sense a threat to their authority when they begin to catch on that a woman is developing some real skills in some area? she wondered. Are men afraid of any moves toward independent action on the part of their wives? And do they consider a woman reaching independence and working toward her own goals an illegal offense against the religious rights of leadership God bestowed upon men? And so Gamrah discovered a crucial principle in dealing with men. A man must sense the strength of a woman and her independence and a woman must realize that her relationship with a man shouldn't just be built on needs: her need for his money, his share of domestic responsibilities, his support of her and her kids, and her need to feel her own significance in the universe. It is very unfortunate, isn't it, that a woman has to have a man to make her feel this sense of importance? Sitting at the computer, Gamrah was going through some files containing screensavers when her eyes fell on a file that appeared to hold a great many photos of an Asian woman. She was Japanese, Gamrah learned later. Her name was Kari.

Kari was petite and slim and appeared to be about Rashid's age or perhaps a little older. In some photos they were side by side. In fact, in one photo they were draped across the sofa in this very apartment in which Gamrah was living.

Here was something that didn't require any deep analysis! These photos were the missing link in Rashid's inexplicable behavior toward her. Rashid had had an affair with this girl before marrying her, Gamrah saw, and it wasn't a stretch to think that he was still having a relationship with her.

After that, the evidence mounted. In addition to the time he spent with Kari every day on the Internet or the phone when he was at school, Rashid was in the habit of spending two days every month away from the apartment with his "friends" on some excursion. She had welcomed those trips because they seemed to have had a magic effect on Rashid; he always returned to her in a state of delirious rapture, in a good mood and outdoing himself to show his affection, to the point where she had felt real gratitude toward those friends and would await the next month's trip impatiently!

How had he managed to hide his relationship with this woman for all these months? And how could Gamrah have been oblivious to her husband's affair with another woman? The first month after their wedding had been really difficult, for sure; but then he had changed gradually, turning into a traditional Najd husband very much like her sister Hessah's husband. How had he been able to keep up this acting in front of her for all this time? Did he meet that woman regularly? Did she live in the same state or did he travel somewhere every month to see her? Did he love her? Did he sleep with her and make her take birth-control pills like he made his wife do?

If anyone had told me that this resigned and unassertive woman Gamrah would do what she did, I would not have believed it. Not before I saw it with my own eyes, anyway. This young wife took up arms, intent on fighting to defend her marriage and struggle for the sake of its survival. She told no one of her painful discovery except her friend Sadeem, who had let her know about her abandonment by Waleed. This friend of hers who had fled into a London exile, Gamrah felt, was the person most capable of really understanding her feelings at such a time, even though she didn't know why Waleed and Sadeem had split up until a year later.

In their daily phone conversations, Sadeem cautioned her not to say anything to Rashid about her discovery. Follow a defense strategy, Sadeem advised, rather than an attack plan for which she had not amassed a large enough stock of weapons.

"You don't have any choice. You'll have to meet her and come to terms with her."

"What would I say to her? 'Stay away from my husband, you husband thief'?"

"Of course not! Sit down with her and try to find out what sort of relationship she has with your husband and how long it's been going on. You don't know! It may be that he's even hiding from her the fact that he's married."

"I'd die to know what he saw in her, this hussy with slitty eyes!"

"More important than finding out what he saw in her looks is finding out what he saw in her personality. Don't they say, Know your enemy?"

Was Gamrah right when she decided to fight for her marriage? Or is a successful marriage fundamentally a relationship that doesn't need war to guarantee its preservation? Is a marriage that demands warfare one that is preordained to fail?

Gamrah came upon Kari's telephone number and address in Rashid's pocket diary. She had a number in Japan. She also had a number in the next state over, Indiana, where Rashid had studied for his MA. Gamrah called Kari at the second number and asked to meet her. She introduced herself first. Kari answered calmly, saying she was willing and ready to come to Chicago to see her at the next available opportunity.

That was about two months after Gamrah had discovered this illicit relationship between her husband and that woman. In the interval, Gamrah had worked very hard to control her clashing emotions. She did not want Rashid to sense any change in her before she had her appointment with his lover.

During those two months, Gamrah stopped taking pills without consulting her mother, whose opinion she knew anyway: "All you've got is your children, my dear. Children are the only way to tie a man." Gamrah did not want children to be the one tie between them—or, to put it plainly, the one thing that forced Rashid to stay with her. But he was forcing her into this—let him bear the consequences of his own deeds! And let their children bear the consequences of the deeds of them both.

Dizziness, queasiness in the morning and even vomiting, which was really annoying: here were the well-known signs of pregnancy for which Gamrah had been waiting impatiently. She wanted these symptoms to appear before she called Kari. She went to the supermarket on the ground floor of their building to get something that would confirm her suspicions. She did not know exactly what she was looking for, so she turned to one of the girls who worked there, pointing at her belly with both hands and sketching a round tummy in the air.

"*I . . . I . . . I bregnent!*"

"Oh! Congratulations, ma'am."

Gamrah had never liked the English language and she had never gotten as good at it as her friends. Every year she had passed English class with difficulty, and one year she had to retake her final exam and then only passed because the teacher felt sorry for her and gave her marks higher than she deserved.

"*Noo! Noo! I . . . bregnent . . . haaw?*" She flattened both of her palms in a gesture as if to ask, *how?*

The shop attendant's brown face showed bewilderment. "Sorry, my dear, but I don't get what you mean!"

Gamrah kept pointing at herself with her index finger. "*Mee . . . mee . . . haaw bregnent? Haaw baby? Haaw?*"

The shopgirl called over two of her colleagues, and they, together with a shopper who had overheard the exchange, labored to solve the riddle of what Gamrah was trying to say. After ten more minutes of effort, Gamrah finally obtained what she was looking for: a home pregnancy test!

13.

To: seerehwenfadha7et@yahoogroups.com

From: "seerehwenfadha7et"

Date: May 7, 2004

Subject: The Face-off: Between She Who Is Worthy and She Who
Is Worthless

> *The Prophet—the blessings and peace of God be upon him—did not*
> *beat a single servant of his nor a woman, nor did he strike anything*
> *with his hand.*
>   —The hadith collection of Ibn Maja, verse 2060

I heard that King Abd Al-Aziz City* is trying to block my site to dam up the channels of communication and ward off malicious acts, scandalous deeds and all causes of corruption or evil. I know that most of you know a thousand ways to get into blocked sites. But I just might die of electrocution if this blockage happens before I can empty out (and load onto you) the charges—positive and negative—I carry in my chest, which have refused to balance each other out to neutral inside of me. I only ask for a small space on the World Wide Web to tell my stories through. Is that too much to ask?

*The Internet provider company in Saudi Arabia.

After spending several long hours at the hairdresser's and after putting on some of her expensive jewelry that she had not worn once since leaving Riyadh, Gamrah headed for the hotel where Kari was staying. On her way there, she warned the wicked little demon in her head against persuading her to strangle this fallen woman the moment she saw her.

Kari—and Gamrah later showed me a picture of the Chinese actress Lucy Liu, telling me Kari was the spitting image of Lucy—came down into the lobby. The waiting had been killing Gamrah. This woman put out her hand, but Gamrah didn't take it. Gamrah was still fighting a battle with the little devil in her head.

The meeting took a direction that wasn't exactly the one Sadeem had predicted. It was Kari who steered the conversation, beginning and ending her words with firmness and confidence, without any sign of confusion, and without stumbling over her English even a little. Unlike her adversary.

"I am happy to meet you. I have heard a lot about you from Rashid. I think your wanting to meet me shows wisdom on your part."

This blasted woman! How dare she!

"It pleases me, naturally, for you to see me, so that you can form an idea of what your husband loves. Rashid has suffered a lot, and you must work to improve yourself, from the inside and out, so that you can move up to the standard he wants and needs. So that you can come up to my level."

Gamrah, who had never expected an offensive such as this, found that the cat had gotten hold of her tongue. Even without understanding Kari's speech completely, what Gamrah did absorb was enough to make her suddenly snap out of her stunned silence and explode in Kari's face, cursing in weak English and in Arabic, too. Kari burst into shameless laughter at the furious sentences that made absolutely no sense, and Gamrah felt herself getting smaller and weaker in front of her. Utterly brazen, Kari took out her cell phone and called up Rashid while his wife watched. She told him that she was in Chicago and was on her way to see him, and would come to wherever he was.

Gamrah didn't need any astrology book to tell her what sort of an expression Rashid the Leo would have on his face when he showed up at home after his lover had personally told him everything that had taken place between her and his wife. That was the reason Gamrah had delayed meeting the fallen woman until she was sure that she was pregnant. She had long heard her mother and female relatives repeating the wisdom of previous generations, that if all else fails, pregnancy was the only way to ensure that a marriage continues. (Notice that I say *continues* and not *succeeds*.)

Less than an hour after Gamrah had seen Kari, Rashid came home. If only he had not.

"C'mon. Get up!"

"Where are we going?"

"You're going to apologize to Kari for what you did to her and for the garbage you said to her. These stupid things you do aren't going to work with someone like me. Got that? If your family didn't know how to raise you, well, then I'll have to do it myself!"

"You're not going to tell me what to do! I will *never* apologize to that Filipino! And for what? And who should do the apologizing?"

Rashid grabbed her arm and yanked. "Look, lady! You're the one who is going and you're the one who is apologizing. And after that you are getting on the first airplane out of here and you are going back to your family and I don't want to see your face here ever again. I'm not a man that a woman like you is going to order around!"

"Yeah, right! So I'm *the one who wasn't raised properly!* And what about you, mister? Cheating on me with that Asian housemaid!"

The slap landed on her right cheek, and the sound of it echoed in her head.

"That 'maid' is as good as you, and she's worth your whole family, too, do you understand? At least her father didn't come kissing up to my father so he could marry his daughter to a man who he knew loved someone in America and had been living with her for seven years! This housemaid loved me and stood next to me and gave me a place to live when I wasn't getting a penny from home, when my family refused to let us get married and cut off my money for three years! *She* didn't run after me because of money and my family's reputation! The one you hate so much is more honest and more honorable than you are and more than your family is, much, much more!"

After the painful slap, Gamrah's mind stopped taking anything in. Everything Rashid said after that, all the insults, were just a continuation of that never-ending slap. Without realizing what she was saying and that the timing was all wrong to confess such a thing (is it ever okay to use children as human shields during marital wars?), she said, amid her tears, touching the spot on her cheek with one hand and putting the other on her belly, "I'm pregnant."

Gamrah's voice started to fade as the scene grew more tense, while Rashid's voice got louder. Rashid had become a mass of anger, his eyes glowing like a pair of bright-red coals. His voice boomed out:

"What? Pregnant? You are pregnant! How did that happen? Who gave you permission to get pregnant? You mean you're not taking the pills? Didn't we agree there would be *no pregnancy* until I finish my PhD and we go back to Saudi? You figured you could twist my arm with these filthy tricks!"

"*Me?* I'm the one with dirty tricks? Am I the one who wanted to keep an innocent wife dangling for two years, having her work for you as a servant until you get your diploma, and then planning to throw her out like trash? Was it me who married a good girl from a good family while I was playing around with a cheap *whore?*"

The second slap came and she fell to the floor, sobbing painfully. Rashid left the apartment to run into the arms of the "unworthy one," leaving Gamrah cursing and slapping her cheeks and spitting at him, in a state of hysteria, close to madness.

14.

To: seerehwenfadha7et@yahoogroups.com

From: "seerehwenfadha7et"

Date: May 14, 2004

Subject: Of Michelle and of Faisal I Will Tell You

Love is a matter of the heart, and a person has no control over it. Human hearts lie between two fingers—the fingers of Allah the merciful—and He tilts them as He wills. If love were not so very precious and fine, then so many people, ever since the time of the prophets, would not have ventured there. The Prophet—may the blessings and peace of God be upon him—stressed that the flame of love can only be quenched by marriage. For love which is bound by the reins of chastity and piety gives no cause for shame. But if the marriage does not occur, then patience with the bitterness of disappointment is the only solution.

We have to distinguish between love as a practice and a behavior, on the one hand, and love as an emotion, on the other. It is right Islamic practice i.e., Halal to feel love, but if love turns into acts of love, such as a touch or a kiss or an embrace, it is against the law of Islam i.e., Haram. Many bad things will result, because it is difficult

for the person in love to keep that love in check. So what is the love
that we do want? We want love that changes hearts and souls. We
mean love that pushes those who have it to perform deeds that will
then get documented in history as a beautiful love story.

—Jassem Al-Mutawa'*

I have begun to get really engrossed in reading your comments on the story,
all of you out there! After my last e-mail, I received nearly one hundred messages! And I read every last one. That is because I want to be sure that we are
a people who agree to disagree. From the one who sympathizes with Gamrah
to the one who finds her pitiful, and from Rashid's supporters to those who
are really angry at him and ready to swing a blow, I can assure you that I
thoroughly enjoyed reading every one of your varied opinions, even those
I disagree with. But to those of you who ask about Michelle and say I have
neglected her for too long, I must say that I agree, and I apologize. Things
are looking good for Michelle, and how easy it is to ignore happy people!

In Faisal, Michelle found everything she had been looking for in
a man. He was not like any of the young men she had met since
settling in Saudi Arabia. The strongest indication of this difference was
that their relationship was still going strong after nearly a year, when
the longest of her relationships before Faisal had not lasted more than
three months.

Faisal was a truly cultivated guy. He knew exactly how to treat a
woman, and he didn't jump to exploit opportunities like all the other
guys did. He had quite a few friends who were women, just as Michelle
had male friends, but they both made it clear to everyone that they were
a serious couple.

*Sheikh Jassem Al-Mutawa', a famous Kuwaiti Muslim televangelist who hosts a very
well-known Arabic TV program called *Happy Nests* and is the chief editor of several
magazines and the author of many Islamic books that discuss relationships between men
and women, marriage and family matters.

Faisal's gentleness and refined behavior made Michelle rethink the bad impression she had initially formed of young men in her home country, following a number of very short-term relationships. Before getting to know Faisal, it did not even occur to her that a young Saudi man could be as romantic as young men everywhere else in the civilized world. For example, every morning when her driver took her to the university, Faisal would follow them in his own car as a sign of his devotion. She had to admit to herself that seeing him at seven-thirty in the morning maneuvering the streets of Riyadh and working hard to fight off his drowsiness just so he could be *almost* in her company tickled her heart and filled it with joy.

Michelle had never been able to explain to any of her friends, not even her close girlfriends, the sense of loss she had felt when she had to move back to Saudi Arabia from America. Even though her girlfriends understood how intensely she loathed Saudi society and its severe traditions, and even though they knew how much she mocked the restrictions that the society placed on young women, the battle of two civilizations that raged within her was so contradictory and complex that only someone with an acute intelligence and an enlightened, open-minded thinking could truly comprehend it. And then Michelle found herself in the company of Faisal, who seemed to understand exactly what she was going through. Soon, every time they were together, she told him more and more about what troubled her. After finally stumbling across a young man who understood her, after years of groping around for something that didn't seem to exist, how could she not grab the opportunity to reveal who she really was to someone?

She would meet him at Um Nuwayyir's house. Um Nuwayyir believed in love and never once tried to represent it to the four young women as something that one should be ashamed of. She was well aware that genuine love had no outlet or avenue of expression in this country. Any fledgling love relationship, no matter how innocent or pure, was sure to be seen as suspect and therefore repressed. And that, in turn, might well push the lovers over the edge and into a whole lot of bad choices. So when Michelle told Um Nuwayyir that she was determined to invite Faisal to her home in her parents' absence, since she had gotten so tired of meeting him in cafés and restaurants where they had to hide behind protective curtains as if they were fugitives, Um Nuwayyir opened the door of her own home to the hapless lovers. She did this to keep their heretofore innocent and respectable relationship from turning into something bigger before any official acknowledgment of their union was established.

Faisal grabbed Michelle's pampered little dog, Powder, and played with the tiny white poodle as he listened to Michelle tell one of her stories. She spoke English, because she felt less constrained that way.

"When I was five and we were still in America, the doctors discovered that Mama had cervical cancer. She had to have chemotherapy and then she had a hysterectomy. So she couldn't have any more babies.

"We returned to Riyadh after she finished the radiation therapy but before her hair had grown back in. As soon as we arrived, instead of consoling us, my aunt—that's my father's sister—suggested, right in front of my mother and me, that my dad should marry another woman who could give him a son to bear his name. As if I'm not enough! What's the use? If I were to try to talk about every crime committed in this hypocritical society, I would never stop talking! Daddy stood his ground and refused to marry another woman. He loved Mama and was totally attached to her, he loved her from the first time he saw her, in America, on New Year's Eve, which he was spending at a friend's. He met her that night and married her two months later. My father's family was never reconciled to that marriage, and my grandmother would grumble every time my mother visited—and she still does.

"Less than a month after we left America my father moved us back there—my father, who had dreamed of returning to his homeland so that I would grow up as a Saudi girl! But he couldn't get his relatives to respect his privacy and stay out of his business. So he emigrated again."

Every so often, Um Nuwayyir came in to check on things. She was so sweet and kind. Even though she didn't care much about tradition, she was always as protective of the four girls as if they were her own daughters, and she was completely committed to them. Um Nuwayyir would sit with the two of them for a few moments, asking Faisal about the health of his mother and siblings, none of whom she knew, of course. She wanted him to know that she cared about Michelle and that he would have to be on his best behavior. She did not want him to get "too close" to Michelle physically, either. He had to feel that they were not left alone in the house, that the caring auntie could come in at any second. After Um Nuwayyir left the room, Michelle returned to her story as the two of them munched on the special mixed nuts that Um Nuwayyir had brought from Kuwait.

"Three years later, when I was thirteen, we returned to Riyadh, and Meshaal was with us. Can you believe that it was me who chose him, from out of hundreds of children, as my brother? I really had the feeling, at the time, that I was shaping fate! I loved his black hair, which was nearly the color of mine, and his little innocent face. I felt somehow that he was close to me. He was seven months old when we adopted him. He was so cute. As soon as I saw him, I told my mother and father that this child was my brother, he was the one they were looking for.

"When we returned to Riyadh, my father had a meeting with his parents and brothers and sisters. He said to them straight out that little Meshaal was the son God had not wished to give him through Diane—my mother—and that they were all to respect his choice, and that they were not to reveal this secret in front of Meshaal, ever. Close relatives were the only ones who knew about my mother's illness because no one had seen her here throughout her illness and treatment, and my father did not permit the news to get out.

"My father gave his family a choice: if they wanted him to stay, they could accept his decision and his family. If they didn't accept, he would return to live in the States. After a week of family conferences, the family agreed to accept little Meshaal as one of their own. My father was sure that they would agree, not because they loved him but because the family business urgently needed my father's expertise. We went back to America just to tie up everything there, and one year later, the four of us were back in Riyadh, beginning a new stage of our lives."

She had gotten used to Faisal's silences when she was speaking, especially if it was something moving and sad like this, but she was a little afraid of his silence this time. She started searching in his eyes for some reaction, some response that would hint at what he was thinking about after hearing her story. When she didn't find anything to reassure her, she added sadly, "We're not afraid of anyone. We didn't hide where Meshaal came from out of embarrassment or anything. Believe me, my father was ready to broadcast the truth on the pages of national newspapers and magazines, if it were not for his sure sense that his society in Saudi would not accept his adopted son with the same welcome that his wife's society in America would welcome him. Isn't it sad to have to hide a truth like this from Meshaal and from my friends? I wish I could tell them, but they wouldn't understand. They would call him painful names behind his back and treat him badly. And that is what I won't accept! It is my father's and mother's life and they chose to live it in this way, so why did everyone try to interfere in their business? Why am I forced to act a part in front of others? Why doesn't this society respect the difference between my family and other Saudi families? Everyone considers me a bad girl just because my mother is American! How can I live in such an unjust society? Tell me how, Faisal!"

She burst into tears, which she had found she even enjoyed when she was with him. He was the only one who knew how many tears exactly he had to let her spill before he could gently tease her to get her to stop crying. He was the only one who knew that she would laugh in spite of herself if he brought her the soft butter milk candy of her childhood or a can of her favorite strawberry soda from the nearest grocery shop.

Faisal, this time, was keeping his thoughts to himself. He comforted her gently as he imagined the conversation he would have with his mother as soon as he returned home. He had tried to postpone this conversation many times, but this time he was determined to open (or close) the subject with his mother once and for all.

God help us! he said to himself, and left.

15.

To: seerehwenfadha7et@yahoogroups.com

From: "seerehwenfadha7et"

Date: May 21, 2004

Subject: My Heart! My Heart!

I know that all of you are dying to know what happened between Faisal and his mother, and so we return today to the chapter of Faisal and Michelle. Dear Michelle, who is such a source of gossip because people are convinced that I am her (if I am not Sadeem)! It seems that I am Michelle whenever I use English expressions. But then, just the next week, when I type out a poem by Nizar Qabbani, I become Sadeem. What a schizophrenic life I lead!

The minute Um Faisal heard the English name *Michelle*, one hundred devils swarmed into her head. Faisal hastily tried to correct his mistake. People called her Michelle but her real name was purely Saudi, Mashael, he assured his mother.

"She is Mashael Al-Abdulrahman."

A searing look from his mother's eyes scared him and halted his tongue. He worried suddenly that some ancient quarrel existed between the two families. But it quickly became clear to him that the problem was that his mother had never before heard the name of this family.

"Who do you mean, *Al-Abdulrahman*? Abdul is the servant and Rahman is the Merciful, one of Allah's several names. So she comes from the family of the servant of God, just like any Abdullah or Abdullatif or Abdulaziz. All are names of God. But do you know how many servants of God there are? We all are! So what makes this Abdul Rahman special?"

Michelle's family name—"Servant of the Merciful"—was as common as the epithet suggested it could be. Apparently, the name had never ascended to the ranks of families who formed alliances with—or even mixed with—the family of Al-Batran. Faisal tried to explain to his mother that Michelle's father had only been settled in the country for a few years, and maybe that was why his name was not yet known to many in Riyadh society.

His mother didn't get it. "Who are his brothers?" she demanded to know. Faisal answered energetically that Michelle's father was *the most successful* of the Al-Abdulrahmans. It was just that, since returning from America, where he had lived for many years, this Al-Abdulrahman had customarily mixed only with people who had the same cultural outlook and ideas.

That just made his mother angrier.

The family of that girl was not of their sort. They must ask Faisal's father, since he knew infinitely more about genealogies and families. But from the start, his mother suggested, this line of conversation did not augur well. The girl had tricked him! *Aah,* the girls of this generation! How awful they were! And *aah,* for her young, green son—she never would have expected *him* to fall into the trap of a girl such as this! She asked him who the girl's maternal uncles were and as soon as she heard that the girl's mother was American, she decided to bang the door shut *for good* on this fruitless dialogue around this utterly ridiculous topic. So, like countless mothers before her, she resorted to the oldest trick in the book:

"Quick, son! Get up, hurry, get me my blood pressure medicine! My heart, oh, my heart! I think I'm dying . . ."

Faisal tried hard. It must be said that he really tried hard to convince her, to get her to see Michelle's many exceptional qualities, or, in the horse-trading language of mothers looking to make a match, her "fine attributes." He went on and on about things that meant nothing to her. Mashael was a cultured, educated girl; she was a university student whose potpourri of Eastern and Western thinking he really liked and admired. The girl understood him; the girl was sophisticated and not straight out of the village like all of the other girls he had met or those his mother had hinted strongly about marrying him off to. The simple truth of it was the one thing that he could not say plainly to his mother: the girl loved him and he loved her. He loved her even more than she loved him, he was sure.

Faisal's mother gulped down her pills. (If they didn't help, at least they didn't hurt.) She wept hot tears and she stroked his hair gently as she talked about her great hopes to marry her youngest son to the best of girls, to give him the best home there ever was, and the best automobile, plus all-expense-paid tickets to spend the best honeymoon ever.

Poor miserable Faisal! He cried, too, poor Little Faisal under the feet of his cherished mother. He loved no one in the universe more than his mother, and he had never opposed her, never ever, never in his life. He wept also for the sophisticated girl, his beloved who understood him and whom he understood, more than any two people in this world could ever understand each other, Michelle with her Najdi beauty and American personality, who would not be his.

16.

To: seerehwenfadha7et@yahoogroups.com

From: "seerehwenfadha7et"

Date: May 28, 2004

Subject: Is *This* Emotional Stability?

Lots of you folks out there simply did not believe what Faisal did. Or, to put it more accurately, what he did not do. Let me assure you, though, that this is exactly what happened. He told Michelle the sordid details of the back-and-forth with his mother—which I in turn conveyed to you—but only after several weeks of confused mental meandering, several weeks of self-punishment, several weeks of war between a passionate heart and a head that knew exactly what the limitations—set down long ago by his family—were in the choices he would have in life.

I can't understand why all of you are so surprised! Such tales happen among us every day, and yet no one has an inkling of it except the two people who get scorched at the scene of the fire. Where do you think all of these sad poems and wailing, melancholic songs of our heritage came from? And today, poetry pages in newspapers, radio and TV programs, and literary chat rooms on the Internet all draw their nourishment from such tales, such heartbreaks.

I will tell you the things that happen inside our homes and the feelings that grip us—we, the girls of Riyadh—when such things happen to us. I will not attempt to access the contents of the manly crocodile chests out there because to put it simply, I don't know enough about the nature of crocodiles. Frankly, crocodiles are not among my spheres of expertise or interest. I speak only of my female friends; the rest is up to someone who is feeling crocodilish enough to want to say something about his friends. That crocodile should definitely write to me and inform me of what goes on in the swamps they inhabit, because we—the lizards—are in truly desperate need! We really do long to know their thoughts and understand their motives, which always seem to be so deeply hidden away from us.

All hell broke loose for some after my last e-mail about Faisal and Michelle. Unfortunately, some people can always be heard over everybody else because they are proud practitioners of the questionable philosophy that the loudest voice beats all. If they are so eager to stir things up, wouldn't it be a better use of their time for these vengeful types to wag their tongues against repugnant ideas and outdated traditions like tribal prejudice,* rather than against people who merely try to get some discussion going about how offensive these practices are?

Everyone is condemning my bold writing, and perhaps my boldness in writing at all. Everyone is blaming me for the fury I have stirred up around "taboo" topics that in this society we have never been accustomed to discussing so frankly and especially when the opening salvos come from a young woman like me. But isn't there a starting point for every drastic social change?

And this I believe: I might find a few stray people who believe in my cause right now, or I might not, but I doubt that I would find many people opposed to it if I were to look half a century into the future.

*Among the different subclassifications of Saudi society, there are the tribals and the nontribals. Between those two classes/sectors there can be no marriages. A tribal family is one that can be traced to one of the well-known Arabic tribes.

G amrah's permanent return to her family's home was billed as a routine visit. Her mother, who knew everything that had happened, thought it wisest to hide the truth from everyone. "A summer cloud"—that was how she described her daughter's quarrel with Rashid and his threat to divorce her. Her mother decided not to tell even Gamrah's father, who was in North Africa on holiday. After all, the man had never taken any interest in the personal lives of anyone in the household and he never would. Gamrah's mother had always been the organizing mastermind, the mover and shaker of the household, and she always would remain so.

When various women visited, pouring out their congratulations on her pregnancy, Gamrah repeated what she had rehearsed with her mother:

"Rashid, poor man, is at the university night and day—he won't even take any time off on holidays. The minute he realized I was pregnant, he insisted that I must give my family the good news in person, the darling! A month or so here, and I'll go back. I know he can't stand waiting for me any longer than that!"

In private, her mother would say, "There will be no divorce in our family. I don't care if your brother did divorce his wife. *Al-Qusmanji girls* never get divorced!"

But Rashid the jerk did not let things go long enough to give Gamrah's mother time to think of a solution. In a virtual reenactment of Sadeem's tragedy, the divorce papers were delivered to Gamrah's father two weeks after Gamrah landed in Riyadh, effectively blocking all possible maternal machinations. It appeared as though Rashid had just been waiting for the moment in which he felt he could justifiably rid himself of the wife that had been imposed on him by his family.

The divorce document was not particularly gruesome-looking in itself, but its contents were indeed pretty horrifying. When her brother handed it to her, Gamrah read the lines of script and collapsed onto the nearest chair, screaming, "*Yummah!** *Yummah*, Mama, he divorced me! *Yummah*, Rashid divorced me! It's all over, he divorced me!" Her mother took Gamrah into her arms, weeping and cursing the wrongdoer with vile invectives: "God burn your heart to ashes and the heart of your mother, too, Rashid, like you've burned up my heart over my little girl."

GAMRAH'S SISTER HESSAH, who had gotten married a year before Gamrah and had been eight months pregnant at Gamrah's wedding, joined her sister and mother in hurling curses, but in her case they were directed at all men. She, too, had suffered since getting married. Her husband Khalid, who had been mild-tempered and tender through the entire engagement period, had turned into another person immediately after marriage, when he became completely aloof and uninterested in her. Hessah complained constantly to her mother about his neglect. When she got sick, he would not take her to the doctor. And when she got pregnant, it was her mother who accompanied her to the standard pregnancy checkups. Once the baby girl arrived, her older sister Naflah had to go with her to buy the necessary baby products. What infuriated Hessah most in Khalid was his lack of generosity with her, since she knew he had a lot of money and he certainly was not stingy about his own expenditures. He refused to give his wife monthly expense money the way her sister Naflah's husband did and the way her father did for her mother. Instead, he handed money over for each specific item she wanted to buy, and even then only when she had harassed him to the point where she felt humiliated.

If she needed a new dress to wear to her cousin's wedding and asked him for three thousand riyals, he would come up with whatever excuse he could find to avoid giving her the money: "No need for the dress, you have lots of dresses." Or, "Didn't I buy you a dress six months ago?" Or, "I have barely enough money. Go and get it from your father, he's always

*"Mama" can also be used as an expression to indicate surprise or fear ("Oh, God!").

buying one of your brothers a new car, or did they dump you on me so they could rid themselves of your ridiculous demands?" Or some other equally outrageous comment that generally succeeded in getting her to turn her eyes away from whatever it was she happened to need or want. On those rare occasions when he did give her money, he would give her five hundred instead of the three thousand she had asked for, or fifty if, hoping to spare herself his humiliating response, she had only asked for the five hundred in the first place. And for some reason that escaped her, his mother encouraged him. In fact, the Scorpion (as she had nicknamed her mother-in-law) positively applauded her darling son Khalid for being so stingy with his wife. That's how a good Najdi man should be. It was how her husband, Khalid's father, treated her all those years.

Gamrah suffered a great deal of pain as a result of her divorce from Rashid. Though Sadeem had told her how excruciating her official separation from Waleed had been, Gamrah was overwhelmed in a way that Sadeem had not prepared her for. Nighttime was the worst. Since returning to the family home, she had been unable to sleep for more than three hours a night—she, who had never found it hard to sleep ten—or twenty—hours at a stretch before her marriage, and even during it! Now she would wake up tormented in anguish. Was this the "emotional instability" that was such a popular topic of conversation among her unmarried girlfriends? She had never once been aware of the importance of Rashid's presence in her life until he left it.

Lying in bed on her side, she would extend her right leg full length and when her foot would not collide with Rashid's, she would turn over restlessly. She would recite the two talismans and the protective Throne Verse from the Qur'an and all of the bedtime prayers she had ever memorized, and then she would clutch her pillow and lie on her stomach. Finally, she would doze off, her head at the upper right corner of the mattress and her feet stretched down to the bottom left corner. Only when she lay down on the diagonal like this could she fill the big emptiness that Rashid had created in her bed, but only a small part of the emptiness that he had created in her life.

17.

To: seerehwenfadha7et@yahoogroups.com

From: "seerehwenfadha7et"

Date: June 4, 2004

Subject: All I Need Is Another Saudi!

Have We not laid your chest open for you, and put aside your burden
for you, that burden which weighed heavily on your back even as it
exalted your mention among people? For with hardship comes ease;
indeed, with hardship comes ease.
   —Qur'an, Surat Al-Sharh
   (chapter of easing), verses 1–8

During the past few weeks, I have been reading news stories that
talk about me, or let's say, about my e-mails! Eminent national newspapers are writing about

   a prevailing uproar here, and behind it is an anonymous young
   woman who sends an e-mail every Friday to a large number of Internet users in Saudi Arabia. In these e-mails, she tells the stories of
   her four female friends, Gamrah Al-Qusmanji, Sadeem Al-Horaimli,

Lamees Jeddawi and Michelle Al-Abdulrahman. The girls belong to society's "velvet class," an elite whose behavior is normally kept hidden to all but themselves.

Each week, the writer reveals new and thrilling developments, leading her ever-widening circle of eager readers to await Friday noon prayers breathlessly. Every Saturday morning, government offices, meeting halls, hospital corridors and school classrooms metamorphose into arenas for debate about the latest e-mail. Everyone weighs in. There are those who support this young woman and those who object to her. There are those who believe that what these girls are doing is perfectly natural (and also is no secret) and there are others who boil with rage at the revelation of what they consider to be the excesses that are going on around them in our conservative society.

Whatever the outcome, there is no doubt whatsoever that these strange and unusual e-mails have created a furor in our society, which has never before experienced anything like this. It is clear that these e-mails will continue to furnish fertile material for exchange and debate for a long time to come, even after the e-mails cease to appear.

Sadeem began to enjoy her job at the HSBC Bank. Everyone treated her affectionately and politely. She was the youngest worker there, and people went out of their way to offer her help and advice. She was especially comfortable with Tahir, a Muslim Pakistani colleague who was the cheeriest and most fun of everyone.

The work was not burdensome. Her duties were limited to receiving people who came into the bank for information and helping them to fill out forms, or sorting and filing papers.

She wasn't attracted to any of her fellow workers, so she behaved unself-consciously with everyone. Even better, there wasn't a single other Arab among them, so she felt free to act as if she were one of them, joking with this one and laughing with that one, and putting no constraints on herself as she normally did when she was with a group of Arabs, especially people from the Gulf and particularly Saudis.

One day as the bank was closing, Edward, a colleague with blue eyes, black hair and a charming Irish accent, suggested that they all go to the Piano Bar on Kensington High Street. Sadeem agreed to come, since a whole group of people including Tahir was going and since the bar they were heading for was not far from her apartment. Tahir had planned to meet a friend at the bar and then go on to the movies. Sadeem announced that she would leave whenever Tahir did. He had become like a big brother in whose presence she felt relaxed and secure.

At the bar, Sadeem's eyes kept straying over to the piano. A line of glasses sat on the piano's transparent glass cover. The piano made her think of the white piano in her aunt Badriyyah's old home in Riyadh. Tariq, her aunt's son, had taken piano lessons and had taught her everything he learned.

Sadeem made the bold decision to try to play the piano even though it had been seven years since she had last played. She apologized in advance and began to attack the keys almost at random until she found the right note. She went back to the beginning and this time played a recognizable tune, a piece by Omar Khayrat, her favorite composer.

About to enter the pub where he was to pick up Tahir, Firas was stopped in his tracks by the familiar Arabic melody coming from within. From his position on the stairs, he peered through the glass window and caught sight of a very attractive young woman sitting at the piano. He stayed where he was, listening to her play until the sound of applause rose and the girl returned to her seat.

Firas descended the remaining steps and walked over to his friend's table. He gave a quick greeting to the group and asked Tahir to hurry up so that they could get to the film in time, leaving no time for Tahir to introduce him to the group.

Tahir turned to Sadeem and asked if she was sure she didn't want to come to the nearby Cinema Odeon with them. She declined, wishing them a pleasant time, but gathered her things to walk out with them, as she didn't want to stay at the bar without Tahir. Outside, they headed left toward the cinema while she turned right, walking toward her flat.

A WEEK LATER Tahir threw a party for his thirtieth birthday at the Collection Pub and Bar at South Kensington. There, Firas saw Sadeem for the second time. He walked over to her just as she settled herself down on one of the chairs.

"My sister here is an Arab?"

Sadeem's eyes flew open. "You're an Arab?"

"Saudi, in fact. My name is Firas Al-Sharqawi."

"I'm Sadeem Al-Horaimli. I'm so sorry, I assumed you were Pakistani like Tahir."

He laughed at her embarrassed frankness. "What about you? Anyone looking at you would swear you're Spanish! Even your English—*ma shaa Allah!* It's perfect."

"I'm Saudi, too."

He smiled. "It's an honor to meet you."

Sadeem was not at all so thrilled to meet him, now that she knew he was Saudi. "Yes, well, hello; nice to meet you, too."

"I heard you the other day playing the piano and I knew you must be Arab, and then when I asked Tahir he told me you're Saudi."

"Really? I don't recall you being there when I was playing."

"I stayed hidden on the stairs and watched you through the glass. It's the first time I've heard Eastern music in the Piano Bar. I thought your playing was amazing."

"Thank you— that's very kind." Sadeem picked up her handbag from where it was resting on the chair next to her. "Well, I have to go now. Excuse me."

"It's early!"

"I have an appointment."

"Okay, but why don't you wait a little—at least until you have had a chance to say good-bye to Tahir? He's probably downstairs at the bar."

"I can't. Please, if you see him, give him my best and tell him I'm sorry, I had to leave."

"Good-bye, and I hope I didn't bother you. Anyway, it was nice to have a chance to see you again."

Bother me? You could say that! Just a few words from you and I can feel all my old bitterness rising up inside me like a volcano. What do you expect, though? You're Saudi!

"It was very nice indeed. 'Bye."

Sadeem returned home, cursing her luck at the revelation that Tahir's friend was Saudi. She began reviewing in her mind every single thing that had happened that night at the Piano Bar the week before. Had she committed any of the transgressions that a young Saudi guy must not see coming from a daughter of his country? Had she said anything opinionated, bold, inappropriate? Had she been wearing something that was respectable enough?

God pluck him from this earth! What brought him here anyway! So, even in this place I can't relax and behave naturally? These Saudis are always after me! Always in my face! Almighty God. I bet he makes a scandal out of what he's seen, and tomorrow every breath of mine will be broadcast in Riyadh! God not spare you, Tahir, you and your friend. What was it he said: Our sister here is an Arab? Ahh, what a line!

Early the next week, Sadeem asked Tahir about Firas and scolded him for not telling her where he was from. Tahir vehemently denied that he had done it deliberately. Firas was not the type of guy that should worry her, he reassured her. He had known Firas, he said, for a long time—they had gone to the University of Westminster together. Firas had been studying for a doctorate in political science while Tahir was finishing his master's thesis in accounting. They had shared a room in the university housing in Marylebone Hall for six months. What they liked best about the residence hall was its closeness to the major mosque in Regent's Park, where they were regulars at Friday prayer service. After Tahir had gotten his degree he moved to his own flat in Maida Vale. A bit later, Firas also moved, to live in the rooms he still had in St. John's Wood. Firas had remained a dear friend and Tahir felt lucky to have him.

In the days to follow, Tahir did not volunteer any more information about Firas and Sadeem did not ask. She was apprehensive, though, that Tahir had told Firas of her discomfort at the birthday party. How mortifying that would be for her! In general, everyone understood that Saudi girls were more at ease mixing with men who were not Saudi. Firas would not be the first, or the last, to experience the shock of finding that a girl from his home country would much rather hang out with his Pakistani friend than with him.

Though Sadeem was, relatively speaking, free of the kinds of constraints and worries of most Saudi girls because she had a *somewhat* liberal father and though normally she really couldn't care less about what others said or thought, she did wish, this one time, that she could have the opportunity to meet this particular man again so she could get a sense of the impression she had made on him. It troubled her to think that perhaps he thought badly of her, for even though she didn't know him, he was a Saudi, after all, and he might just stir up a storm of talk around her that could blow from London as far as Riyadh.

Sadeem had gotten into the habit of spending every Saturday morning shopping in the stores on Oxford Street and then spending a few hours at Borders. She liked to browse through all the nooks and crannies of the enormous five-story bookstore, reading magazines and listening to the latest CDs, after getting a light breakfast at the Starbucks inside.

That's where she found him. For the third time in a row, fate had arranged a suitable and respectable chance meeting for her with this stranger. *That must mean something,* thought Sadeem, and one of Um Nuwayyir's favorite expressions popped into her head: *The third time's a charm.*

Firas was absorbed in reading a newspaper, a cup of coffee in his right hand. Papers and a laptop lay in disarray on the table in front of him.

Should I go over and say hi to him? What if he decides to be rude and pretends he doesn't know me? Yallah, *whatever. I haven't got anything to lose, so . . .* She turned toward him and greeted him nicely. He got up and shook her hand respectfully, and his "How are you, Sadeem? How nice to see you" erased whatever ill thoughts she had had of him. They stood beside his table chatting. After a few minutes, he helped her move her coffee and cheese croissant from her table to his so that she would not have to eat alone.

Their conversation flowed easily and pleasantly. Somehow, over the course of the conversation, she forgot that this was the very guy, the very Saudi, whose tongue she had wanted to cut out before he could start spreading gossip about her. She asked him about his university and the topic of his dissertation, and he asked her about her studies and her summer job. When she asked what all the scattered papers in front of them were, he confessed that he had intended to read more than two hundred pages this morning, but, as usual for him, he had not been able to resist the temptation of a fresh, crackly newspaper. With childish naughtiness, he hid from her what was sitting on the chair next to his—another stack of newspapers. She laughed at him. He claimed that all he had bought this morning was *Al-Hayat, Asharq Alawsat,* and the *Times,* which he had read cover to cover instead of reading his mountain of academic papers.

As their conversation continued, Sadeem was stunned by his sophisticated appreciation of and familiarity with music and art. When he made her promise to listen to the soprano Louisa Kennedy's rendition of the "Queen of the Night" aria from Mozart's *The Magic Flute,* she thought that he was one of the most cultivated men she had ever met.

Their conversation shifted to the topic of the amount of Gulf tourists who flowed into London every year in that season. Sadeem let her biting, critical humor go unrestrained. Firas, it turned out, loved nothing more than a good joke. Together they filled the café air with their warm laughter.

The chemistry between them became so thick that it hovered and swooped around their heads like cartoon sparrows. Sadeem noticed that a hard rain had started to pelt the sidewalks, even though the sun had been shining brightly just before. Firas offered to drive her to her flat— or anywhere else she wanted—and she refused politely, thanking him for the nice offer. She told him she would finish her shopping nearby and then take a taxi or bus home. He did not insist, but he asked her to wait a few minutes while he went to get something from his car.

He came back carrying an umbrella and raincoat, and he handed them both to her. She tried to convince him to keep one of them, but he stood firm, so she accepted them with thanks and good wishes.

Before they parted, Sadeem hoped he would be bold enough to ask for her telephone number so that they wouldn't have to leave the next meeting to chance, especially since she only had a few days left in London before she had to return to Riyadh to resume her studies. He disappointed her, though, putting out his hand to say good-bye and thanking her pleasantly for her company. She went back to her flat, every step carrying her farther away from the happy ending to a story that had not even had a chance to begin.

18.

To: seerehwenfadha7et@yahoogroups.com
From: "seerehwenfadha7et"
Date: June 11, 2004
Subject: A Society Riddled with Contradictions

> *The noble Prophet, God's blessings and peace be upon him, married Arab women and non-Arab women; women of his tribe, Quraish, and women who were not of Quraish; Muslims and non-Muslims; Christians and Jews who converted to Islam before he consummated the marriages; women who had been married before and virgins.*
> —Amr Khaled*

I've noticed that recently my e-mails have (finally!) begun to get approval from members of my own sex, although most of the encouraging letters I get are from males, bless them! I can just imagine the scenario: your average girl, week after week, sits hunched over her computer every Friday after prayers waiting for my e-mail to come up, and the minute it does she

---

*Amr Khaled is an Egyptian Muslim activist and preacher. His popularity has now grown all over Arab countries. He is one of the most influential televangelists and authors in the Arab world.

frantically scans it for any sign of resemblance to herself. When she doesn't find any, she breathes a sigh of relief and then calls her friends to make sure they're also in the clear, and they all congratulate each other for having safely avoided scandal for yet another week! But should she find anything that remotely resembles an incident she went through some years ago, or a street that one of my characters walked on sounded like the street near her uncle's house in the suburbs, then all hell would break loose on me.

I get a lot of e-mails that are threatening and scolding: Wallah, we will reveal you the same way you revealed us! We know who you are! You're that girl, the daughter of my sister-in-law's uncle's niece! You're just jealous because your cousin proposed to me and not you! Or, you're the big-mouth daughter of our old neighbors in Manfooha, so jealous because we moved to Olayya and you're still stuck in that awful place.*

Faisal told Michelle half the truth. Sitting across from her in their favorite restaurant, he told her that his mother had not supported the idea of his marrying her, and he told her about the dramatic nature of the exchange, but he left it for Michelle to deduce the obvious reasons behind his mother's anger. Michelle could not believe her ears. Was *this* the Faisal who had dazzled her with his open-mindedness? Was he seriously letting go of her as easily as this just because his mother wanted to marry him to a girl from their own social circles? A stupid naïve little girl who was no different from a million others? Was this how Faisal was going to end up? Was he really no different from the other trivial young men whom she despised?

It came as a severe shock to Michelle. Faisal didn't even try to make any excuses for himself because he knew that he wouldn't be able to change anything no matter what he said, so his position seemed weak and his reaction cold. All he said was that he hoped Michelle would consider

*Manfooha is a very old and urban area south of Riyadh, and Olayya is a bustling area in Riyadh where real estate prices are high.

what the consequences would be if he were to challenge his family; there was no power on earth, he said, that could block or lessen the awful things they would do to hurt both him and her, if he insisted on marrying Michelle. She would never be accepted by his family, and their children would suffer for it. He had not even made an attempt to object to his mother because of the utter futility of it. It was not because he didn't love her, he said. But *they* didn't believe in love! *They* believed only in their inherited beliefs and their traditions from across the generations, and so how could one possibly hope to convince them otherwise?

Michelle remained absolutely silent and still, staring across the table into the face which she seemed no longer to recognize. He held her hands to his face, moistening her palms with his tears before he said good-bye and stood up to leave. The last thing he said to her before he left was that she was lucky, because she was not from the kind of family he was from. Her life was simpler and clearer and her decisions were her own, not those of the "tribe." She was better off without him and his family. Her wonderful free spirit would not be sullied by *their* rules; *their* poisonous thoughts and insidious ways would not destroy her goodness.

Faisal distanced himself from his beloved Michelle. He put before her the ugly truth and then he fled even from his responsibility to deal with her reaction. He left her sitting in the restaurant silent and alone so he would not see the reflection of his own disfigured image in her eyes. Poor Faisal! It wasn't his pride that made him abandon her. It was just that in spite of everything he wanted to preserve a beautiful memory of her love for him.

With a great deal of patience and will and a sincere desire to surmount grief, and with the help of God, who knew how harsh her suffering was, Michelle began the process of peeling away the pain. Aided by her righteous scorn and her stubbornness, she decided to let the trailing hems of their beautiful past slip through her hands.

She hoped that time would heal her and that her joy in simple things would return to her life. When this did not happen, she took the uncommon step of seeing a shrink. She went to an Egyptian psychiatrist referred to her by Um Nuwayyir, who had seen him during the first stages of her divorce.

She found no chaise longue to stretch out on there; there would be no "free association" allowed. The shrink seemed quite conservative in the way he dealt with her, and he didn't appear able to handle her grief-filled question whose answer would remain hidden from her for as long as she lived: What more could I have done or said to make him stay?

After four visits, all Michelle discovered about herself was that she needed a more profound cure than anything she would find in the words she heard from this primitive physician. In discussing Faisal's deception, the good doctor said it all boiled down to the story of the wolf enticing the ewe to his lair before devouring her. Well, she was no bleating sheep and her darling Faisal was certainly no wolf. Was this the most brilliant and cutting-edge insight that the discipline of psychology had produced among the Arabs? And how could a male Egyptian shrink understand the dimensions of a problem that afflicted her female Saudi self anyway, with the enormous gap in social background that their nationalities entailed, since Saudi Arabia has a unique social setting that makes its people unlike any others? In spite of the wound that Faisal had inflicted, Michelle was sure that Faisal had loved her truly and fiercely, and that he still loved her as she loved him. But he was weak and passive and submissive to the will of a society that paralyzed its members. It was a society riddled with hypocrisy, drugged by contradictions, and her only choice was to either accept those contradictions and bow to them, or leave her country to live in freedom.

This time when she proposed the idea of studying abroad to her father, she did not face an immediate refusal as she had a year ago. It may be that the weight she had lost and the paleness that taken hold of her face in recent weeks had an effect on his decision. The atmosphere of their home had become very bleak with her depression and the departure of her brother Meshaal to Switzerland for his summer boarding school. Her parents agreed to let Michelle go to San Francisco, where her uncle lived. On that very day, she wrote to all of the colleges and universities in San Francisco; she was determined to not lose the opportunity to register before the beginning of the new school year.

All Michelle wanted was to hear that she had been accepted in one of the schools there so that she could bundle up her belongings and turn her back on a country where people were governed—or herded—like animals, as she said to herself over and over. She would not allow anyone to tell her what she could and could not do! Otherwise, what was the point of life? It was her life, only hers, and she was going to live it the way she wanted, for herself and herself only.

19.

To: seerehwenfadha7et@yahoogroups.com
From: "seerehwenfadha7et"
Date: June 18, 2004
Subject: Among the Stars . . . Above the Clouds

My inbox is on fire with exploding e-mails. Some have warned me that I'm getting too close to the red line. Others tell me that I've already crossed it and that I will surely be punished for interfering in other people's affairs, and (worse) for becoming a role model to others who might be tempted to challenge our society's traditions with such audacity, brazen insolence, and self-assurance.

Hey, don't shoot the messenger!

On the walkway into the airplane Sadeem wept, as if she were trying to rid herself of whatever tears remained inside before going back to Riyadh. She wanted to return to her old life there, her life before Waleed. She wanted to go back to her university and her studies and her hard work, to her intimate friends and the good times at Auntie Um Nuwayyir's house.

She took her seat in the first-class cabin, put the earphones to her Walkman on and closed her eyes, as the beautiful music of Abdulmajeed Abdullah, one of her favorite Saudi singers, washed over her.

Among the stars up here,
above the clouds serene
I wash blues with hues of joy
all the anguish I wash clean.

To occupy her time as she flew toward her homeland, Sadeem had chosen a collection of songs that could not have been more different from those that took her to London. This time, she intended to say fare-well to the sadness that overtook her when she broke with Waleed. She had decided to bury her grief in London's dirt and return to Riyadh with the high spirits a young woman of her age ought to have.

After the seatbelt light went out, Sadeem headed—as she always did on any international flight—to the WC to put on her *abaya*. She could not bear putting this task off until just before the plane landed in the kingdom, when the women were all lined up, and so were the men, down the aisle, waiting to get into the toilets to put on their official garb. The women would put on their long *abayas,* head coverings and face veils, while the men stripped off their suits and ties, including the belts that they always tightened under their bellies so that one could see how rippling-full of flesh and fat and curds and whey they were, to return to the white *thobes* that concealed their mealtime sins and the red *shimaghs* that covered their bald pates.

As she made her way back to her seat, she caught sight of a man who, it seemed to her, was smiling at her from a distance. She squinted and frowned to make out his features more clearly. How much easier it would be if she were able to put in her corrective contact lenses herself instead of depending on the eye specialist at the shop to put them in for her! When she reached her seat, though, only four steps separated her from that young man's row. She saw who it was! A gasp escaped her, louder than it should have been, loud enough to embarrass her. It revealed her enthusiasm, which of course would have been hard to explain in public.

"Firas!"

She went the rest of the way to him. He rose, welcoming her with obvious delight and then asking her to sit in the seat next to his, which fate had decreed would be empty.

"How are you, Sadeem? What a wonderful coincidence!"

"God sweeten your days! *Wallah,* seriously, a lovely coincidence. I never imagined I would see you after that day in the bookstore."

"And you know what? I was on the waiting list for this flight. I mean, I wasn't sure that I would even be traveling tonight! A God-given grace! But then, thank goodness you got up to go put on your *abaya*, or I never would have seen you!"

"It's strange, isn't it?! And look at you! You've got your *thobe* on before you even get on the airplane."

"Yeah, well, I don't like to change my clothes on the airplane. Makes me feel like I'm schizoid. As if I'm Dr. Jekyll about to change into Mr. Hyde."

"Ha ha! It's pretty impressive that you recognized me even though I was in my *abaya* and hair cover."

"As a matter of fact, you happen to look terribly cute in your *abaya*."

Was this man serious? Was his taste really that appalling or did he think she was so hideous that he preferred it when she was covered and wrapped in her *abaya* to spare him the sight?

"Oh, thank you. I guess beauty is in the eye of the beholder. By the way, I still have your umbrella and raincoat, you know!"

"Of course. I gave them to you to keep."

"I hope you didn't get sick that day because of me."

"No, *Alhamdu lillah*, thank God. When you live in London, you get used to leaving your umbrella and raincoat in the car because the weather changes all the time. Anyway, on that day I got right into my car and went straight home. I was more worried about you getting sick from walking in that bad weather."

"No, nothing, *Alhamdu lillah*. And it's all because of your umbrella and raincoat; now I don't go anywhere without them!"

"Enjoy them!"

"Thanks. By the way," Sadeem asked hesitantly, "are you staying in Riyadh this time or planning to return to London?"

"*Wallah,* I still haven't made up my mind, but until things get a little clearer my time will be divided between Riyadh, Jeddah and Khobar. It makes a certain sense, since Riyadh is the official capital and Jeddah is the unofficial capital and Khobar is the family's capital."

"You're from Khobar?"

"Yup. I mean, originally we are from Najd, but we settled in the eastern region a very long time ago. You know how they say there are no native citizens in the eastern province. Most of us come originally from Najd."

"Isn't it tiring to do that, move around so much? Aren't you kind of beyond that, so much coming and going every week?"

Firas laughed. "It's nothing. My chauffeur buys the plane tickets for me, I have clothes in both places and even the little things, like toothbrushes, one in each house. At least after all this practice, I won't have any problems juggling two or even three wives."

"Ha ha, very funny! So the real you is wicked after all, eh? What's your birthday?"

"Why? Are you planning to buy me a present? You can bring it by anytime!"

"Now, why would I bring you a present? You're too old for that kind of stuff. Leave that to the youngsters like me!"

"Thirty-five isn't so old."

"If you say so. So, tell me, what's your star sign?"

"You know about that stuff?"

"No, not much, but one of my friends is an expert, and she got me into the habit of asking everyone I meet."

"I'm a Capricorn. But I don't believe in those kinds of things. As you said, I'm too old for that, right?"

During the flight, Sadeem noticed Firas's care in making sure that none of the flight attendants mistakenly offered her any alcohol or food with pork in it. He didn't have any, either. But it surprised her that he was so concerned about what she did. She really enjoyed his solicitous attention. And being a Virgo (as Lamees had explained), she was bound to appreciate someone who cared about little details as much as she did.

"I'm sure you'll find your mother leaping for joy that you're coming home," Sadeem said warmly.

"Yes, she would, but actually, she's still in Paris with my sisters. Poor thing, she was so miserable the whole time I was away studying. She called me every day with the same questions: 'Are you happy? Don't you want to come home? Haven't you had enough? Don't you want to get married?' "

"Well, she has a point there. Don't you want to get married?" Sadeem's question was impulsive and her eyes were fixed on the gap between his two front teeth.

"Hey, this is the second beating—after that you're too old remark— I've gotten in the space of a minute! Can't a guy get a break? Am I really that old?"

"No, no, I didn't mean that, please don't misunderstand me! It's just that, I mean, I'm not used to seeing a Saudi guy over thirty who isn't married. Usually our boys start nagging their mothers to find them someone to marry even before they have the faintest shadow of a mustache!"

"I'm a little difficult, I guess. I have very specific qualifications that are hard to find in many girls these days. Frankly, it has been years since I gave my family my description of the girl I would want to be with. I told them, look around but take your time. But they still haven't found me the right one. Anyway, I'm fine as I am, perfectly content, and I don't feel like I'm missing anything."

"So, can I hear what these impossible qualifications are, since no one can find anyone with them?"

"At your command. But before I forget, can I make a small request?"

She was studying his white teeth, deep in serious thought. It really was the cutest little gap. Would her little pinkie finger fit in it? "Sure."

"Can I call you later? I'd like to hear your voice tonight before I go to sleep."

20.

To: seerehwenfadha7et@yahoogroups.com
From: "seerehwenfadha7et"
Date: June 25, 2004
Subject: Return to Um Nuwayyir

One reader who says she has followed my e-mails from the beginning was extremely thrilled by the ending of my previous e-mail and sent me the following message: YAAAAAAAAAAAAY!! Finally! What we've been longing for! We were running out of patience waiting for this Firas to make a move! *Alf mabrook,* many congratulations to Sadeem!

How enchanting this give-and-take is! It compels me to forge ahead with this series of mine, this scandal-mongering, highly committed and seriously reform-minded series. Aren't messages like this a thousand times nicer than the others I get every day telling me how liberal and how decadent I am?

Some say I speak of the faults of others but claim to be faultless myself by simply removing myself from the events told. No, I'm not making any such claim. I'm not pretending to be some kind of paragon of perfection, because I don't consider the actions of my friends to be wrong or sinful in the first place!

I am every one of my friends, and my story is their story. And if I have refrained from revealing my identity at present for my own private reasons, I will reveal it someday when those reasons no longer exist. Then I will tell you my whole story, just as you want to hear it, with complete sincerity and transparency. As for now, let's return to our darling Gammoorah.

All this time Gamrah had been anxiously pondering her unknown future. As Sadeem had done with Waleed, for many weeks Gamrah went on dreaming that Rashid would return to her or at least would make some attempt to contact her after coming to regret how awful he had been, and how terribly he had wronged her. But when that didn't happen she began to worry about her future. Would she remain parked in her father's house like an old piece of furniture in the back storeroom? Would she return to the university to finish her studies? Would the university administration even allow that, now that she was a whole year behind her classmates? Or should she sign up for one of the courses offered by private institutes and women's associations to fill her free time and obtain some kind of certificate? It didn't really matter what it was.

"Mama, I want some more limes with salt."

"Too much lime isn't good for you, my dear. You'll get a tummy ache."

"Ufff! I'm just asking for some lime and salt, for God's sake! What if I was craving something *really* hard to get? Then what would you have done?"

"I seek God's refuge from your tongue!" Gamrah's mother turned to her housemaid. "Bring her this lime, may she get acid tummy for it, then maybe she'll know how to control her temper!"

Gamrah's younger brothers, Nayif and Nawwaf, were delighted that she had come home. They were always trying to divert her and cheer her up, inviting her to come and play Nintendo or PlayStation with them. But the severe mood swings that Gamrah suffered—brought on by Rashid and by Rashid's child, who had begun to rule her life even before he was born—made her tense and ready to argue at the drop of a hat.

"Is this the way I'm going to be for God knows how long? God give you no rest, Rashid! May the Lord not absolve you, wherever you go and whatever you do! May what you have done to me be done to your sisters and daughters! O Lord, make my heart cool down and make his burn and take away the pain from me and put it all on him and his cheap mistress."

SADEEM GOT in touch with her friends the minute she arrived in Riyadh, and the four girls agreed to meet the next day at Um Nuwayyir's house. They hadn't all gotten together for a long time—after all, each of them had been caught up fully in her own circumstances.

Um Nuwayyir offered them cups of chai tea with milk and cardamom sweetened with lots of sugar in the Indian-Kuwaiti style, as she scolded them for neglecting to visit her. Sadeem was the only one who had remembered Um Nuwayyir during her travels: she brought her a luxurious cashmere shawl that absolutely delighted Um Nuwayyir, and she congratulated her on the return of her son Nuri from America, where she had enrolled him two years before in a special boarding school for troubled teens.

When the counselors informed Um Nuwayyir that Nuri's condition was psychological rather than physiological, and that it was a temporary phase any adolescent might go through—especially one who was experiencing family problems—Um Nuwayyir breathed an enormous sigh of relief. She was well aware that even if showing signs of being homosexual might not be considered an illness in America, in Saudi Arabia it was an utter calamity, an illness worse than cancer. She had almost fainted when the doctors told her, at the start of it all, that her son was "defining his sexual identity." Over time, they said, he would choose between masculinity and femininity. And when Um Nuwayyir asked what would happen if his choice rested on femininity, she was aghast to hear them say that at that point it was possible to intervene medically to help him with a surgical operation and hormone treatment along with psychological counseling.

Nuri stayed in that school for two years, before deciding on masculinity, at which point he was promptly returned to his mother's embrace. Her spirits soared when she saw that her only child had grown into a man she was proud of, someone she could stick in the eyes of his father and everyone else who had slandered and despised her and her son. Especially all those female relatives and neighbors and coworkers!

Once the girls were reunited, Michelle could talk of nothing but the corruption of Saudi society, its backwardness, its benighted rigidity and overall reactionary nature. She was bursting with enthusiasm about traveling in two days' time to begin a new life in a healthy place—somewhere other than "this rotten-to-the-core, toxic environment that would make anyone sick," as she put it. Sadeem, meanwhile, cursed Waleed after every sentence she uttered. As for Gamrah, she kept up a steady stream of complaints about her mother's constant harassment; she moaned that her mother forbade her to go out the way she used to, just because she was now a divorcée and, her mother claimed, all eyes were fixed on her, waiting for a single misstep and prepared to spread the most lurid rumors about her.

Gamrah believed her mother trusted her but was too concerned with what other people thought. Her mother had never learned the truth of the old adage that anyone who tries to watch all the people all the time will die of exhaustion. Dozens of times every day, Gamrah was told the same thing: "What? Did you forget you are a divorcée?" Of course she hadn't forgotten it, not for a single second. But wasn't that painful enough without having her freedom so horribly curtailed? And without spending so much time worrying about all the busybodies and their stupid chatter? Believe it or not, this was the first day that she had been allowed to leave the house since her return from America three weeks before, and she did not think her mother would let her repeat an outing like this anytime soon.

Late as usual, laid-back Lamees had pranced in balancing a platter of lasagna in one hand and a pan of crème brûlée in the other, and swearing they would love both. The three girls glared at her as Um Nuwayyir got up to help her carry her load to the kitchen. Lamees asked her why everyone was in such a bad mood.

"Honey, look, these girls—every one of them is up to her eyebrows in troubles, and then you come sailing in without a care in the world and bugging them with trying your macaronis and your sweets? You never quit, do you?"

"What harm can a little comfort food do? So, am I supposed to be like them and act suicidal, too? May God give them something better, sure, but this is no way to be! Look at them, every one of them sitting there with a scowl on her face. Reliving their stories only brings more grief!"

"Don't say that. You don't know how heartbroken each one of those girls is. Damn men! Bastards! They have always been such a pain and headache!"

But Lamees was determined to snatch her friends from the abyss of misery. She pulled from her handbag the latest hot-off-the-press, thin-as-toast book by Maggie Farah on the zodiac, which she had ordered from Lebanon. The girls immediately became more animated when they caught sight of their source book for love. They began their usual give-and-take.

SADEEM: Lamees, please check out the traits of the Capricorn man for me.

LAMEES: "The Capricorn man is emotional by nature, but he has very little ability to awaken feelings and emotions in the other partner. He is a rational creature who does not react quickly, but when he does react he loses his senses completely and he can't control his behavior. The Capricorn man is exacting; he holds fast to customs and traditions and doesn't go in for adventure and risk. He is never led by sentiment and rarely influenced by his feelings. Family attachments are important. Among his flaws are pride, egotism, and careerism."

MICHELLE: What's the success rate for a Leo woman and a Cancer man relationship?

LAMEES: Eighty percent.

SADEEM: Is Virgo a better match with Aries or with Capricorn?

LAMEES: With Capricorn, *of course!* I don't even have to go to the book to know that! Look—see what's written here. "The degree of harmony for the Virgo woman with the Aries man doesn't get any higher than sixty percent. Between the Virgo woman and the Capricorn man it won't go lower than ninety-five percent." Way to go, girl! Obviously, you are getting over Waleed in no time! C'mon, spell it out, *Yalla,* who's this Capricorn you're interested in?

GAMRAH: Listen to a little advice from me, girls! Just stop dreaming. Forget all this and leave it to God. Don't get your hopes up when it comes to men, because you'll get the exact opposite of what you were hoping for! Believe me.

LAMEES: So if he's the opposite of what I hope for, what's going to force me to take him?

GAMRAH: Fate, I guess.

MICHELLE: Let's be honest with each other here. If Rashid hadn't appealed to you, you wouldn't have accepted him. You had the right to say no, but you didn't. So you better drop all this "fate" theory, all this stuff about us not having any hand in any of our life paths. We always act the role of the helpless females, completely overcome by circumstances, and as if we don't have a say in anything or opinions of our own! Utterly passive! How long are we going to keep on being such cowards, and not have even the courage to see our choices through, whether they're right or wrong?

The atmosphere immediately turned electric, as it always did when Michelle jumped in with her sharp views. Um Nuwayyir, as usual, intervened to try to calm them down with her jokes and comments. This was the last evening the three of them would be with Michelle before she left to study in America, and so everyone was managing to overlook her biting candor. But Gamrah found herself shrinking, secretly and silently, from the painful remarks Michelle always directed at her whenever the two of them were with the rest of the clique.

21.

To: seerehwenfadha7et@yahoogroups.com

From: "seerehwenfadha7et"

Date: July 2, 2004

Subject: Fatimah the Shiite

I am dedicating this e-mail to two Shiite readers, Jaafar and Hussein, who both wrote in to inform me that even the Shiite community is devoutly following my story every week. It got me thinking how hard it must be to be different in a unicultural, uniethnic, unireligious country like Saudi. I feel sorry sometimes for those of us who are in some way . . . different.

Lamees's move to the College of Medicine in Malaz put a serious strain on her friendship with Michelle. Each tried to ignore the new tension, but some pervasive, negative thing had begun to seep into their relationship. It all came to a head over Lamees's new friend: Fatimah.

"Fatimah the Shiite"*——that's what the *shillah* called her. But Lamees

*After the death of Prophet Mohammed——peace be upon him——Muslims were split on who should lead them. Khalifah Abu Baker Al-Siddeeq, Prophet Mohammed's loyal friend, was nominated, but there were those who rejected the choice and

was completely confident that deep down none of her friends really cared whether Fatimah was Shiite or Sunni or a Sufi Muslim mystic or Christian or even Jewish; what bothered them was that she was just different from all of them, the first Shiite they had ever met, a stranger in their midst, an intruder in their close-knit Sunni circle. The long and short of it was that for people in their society, hanging out together went way beyond the simple matter of friendship; it was a big deal, a deep commitment that aroused all kinds of sensitivities, a social step more akin to engagement and marriage.

Lamees recalled her childhood friend Fadwa Al-Hasudi. Lamees did not usually gravitate toward people like Fadwa; she tended to befriend girls like herself who were lively and spirited. But one morning Fadwa surprised her with a question.

"Lamees, will you be my best friend?"

The proposal came just like that, without any preliminaries, like a marriage proposal in a Western country. And just as quickly Lamees agreed. She couldn't have imagined that Fadwa would become the most jealous girl around.

Lamees "went with" Fadwa for several years and then she met Michelle. At first her relationship with Michelle was based on little more than sympathy for a new student who knew no one, but then they grew close. Fadwa became maliciously jealous and began to launch attacks on Lamees denouncing her around the school. The reports quickly reached her: "Fadwa says you talk to boys!" "Fadwa says your sister Tamadur is smarter than you are and you cheat off your sister to get better grades." What really embittered Lamees was that Fadwa was two-faced; she kept proclaiming her innocence to Lamees's face. There was nothing that Lamees could do except be cold to her until finally they graduated from high school and went their separate ways.

---

wanted Prophet Mohammed's cousin and son-in-law, Ali Bin Abi-Taleb, to succeed. Shiite Muslims are of the opinion of the last group and thus are referred to by some Sunnis as rejectionists.

Lamees's relationship with Fatimah was altogether different. It was founded on mutual attraction. Lamees marveled at Fatimah's strength and sparkle, while Fatimah loved Lamees's boldness and quick mind. All it took was a short while until, somewhat to their surprise, each had become the other's closest friend.

After screwing up her courage, and then wondering how to phrase it, Lamees gently asked Fatimah about some things that baffled her when it came to Shiites. One day during Ramadan Lamees took her Fotoor* meal to Fatimah's apartment so that they could break the fast together once the sun had gone down. On the way Lamees remembered (with a smile on her face) the days when she was afraid to eat any of the food offered to her by her Shiite classmates at the university. It was Gamrah and Sadeem who were always warning her to avoid the food; they insisted Shiites spit in their food if they knew a Sunni was going to eat it, even going so far as to poison it to obtain the blessing due to someone who slays a Sunni! So Lamees would accept the sweet pies and pastries from her Shiite classmates politely and then once out of sight toss them into the garbage can. She was even afraid that wrapped candy and pieces of gum had been doctored. Lamees never trusted any food from a Shiite until she met Fatimah.

Now Lamees put a small plate of dates in front of Fatimah to break the fast. But after the dusk call to prayer signaling the end of the fast, she noticed that Fatimah didn't tear into the dates as she had expected. In fact, she was so busy preparing the Vimto** drink and the salad that she didn't break her fast with so much as a single bite until twenty minutes later. Fatimah could see Lamees's surprise. Sunnis break their fast as soon as the sound of the Athan*** makes its way to their ears from the nearby mosque. But Fatimah told her friend that their custom was not to eat the moment they heard the call to prayer by a Sunni Imam,§ but to wait awhile in order to be certain of nightfall, in a way of striving for accuracy.

*Breakfast meal in Ramadan.
**A popular Ramadan drink; juice of grapes, raspberries and black currants.
***The call for prayer.
§The religious sheikh who calls for prayers at a mosque.

Now Lamees's curiosity about Shiite traditions was really roused. She plunged in, asking her friend about the decorations hung on the walls in her apartment. The elegant Arabic script suggested some religious meaning. Fatimah explained that the decorations were hung for some rites that the Shiites celebrated every year halfway through the Arabic month of Sha'ban, the month right before Ramadan.

Then Lamees asked Fatimah about some photographs she had seen in the wedding album of Fatimah's older sister. At the time, she thought they were strange but refrained from asking about them. There were photos showing the bride and groom dipping their bare feet in a large silver basin, coins scattered around the bottom. Two grandmothers were pouring water over the couple's feet. This was just one of their wedding traditions, Fatimah told her, akin to the practice of drawing patterns in henna on the bride's hands or the elaborate unveiling ceremony. They would rub the bride's and groom's feet in water that had been blessed by having verses from the Qur'an and certain prayers recited over it. Coins were tossed in front of their feet as alms to bless their marriage.

Fatimah answered her friend's questions simply and directly, laughing at the surprise and wonder on her face. When the conversation started to go too far, though, they both sensed the tension in the air. Either one of them could at any moment say something that would appear to disparage the other's version of her faith. So they stopped the question-and-answer session and moved quietly into the living room to watch the popular sitcom *Tash ma Tash* the Saudi TV aired every Ramadan after Fotoor time. At least that was something that both Sunnis and Shiites in Saudi Arabia agreed on!

Tamadur was first to reject her sister's relationship with this rejectionist. She made it very clear to Lamees that all of the girls she knew at college were making fun of the friendship.

"Lamees, *wallah,* I heard the girls saying things about her that are really bad! She lives by herself! Her family is in Qatif* so she can do what-

*A city in the east coast of Saudi Arabia, with a big Shiite population.

ever she wants while she's in Riyadh for school. She goes out whenever she wants and comes home whenever she feels like it. She visits whoever she wants to, and whoever she wants visits her, too."

"They're lying. I went to her place and I saw how tough the security men were over there. They don't let anyone in, and she can't leave the place on her own, no way. Her brother has to be there for her to get out."

"Lamees, whether it's true or not, why do we need to be involved in this? If everyone is talking about her today, tomorrow they'll talk about you, and they'll say you're a bad girl just like her! What is it with you? From Fadwa the psycho to Sarah the princess to Fatimah the Shiite? And the best friend you ever had is an American rebel that doesn't worry about what people think!"

Lamees frowned at her sister's mention of Sarah, the girl from the Saudi royal family who enrolled at their high school for senior year. Lamees had genuinely adored Sarah. The princess bewitched her with her modesty and her high principles—bewitched her in part because Lamees had never expected a princess to be anything but arrogant and pushy. She didn't care in the least about what the girls said about her relationship with Sarah. They snickered about the fact that Lamees gave the princess wake-up calls every morning. But there was a perfectly good reason for it: Sarah was afraid that, with the huge palace she lived in and the large number of people in it, the servants would forget to wake her up on time. Lamees also used to finish some of Sarah's homework for her—but not on a regular basis, as certain people claimed. And she only did it when she observed that Sarah was occupied with more important matters, official occasions and family rituals and social duties that Sarah would tell her about in advance. Lamees would invite Sarah to study in her own modest home on the days preceding the exams they had every month, so that Sarah could concentrate on her studying more than she could in the palace. As for the hurtful rumors going around among the girls at school which Tamadur would confront her with—that she was the princess's servant and would do anything for her—they had no effect—if anything, they brought her closer to her new friend and made her even more anxious to prove her devotion.

With Fatimah, Lamees found herself for the first time friends with a girl so much like her that it was almost uncanny! The closer she got to Fatimah, the more she felt as though she were face to face with a soul mate. As usual, what others said about her didn't bother her much, except that this time she did worry about how Michelle would feel. Michelle had forgiven her for her relationship with Sarah when she saw the way Sarah dropped her once they graduated. Sarah traveled to America, and she never again spoke to Lamees. At the time, Michelle had felt her own power, witnessing Lamees's regret, hearing her plea for reconciliation and knowing how badly she wanted to regain the old friendship. But what would Michelle do now, if she felt Lamees had abandoned their friendship a second time? A better solution, as Lamees saw it, was just to hide the relationship from Michelle and the rest of the *shillah*. Her strategy backfired, though, when Tamadur, who had long been aggravated at what she thought of as her sister's perverse ways, took it upon herself to inform the girls of everything.

So Michelle now knew the real reason for Lamees's inexplicable disappearances. For weeks on end Lamees had been hiding behind a host of excuses: that studying medicine was so time-consuming, that the work was so difficult, that she had so much to learn! Now the hurtful truth was out—Lamees had been choosing her new friend's company over that of her old *shillah*.

Lamees tried to justify her position to Sadeem, who was far ahead of everyone else in their clique when it came to being understanding, even indulgent, about such things.

"Try to see my side of things, Saddoomah! I love Michelle. All our lives we've been friends, and we'll go on being friends, but she doesn't have a right to keep me from getting to know other girls! Fatimah's got a few things Michelle doesn't have. You love Gamrah, but she has her faults, too, and if you found what she lacks in another girl, you'd get attached to that girl, right?"

"But Lammoosah, after all these years! It isn't right to dump your lifelong friend just because you suddenly decide her personality is lacking some vital quality that you think you've just found in some other girl. That precious something didn't matter to you before, though, because you lived years without it and you had *no problem*. Besides, the two of you are supposed to stick together through thick and thin. Suppose you were to get married and your husband turned out to be missing a certain something. Do you go and look for in other guys for what he's lacking?"

"Yah, maybe! And if he doesn't like it, then let him go find whatever he's lacking and spare me the effort!"

"Wow, you're one tough lady! Okay, look, I have a really serious question that's bugging me so badly I'm about to burst. It's about the Shiites."

"What is it?"

With a twitch to her lips that gave away her mock-solemn expression, Sadeem asked: "Do Shiite men wear Sunni pants under their *thobes*?"*

---

*Of course they do! All men who wear *thobes* have to wear long white underpants—called Sunni underpants—underneath to prevent the thin material of their *thobes* from shearing. The name "Sunni" underpants is just a funny coincidence.

22.

I'm sitting down in my La-Z-Boy with my feet stretched way out, just like I do every weekend when I write down these e-mails. And yes, my hair is fluffed and my lips are painted red . . .

It was about ten o'clock in the morning when the airplane landed at San Francisco International Airport. This was not Michelle's first visit to the city, but it was the first time she had been there without her parents and her little brother Meshaal.

She breathed in air saturated with moisture and freedom. People in all shapes and colors, from everywhere in the world, were flowing around her in every direction. No one paid any attention to her Arab-ness, or to the fact that the person standing next to her was African. Everyone was minding his own business.

She made sure her visa was in plain sight. That piece of paper confirmed that she was a student from Saudi Arabia who had come to study at the University of California, San Francisco. The woman in Customs told her she was the prettiest Arab girl she had seen in all her years working at the airport.

After Michelle got through all the necessary official stuff, she searched the faces of the people waiting in the reception area. She caught sight of her cousin Matthew at the edge of the crowd, waving to her, and she started toward him, delighted.

"Hi, Matti!"

"Hi, sweetie! Long time no see!"

Matti gave her a warm hug, asking about her mom and her dad and her brother. Michelle noticed that he was the only one from her uncle's small family who was there at the airport to meet her.

"Where is everyone else?"

"Dad and Mom are at work and Jamie and Maggie are at school."

"And you? How come you came to meet me? Don't you have lectures?"

"My morning lectures today were canceled for the express purpose of coming to meet my darling cousin at the airport. We're going to spend the day together until everyone else gets home. Then I have to go give a lecture in the evening. You can come with me if you want to, and I can show you around the campus, and you can get a quick look at your room in the dorm. By the way, are you still insisting on living in the dorm instead of at our house?"

"It's better that way. I'm really dying to try it out—living with some independence."

"As you like, but hey, my condolences. Anyway, I've gotten everything ready. I chose a room for you; you'll be rooming with one of my students who I think you'll like a lot. She's your age and she's as saucy as you are, but you're a lot prettier than she is."

"Matti! Aren't you ever going to stop spoiling me? I'm older now and I can handle things on my own."

"We'll see about that."

He took her on a tour of Fisherman's Wharf. They spent the day walking and window-shopping. Despite the smell of fish clinging to the air, Michelle took pleasure in everything she encountered: the merchandise displayed in open-air stalls and artists and singers everywhere you turned. When they felt hungry they ordered clam chowder and it came in a huge bread bowl. They enjoyed themselves thoroughly.

Later on, Matti helped her organize her things in the dorm and advised her in choosing the courses to take that term. She decided to begin by following in her cousin's footsteps and major in communications, after hearing him praise it. Among the classes she signed up for was the subject he taught, nonverbal communications.

Michelle began to immerse herself in her studies and other university activities. She hoped she would forget what had been, and eventually she got her wish. With so much going on, and a new life in a new country that kept her occupied every day, bit by bit she was finally able to think about Faisal less and less.

23.

To: seerehwenfadha7et@yahoogroups.com
From: "seerehwenfadha7et"
Date: July 16, 2004
Subject: An Adventure Not to Be Forgotten

The Qur'an verses, hadith of the Prophet—peace be upon him—and religious quotations that I include in my e-mails are, to me, inspirational and enlightening. And so are the poems and love songs that I include. Are these things opposite to each other, and so is this a contradiction? I don't think so. Am I not a real Muslim because I don't devote myself to reading only religious books and because I don't shut my ears to music and I don't consider anything romantic to be rubbish? I am religious, a balanced Saudi Muslim and I can say that there are a lot of people just like me. My only difference is that I don't conceal what others would call contradictions within myself or pretend perfection like some do. We all have our *spiritual* sides as well as our *not-so-spiritual* sides.

amees first encountered her friend Fatimah's brother one day when she gave Fatimah a ride to the train station. Ali was four years older than the girls were, and was, like them, a medical student. Because his car had broken down, he decided to join his sister on the train. They met at the station.

Fatimah was not very close to her brother Ali even though they were living within the same city of Riyadh. They seemed to spend very little time together. He lived in an apartment with his friends and his sister lived with her friends in another apartment far away. Ali didn't come to visit her very often and every weekend he took his car or got a ride with a classmate going to Qatif, while Fatimah always took the train with her Qatifi classmates.

The first thing that really pleased Lamees about Ali was his height. At five foot seven, she was taller than most of the guys she came across. But Ali was a full six feet tall, maybe even a little bit more. And then there were his looks! He had a tanned complexion and very thick and dark eyebrows, and he positively exuded masculinity. He even seemed to Lamees to be, strangely, a little magical.

A week after they met, Lamees bumped into Ali in the hospital where she and Fatimah had gone to buy some reference books. It was before they had their rotation in that hospital later on. Many of the girls in the freshman class had met nice guys—colleagues—there by pretending they needed tutoring to understand the difficult medical courses, and Lamees used the same ploy with Ali, who was a senior. They met within the confines of the hospital at first and later on outside in one of the nearby coffee shops.

Somehow none of her friends caught on to their relationship. In front of her friends, Lamees acted as if nothing were going on between the two of them, that he was just tutoring her every now and then. Only Fatimah knew, because her brother told her. It turned out that he had asked her to arrange that meeting at the train station. He had seen Lamees's photo framed in his sister's room at their home in Qatif and he was smitten with her. In the photo, Lamees, Fatimah and some other classmates, all dressed in white lab coats, posed next to a corpse they had dissected in the anatomy lab of the Medical College for females in Malaz—a horrifically depressing room in which you could smell the mingled odors of formalin and cheap *bukhour** that the workers burned all the time in their attempts to mask the strong odor of the preserved bodies.

Ali was in his final year of medical studies and he was supposed to start his internship immediately after graduation. He would be assigned to one of the hospitals in the eastern part of the country. Lamees and Fatimah were still in their second year of university.

One day, as Lamees and Ali sat together in a café on Al-Thalatheen Street, a band of men from Al-Hai'ah** swooped down on them and led the pair off swiftly to two separate SUVs and headed immediately for the organization's nearest bureau.

There, they put Lamees and Ali into two separate rooms and began interrogations. Lamees could not bear the hurtful questions put to her. They asked her in detail about her relationship with Ali. They used coarse language and they forced her to hear words that would have embarrassed her even in front of her most intimate girlfriends. After trying for hours to appear self-confident and completely convinced of the rightness of everything she had done, she collapsed in tears. She really did not believe that she had done anything that was cause for shame. In the next room, the interrogator was putting pressure on Ali, who lost his cool completely when the man asserted that Lamees had confessed to everything and that he might as well come clean.

The senior officers contacted Lamees's father. They told him that she had been apprehended with a young man in a café and was being held

---

*Arabic incense. Wooden sticks that come from particular trees in India or Cambodia, and when burned, generate strong and beautiful lasting fragrance.
**Al-Hai'ah is a short name for the Commission for the Promotion of Virtue and Prevention of Vice, i.e., the Religious Police.

at their headquarters and that he must come and get her after signing a promise that his daughter would never again engage in such an immoral act.

Her father arrived, his face so pale from the sudden call. He signed the necessary papers and then was allowed to take her. On the way home, he tried to suppress his anger and to console, as much as possible, his sobbing daughter. He vowed he would not tell her mother or sister what had happened, on one condition: she must never again meet that boy outside the hospital building. Yes, he admitted, it was true that she was allowed to go out on her own with her male cousins and the sons of his friends and her mother's friends in Jeddah. But in Riyadh, things had to be different!

Lamees worried about Ali. At the headquarters, she had heard a policeman whispering into her father's ear that they had found out the boy was "from the rejectionist sect." He was a Shiite from Qatif and so his punishment would certainly be worse than hers.

That day marked the rupture of Lamees's relationship with Fatimah as well as Ali. From then on, every time their eyes met, Fatimah repudiated her with a burning stare, as if she blamed Lamees entirely for the whole thing. Poor Ali. He had been such a sweet guy, and frankly, if Lamees had been allowed to continue seeing him, and more important if he hadn't been Shiite, she might actually have fallen in love with him.

24.

To: seerehwenfadha7et@yahoogroups.com
From: "seerehwenfadha7et"
Date: July 23, 2004
Subject: Firas: The (Near) Perfect Man!

I am so tired of getting these boring responses that try to dissect my personality after every e-mail. Is that really what matters most to you, after everything I have written? Whether I am Gamrah or Michelle or Sadeem or Lamees? Don't you get that it doesn't matter who I am?

I didn't know that shopping for the baby could be so much fun!" Sadeem said to Gamrah, her voice laced with enthusiasm. "These baby things are *so* adorable! If only you would agree to ask your doctor about the sex of the baby during your next ultrasound—then we would know what we are shopping for!"

Because Gamrah's two older sisters, Naflah and Hessah, were so busy with their husbands and because her little sister, Shahla, was so preoccupied with her high school studies, Sadeem offered to go with her pregnant friend to buy whatever would be needed for the newborn. And occasionally, when Gamrah's mother's arthritis was acting up, Sadeem would take her place and accompany Gamrah to the gynecologist for the periodic checkup.

"It doesn't matter to me if it is a boy or a girl. Let's buy the basic stuff now and the rest can come after it's born."

"Don't you have any feelings about all of this, Gammoorah? You sound so cold. If I were in your place, I couldn't wait to know what sex it'll be!"

"Sadeem, you just don't understand. I'm not eager to have this baby! This little thing is going to change my whole life. And then who will be willing to marry me? Nobody wants a *full package!* So tell me—is this the way my future is supposed to be? I'm going to live out my life saddled with this kid whose father doesn't want it and doesn't want his mother, either? Rashid goes off to live his life free and without any ties. He can fall in love, he can get married, he can do whatever he wants, while I have to live with this aggravation and trouble the rest of my life! I don't want this baby, Sadeem. *I don't want it!*"

They were in the car, on their way back to her house. Gamrah burst into tears of utter despair. Sadeem couldn't find anything convincing to say that might comfort her. If only Gamrah would return to the university to study with her! But Gamrah had been insisting that she didn't have the energy for it. Her body, which used to be so perfectly slender and sleek, was bursting at the seams from so much lying around. Of course, she suffered from boredom, imprisoned in the house as she was. Even her younger sister Shahla had more freedom than her! That's because *she* was not *a divorced woman.* Meanwhile, Mudi, her cousin who came from the conservative city of Qasim to live with them while going to college in Riyadh, never ceased to annoy her with all her criticisms. She disapproved of Gamrah's neatly tweezed eyebrows and the fact that she wore an over-the-shoulder *abaya* instead of the *abaya* that you drape over your head that covers your figure completely. As for her older brothers, Mohammed and Ahmad, they were completely engrossed in their friends and the adventures they had endlessly inundating girls with their phone numbers. There was no one left to entertain her but Nayif and Nawaf, who were only ten and twelve. Pitiful!

What could Sadeem possibly have said to Gamrah? How could she have comforted and distracted her? After all, there was nothing worse than a person who claimed to be filled with sympathy, to be *all there* for someone drowning in grief, when streams of happiness were so obviously glistening in her own eyes! If only she could have faked a little misery, thought Sadeem. But how could she possibly have managed that when she had Firas?

Yes, in Firas, God had answered her prayer. After she went through the breakup with Waleed, how often had she begged God to return him to her. But the fever of her prayers had cooled gradually, until finally, praying for Waleed's return turned into praying for Firas's presence. This Firas was no ordinary man! He was an extraordinary, marvelous and divinely made creature, and Sadeem felt she must offer her thanks to God for him night and day.

What did he lack, after all? He must be missing something. There must be some hidden defect—something, anything, to detract from his total gorgeousness. No human being could be this perfect, for perfection belongs only to God! But Sadeem was unable to figure out just what that crucial defect could be.

Dr. Firas Al-Sharqawi was a diplomat and a politician, widely connected and respected. A successful man with a fertile brain and a forceful personality, he was known to be someone who leads and is not led, who rules and is not ruled. Very soon after his return from London, Firas's reputation spread. In his capacity as a counselor in the king's cabinet, the royal *diwan,* his face often shone out from the pages of newspapers and magazines. Sadeem regularly bought two copies of every newspaper or magazine containing an interview or a news item about him. One copy she bought for herself and the other for him, since he was too endlessly busy to follow his own coverage in the press. Moreover, from what Sadeem could pick up, his parents weren't particularly intent on reading newspaper stories about their son. His father was a very old man who suffered terribly from various physical ailments, and his mother was a housewife who didn't read or write very well. As for his sisters, the last thing to interest them would be politics and its great men.

In Sadeem's eyes, such family circumstances only made Firas's stature seem even higher. Here was the man who had risen by his own efforts, who had crafted so much from nothing! Here was an extraordinary individual who would one day ascend to the very highest positions. She made a point of reading to Firas every single word she could find that anyone had written about him. Secretly, she made a scrapbook of articles and photos of him. She had a plan: she would give him the scrapbook on their wedding day.

It was not in the least bit unreasonable for Sadeem to be thinking of marriage. Even her friends did not think she was rushing ahead of herself. It seemed the inevitable, fated outcome. His allusions were crystal clear, weren't they? Even though he didn't ever say "marriage" right out loud, the idea had been circling around inside his head starting from that day he circled around the Kaaba in Mecca, performing Umrah.*

From inside the sacred enclosure at Mecca he had called her. He was accompanying a small group of VIPs. He asked her what she wanted him to pray for on her behalf. "Pray that God gives me what is in my heart," she said. And then, a moment later, "And you know *who is in my heart.*"

A few days later, he told her that hearing this shy confession of hers had submerged his heart in an ocean of pure delight, a feeling he'd never experienced before. Her boldness led him to grow bolder in his own thoughts. From that day on, he began to float along in private fantasy, always moving closer to an attachment to her. A composed and steady man who considered every step a thousand times before taking it, he was unaccustomed to the emotion of being swept away. He began to show his solicitude, his desire to know every little thing happening in her life. He vowed to her that she was the only woman who had been

---

*A short pilgrimage to Mecca undertaken by Muslims. Unlike Hajj, Umrah can be done anytime of the year.

able to slip into his life, manipulate his precise daily schedule and prod him (with barely any effort on her part) to stay up late, neglect his work and postpone his appointments, all for the sake of spending more time with her on the phone!

What was a little odd about Firas was his utter devotion to religion in spite of having spent more than a decade abroad. He showed no signs of Western influence. He didn't seem at all ill-disposed toward the way things were in the kingdom, unlike many others who spent a few years abroad and came home to despise everything they saw, no matter how fervent they had once been in their praise of their country's customs and practices. Firas's attempts to steer Sadeem this way or that on the path of righteousness didn't annoy her. To the contrary! She found herself strongly inclined to accept all his ideas of making her a better Muslim and primed to embrace them, especially since he didn't make a big deal of anything. That really pleased her. It was simply a matter of delaying a good-night phone conversation because the time for the dawn prayer had come, or maybe an innocent little hint about wearing the *hijab* and *abaya,* like the one he had come up with when they were sitting on the airplane, or an earnest observation about how annoying the young men who followed girls with uncovered faces in the malls must be, suggesting that the face cover protects a girl sometimes from such encounters. That was his way, and gradually Sadeem found herself trying to move closer toward religious perfection so that she would be worthy of Firas, who was so much closer to that perfection than she was.

Firas never made her feel that she needed to work hard to keep him. *He* was the one always making the effort to remain in touch with her and be near her. He never traveled without telling her where he was going and when he would be back, and he always gave her addresses and telephone numbers to contact him. He begged her pardon for calling her so much to see that she was all right. For them, as for so many other lovers in the country, the telephone was the only outlet, practically, for them to express the love that brought them together. The telephone lines in Saudi Arabia are surely thicker and more abundant than elsewhere, since they must bear the heavy weight of all the whispered croonings lovers have to exchange and all their sighs and moans and kisses that they *cannot,* in the real world, enact—or that they do not *want to* enact due to the restrictions of custom and religion, that some of them truly respect and value.

Only one thing disturbed Sadeem's serenity, and that was the relationship she'd formerly had with Waleed.

When they first got to know each other, Firas had asked her about her past and she had immediately poured out everything about Waleed, the only false step she had ever made, the injury whose wounds she hid from everyone. Her explanation seemed to satisfy him; he seemed very understanding and sympathetic. What bewildered her was his request that she never again talk to him about it. Did talking about her past upset him that much? She wished he could turn the pages in her heart with his own hands so he could see for himself that they were blank except when it came to him. She wished she was allowed to share absolutely everything inside of her, including her history with Waleed, but he was as determined and firm in this decision as in any other. That was the way he was.

"So, what about you, Firas? Do *you* have a past?"

She didn't ask in order to uncover a wound in his heart that might match hers and put him on the same footing. Her love for Firas was too strong to be affected by a past, or a present, or a future—and anyway, she knew that of the two of them, she would always be the one furthest from perfection! Her question was merely a simple and perhaps naïve attempt to see if she could find some little scratch on Firas's knee that would prove he was as human as she was.

"Don't ask me this question again if you really care about me."

Just drop it! she told herself. *Who cares about his past? He is mine now. And to hell with curiosity!*

25.

To: seerehwenfadha7et@yahoogroups.com
From: "seerehwenfadha7et"
Date: July 30, 2004
Subject: It's a Boy!

Well! So it is *I* who calls for vice and dissolute behavior! What do you know? *I* am the one who promotes moral corruption and hopes to see fornication and abomination spread through our paragon of a society! Moreover, it's I who has a mind to exploit pure, undefiled and noble sentiments, turning them away from their most honorable intentions! *Me??*

May God be merciful with everyone, and may He remove from their eyesight the grim affliction that compels them to interpret everything I say as morally depraved and wanton. I have no recourse but to pray for these unfortunates, that God might enlighten their vision, so that they would truly see at least some of what is going on around them, as it really is, and guide them to the ways of respectful dialogue, without attacking others as unbelievers, without humiliating them, and without rubbing them in the dirt.

G amrah's labor went on for five shifts, as the position at her bed-side rotated among her mother, her three sisters and Sadeem. It was not really a difficult birth, but it was her first one. And the first one, as her mother was always saying, comes out with more difficulty than the second, or the third . . .

Um Gamrah spent the last seven hours of labor in the birthing room with her daughter, working hard to calm her and make things easier for her. Gamrah screamed with every bout of pain.

"O Lord, may Rashid suffer from whatever I am suffering from right this moment and more!"

"I don't want his son. I don't want him! Just leave him inside of me! I don't want to have a baby!"

"Mama, call Rashid . . . Mama, tell him to come see me . . . Mama, shame on him, how could he do this to me? . . . Wallah, I didn't do a thing to him . . . I'm tired, I'm so tired! Mama I can't stand this!"

And then Gamrah would burst into sobs, bitter sobs, her voice gradually fading as she got dizzier and the pain got worse.

"I want to die! Then I'll be rid of this! I don't want to have a baby and why does this have to happen to me? Why, Mama? Why?"

After thirty-six hours in labor, the cry of a newborn sounded from Gamrah's room. Thrilled, Sadeem and Gamrah's sister Shahla, who were sitting outside the room, jumped up. They were eager to know what sex the baby was. A few minutes later, the Indian nurse told them it was a healthy beautiful boy.

Gamrah refused to pick up her baby when she first saw it, all splattered with blood, its head elongated and its skin wrinkled in a really scary way. Her mother laughed at her and held the baby after the nurse had cleaned him. She repeated the name of God over him. *"Ma shaa Allah. He looks exactly like his darling little mother!"*

Hours later, as Sadeem gazed softly at that tiny person in her arms, that tiny face with eyes shut tightly, and as she searched for his soft fingers to get them to close around her finger, she asked her friend, "So what have you decided to name him?"

"Saleh, after Rashid's dad."

Rashid was still in America when Gamrah gave birth. His mother visited her at the hospital and then later at home, several times, and his father—Saleh—came by twice and was thrilled that the child was named after him. Still, Gamrah sensed that these visits from his family and the gifts and the money were the very most that Rashid was ever going to provide her and their child.

By summer, Gamrah's mother decided to do something to cheer up this daughter of hers who had grown old before her time. They traveled together—with the rest of the family—for a month to Lebanon, leaving the nursing child with his eldest aunt, Aunt Naflah.

In Lebanon, Gamrah submitted to the makeover procedure called "tinsmithing." It began with a nose job. It ended with sessions of facial chemical peeling. The regime also consisted of a strict diet and exercise program under the supervision of an extremely elegant specialist, and Gamrah topped it all off with a new hairstyle and coloring at the hands of the most famous and skilled hairdresser in all of Lebanon.

Gamrah returned to Riyadh prettier than when she had left. To spare herself the disapproval of her conservative relatives, she told everyone who saw her before she managed to strip off the dressing on her nose that her nose had been broken in an accident while she was in Lebanon, which had resulted in reconstructive surgery. Not cosmetic surgery—since cosmetic surgery is against the laws of Islam.

26.

To: seerehwenfadha7et@yahoogroups.com

From: "seerehwenfadha7et"

Date: August 6, 2004

Subject: The Chatting World: A Whole New World

And to Allah belongs the unseen of the heavens and the earth, and
to Him return all affairs (for decision). So worship Him and put your
trust in Him. Your Lord is not unaware of what you do.
   —Qur'an, Surat Hud
   (chapter of the Prophet Hud), verse 123

Everyone, everywhere, seems to be talking about ME, and I love to listen in.
I often enter the discussion and offer up what I expect, what I predict, who
I think it is, just as they do. At home, I print out the e-mail I send all of you
weekly, and I read it out loud to everyone in the house. Mind you, no one
at home knows that I am the one behind these e-mails! In other words, I
do exactly what every other girl is doing at exactly the same time! In those
moments, I feel such intense pleasure. It's as good as the feeling you get
when you are twirling the radio dial in a moment of boredom and suddenly
you are surprised by your favorite song, soaring out of the radio, and you
even get to hear it from the very first notes!

Lamees's relationship with the Internet began when she was fifteen years old, when her father began accessing the World Wide Web via Bahrain. When the Internet was introduced to Saudi Arabia two years later in 1999, her fascination with this seriously cool online world had to take a backseat to her high school studies and maintaining her GPA. But once she graduated, it wasn't long before Lamees was spending no less than four hours every day on the Internet, 99 percent of it in random chat rooms, Yahoo, ICQ, mIRC and AOL.

With her sense of humor and her saucy mouth, Lamees gained quick fame among chat room regulars. Even though she was careful to change her nickname regularly, there were more than a few out there who were able to figure out that "The Caterpillar" was also "The Demongirl," "Black Pearl" and "Daddy's Sweetheart."

It gave Lamees a good laugh to hear the boys she chatted with sounding so skeptical. None of them believed she was really a girl.

"Okay c'mon, stop it! U r NOT a girl!"

"OK, fine, y are u saying that tho?"

"Hey brother, girls r boring and they have NO sense of humor and u r clearly high on some good hash!"

"So, what you're saying is, I have to make myself a pain to listen to so you'll believe I'm not a guy?"

"Exactly! If u r really a girl, let's hear your voice then!"

"LOL! No Way Jose :-p!"

"Gimme a break, just gimme a quick ring and say hi, OK? And if u don't wanna use the phone just go with the mike, how abt it, just 2 prove 2 me you're a girl ur not a guy."

"Forget it sweetheart. That is just a line u guys use 2 hear a girl's voice."

"Ahhhhhh. You make my heart ache! OK. I believe u, I believe u'r a girl! That word sweetheart coming from ur mouth was as sweet as honey."

"Hehehe. No, forget it, just think of me as Mr. better than starting 2 flirt with me!"

"I swear 2 God u r the most gorgeous Mr, I mean Ms, I mean . . . I'm CONFUSED!:–C"

"Best thing :-p"

"Okay, so now lemme ask u a question and then I'm really gonna know if u'r a girl or a guy."

"So ask."

"Are your knees dark or not? :-p"*

"LoooOOooooL! That's a good one! Okay I've got one for you too! :-D"

"Ask away, baby."

"What about your toenails? Are they disgusting or not? :-p"

"HAHAHAHA. OUCH! Good one! Actually, harsh but good! LOL!"

"Look at that! Black knees you say, hah! Get outta here, baby, take care of your own gender's screw-ups first and then you can make fun of our dark knees!"

By this kind of chatting, Lamees got hold of an unbelievable number of telephone numbers from guys who wanted to continue the discussions on the telephone. By the hundreds, they raved about how totally cool they found her personality, and by the dozens, they professed their love. Lamees didn't waver from her firm conviction, though, that chat was only for some silly laughs and light entertainment. It was a great way to meet guys and joke around with them, in a society that didn't provide any other venue for clowning around, but it wasn't anything to take seriously.

With the help of Lamees, Gamrah got to know the world of chatting. In the beginning, Lamees would ask her if she wanted to accompany her

---

*Due to their darker complexions, Saudi girls tend to have darkened knees. Guys always pick on girls because of that, although they have the same problem! However, due to the hot climate of Saudi, dryness and the frequent use of Arabic sandals, *ni'aal,* guys tend to have very dry feet and dirty toenails. Girls pick on that, in return.

into the chat room. That way, Lamees said, she could introduce Gamrah to her friends online. Little by little, Gamrah got addicted to it. Soon she was spending all hours of the day and night chatting away with some guy or other.

From the start, Lamees was up front with Gamrah about the realities and hidden pitfalls of chatting. She made sure Gamrah was wise to the wiles and glaringly obvious pranks of savvy young men, which might trap a newcomer to the Net. Lamees even read out to her friend a few conversation histories with various Web buddies that had been automatically saved on the computer.

"Look here, Gammoorah, dear. All these guys have the same style, but there are some simple variations they use. For example, guys from Riyadh are a little different than the eastern province boys, and *they're* different from the western province and so it goes. Let's start with the boys-of-Riyadh style, since they are your main interest.

"The first thing he'll say to you after *Hi* would be: May I please know your name? And of course you are *not* going to give him your real name, you just give him any name you like, or you say to him, *sorry,* I don't want to give out my name. The way I handle it is, I dig down and I give him some name, whatever comes into my head. But you have to pay attention and remember which name you've given to which guy! My advice is to do what I always do—write them all down in a notebook so you don't get fouled up. Or you just choose one name and stick with it. But I find that pretty tame.

"So then, what happens next is, a few days after he gets this name of yours, he'll say to you, I am really so into you and I have *never* seen anyone like you, so, can we talk on the phone? He's going to pick on you and pester you and of course you are not going to agree, but he is going to give you his number anyway. And then a few more days go by, and he's going to demand that you two exchange pictures, but in the end he'll get impatient and he'll send it along even though you never send yours.

"And *then* you'll see one of two: a guy sitting behind his desk in a nice office, with a Montblanc pen in his hand and a Saudi flag on a pole right behind him, a 'classic picture!,' or a guy who's making himself out to be a big strutting Bedouin and sitting old-Arab-style on the floor with his head wrapped up in a *shimagh*—Bedouin-style—and he'll have one knee lifted off the ground with his elbow resting on it. All he's lacking is a falcon on his shoulder and he'll be ready to go on one of those Bedouin TV series!

"Next, he's bound to tell you that he was really in love with this fabulous girl two years ago and then she got married. She was totally, *totally* in love with him, but a good man proposed to her family and she couldn't say no to it. And *he*—apple of his mommy's eye!—was still so young and fresh and couldn't set up a household and so he didn't have a choice and he stepped back for her own happiness. Anything just to show you what a great, trustworthy and noble man he is!

"Then after all these confessions, he'll start leaving offline messages for you whenever you're not there—a nice song or poem or a URL of a romantic story or an article that talks about love and how wonderful it is, whatever, and then after just a week or so, it will all come out: He will confess that he is in love with you! He'll say, I've been looking for a girl like you for so long and I want to get engaged, but we have to get to know each other better and talk on the phone. What's really on his mind is arranging things so he can go out with you, but of course he doesn't say that to you, all he's trying to do at this point is to get your phone number. That's enough to start with, and he doesn't want to scare you.

"Then it creeps up, slowly. The tiresome stuff starts. You get stuff on your screen like: Why are you avoiding me? Why do you take so long to answer my message? You're not talking to some other guy, are you? I don't want you talking to anyone but me. I warn you, I'm a very jealous man. If you don't find me online, you don't have to stay. Log off!—and other stuff like this that will make you so sick of him that you put him on *block* or *ignore* or even delete him from your buddy list altogether! That will teach him to never use that *manly* attitude with you ever again, 'cause you'd go off and find someone else who doesn't cause you a headache.

"The most important thing, Gammoorah, is that you don't trust anyone and you don't believe anyone. Just keep in mind that it is nothing more than a game and that all these Saudi guys are cheats and all they want to do is fool dumb girls."

Gamrah's chat style didn't have the finesse of Lamees's. All the guys who were so gung ho when they found out she was Lamees's friend disappeared pretty fast once they discovered she didn't have her friend's sense of humor and quick mind.

Gamrah began to form new friendships on her own, though. On-line, she met people from different countries and of various ages. Like Lamees, she didn't want to talk to any females. "We can meet females anywhere!" they used to say. Everyone on their buddy lists was of the other sex.

On one of those boring evenings at home, she met Sultan: a simple, direct, polite twenty-five-year-old guy who worked as a salesman in a men's clothing boutique.

Talking with Sultan on the Internet was a pleasure for Gamrah, and he seemed in turn to really be interested in what she wrote to him. He laughed at her jokes and he sent her lots of colloquial poetry, which he had composed himself.

As the days went by, Gamrah found that talking to Sultan was better than talking to any other online friends, and he felt the same. He called her by her online name: Pride.

Sultan talked a lot about himself, and she thought he seemed perfectly up-front and sincere and legit. She couldn't reveal anything about herself, though. So she made do with the name Pride and a little lie. She told him she was a student in one of the science departments on the Malaz Campus. She had always felt that Malaz girls were smarter than Olaisha girls, since they specialized in scientific fields.

Meanwhile, Lamees had met on the Internet Ahmed from Riyadh—a medical student at her university. They were both in the third year. Ahmed started leaving the notes he took during class in one of the photo-copying shops where she could pick them up later, and she would do the same for him. After an exam she sent him e-mails with the most significant points the doctor had focused on. Male doctors were always easier on female students and female doctors were easier on male students. Although their classes were separate, the reading materials, homework assignments, quizzes, midterms and finals were mostly the same. The best thing to do, medical and dental students quickly have realized, was to get the notes on what the male doctors were teaching from the female students, and vice versa.

As exams were approaching fast, there were purely practical reasons to be able to get quick answers from each other. There were observations and comments to make about exam topics and the style of this or that professor in the oral examinations. And so despite Lamees's strict rules for online behavior, the relationship between Ahmed and Lamees somehow took the momentous and forbidden leap from the computer screen to the cell phone.

27.

To: seerehwenfadha7et@yahoogroups.com
From: "seerehwenfadha7et"
Date: August 13, 2004
Subject: Sultan Al-Internetti

If you aren't up to lovin', don't do it!
　　—Mahmoud Al-Melegi*

Not a week passes anymore without my reading some article about myself in a newspaper or magazine or Internet chat room. Standing in line at the supermarket, it really stunned me to see a popular magazine on the rack with bold letters across the cover that said: "What Do Celebrities Think of Today's Hottest Talk in the Saudi Street?" I didn't doubt for a minute, of course, that I was that hot subject. Very calmly, I bought the magazine. Once I was back in the car, I flipped through it quickly, flying through the roof out of happiness! Four entire pages crammed full of photos of writers and journalists and politicians and actors and singers and sports stars, each having their little say on the burning issue of the e-mails from an unknown source that have been the talk of the Saudi street for months!

*Egyptian actor. The line comes from a famous black-and-white "classic" Arabic movie.

I was most interested in what the literary lions had to say. I didn't understand a thing, naturally. One said I was a talented writer who belongs to the metaphysical surrealistic expressionist strain of the impressionists' school, or something like that. The pundit observed that I am the first to be able to represent all these things. If only this big-mouth knew the truth! I don't have the slightest idea what these words even MEAN, let alone know how to combine them in some meaningful way! But deserved or not, it is indeed gratifying to be the subject of such panegyric. (Hey, at least I can match their vocabulary now and then!) What do I think about impressionist metaphysical surrealism? It's positively, absolutely PUFFSOULISTIC!

Sadeem, do you think there is any hope Rashid will start aching for his son and come see him one of these days? You know, right, that Rashid's dad brought Saleh a namesake gift because I named the baby after him, even though Rashid isn't even anywhere around?"

"Don't waste your time even thinking about him. Didn't he send money with his mother or father? That's it—curtains! As far as everybody is concerned, he's in the clear. What do you want with him anyway, after everything he's done?"

After her phone conversation with Sadeem, Gamrah started looking at the photo album of her wedding. In picture after picture, she noticed how glum Rashid's expression was, while her face radiated happiness and delight.

What brought her up short was a photo of herself surrounded by Rashid's sisters: Layla, married and mother of two children; Ghadah, who was about Gamrah's age; and Iman, who was fifteen years old. For a few minutes she concentrated on this picture, thinking. She reached a decision. She rushed over to the computer and slid the photo into the scanner. In seconds, the picture appeared on the screen. Using the right mouse click, she cut herself, Layla and Iman. Only Ghadah was left.

In the evening, getting together with Sultan on instant messenger as she did every night, she convinced him that she had finally decided to send him her photo in exchange for the many photos of himself that he had sent her.

She sent him Ghadah's portrait through IM, trembling as she hit send. She had already told him that it was a photo of her with some friends taken at someone's wedding. She edited out all the others, she explained, as a loyal and trusty friend who would never expose her friends' pictures to strangers. As soon as the photo was transferred successfully, Sultan divulged how blown away he was by her good looks, telling her he could never have imagined that she was so gorgeous. Gamrah rounded out her little deception by telling him that her real name was Ghadah Saleh Al-Tanbal!

GAMRAH'S SISTER HESSAH called her older sister Naflah to ask her advice about the never-ending problems Hessah was having with her husband, Khalid.

"Sister, would you believe it, now he's on my back all the time because of Gamrah! He started calling her names just because he heard that my brothers set up an Internet connection for her at home."

"He ought to be ashamed of himself, saying things like that! Did you tell Mama?"

"I told her, but you know what she said to me? She said, 'It's none of your husband's business what Gamrah's doing and you can tell him to stop complaining! The poor girl doesn't have anything to entertain her. It's bad enough that she's shut up in this house day and night. At least, spending time on the Internet is better—for all of us—than having your sister roaming the streets of Riyadh out of boredom!"

"Mama is still so upset about poor Gamrah's divorce."

"So, as long as Gamrah has gone and gotten a divorce, do you want me to follow her example and get myself a divorce, too? My Lord, if Khalid hears any gossip at all about Gamrah, anything bad she's doing online with the guys she chats with every day, anything!, he's going to throw me out and my children, too. Out in the street!"

"He'd be the only loser! Anyway, don't you have a family, a home you can go back to, after all?"

"Oh, fine! Just great. Exactly what I want to do, sit around with Mama and Gamrah now! *Wallah,* the more I see the state Gamrah's in and this life she's living, the more I praise my Lord for this creep I have sitting at home. As the proverb says, hold on to whatever you've got, otherwise you will get a lot worse. *Yallah. Alhamdu lillah* and thank God for everything."

FROM THE MOMENT she sent him the photo of Rashid's sister Ghadah (or, ahem, *her* photo), Sultan had hardly left the Net for a minute. He kept after her all the time to let him talk to her over the phone. She stood firm, though. She wasn't "that sort" of girl, she said. The more she turned him down, the more attached to her Sultan became and the more he praised and glorified her moral rectitude.

In truth, Gamrah had given a great deal of thought to this issue of telephone calls. She simply could not go there, she decided. She thought of two reasons. First, her cell phone was in her father's name. That being the case, it was very possible that Sultan could and would find out who she really was. He would know that she lied to him and he might spread the news that he got to know one of Al-Qusmanji girls and the ex of Rashid Al-Tanbal through the Internet. And second, she had never really warmed up to the idea of talking on the phone to a strange guy, even if she did feel a kind of closeness to Sultan and sensed that he was sincere and would stick to his word. Still, something inside of her would not relent. She, like the majority of well-raised Saudi girls, couldn't help but resist the idea and find it improper.

After some long nights of insomnia and many, many tears of contrition over her unforgivable act of exploiting innocent Ghadah's photo to get revenge on Rashid, and after her mother described the problems Hessah was having with her husband on account of her sister's addiction to the Internet, Gamrah made a very difficult decision. She would withdraw from the bewitching world of chat. She would take herself out of the range of the good, upstanding Sultan, who did not deserve to be treated in such a thoughtless and cavalier way. He especially didn't deserve such horrid treatment after he had begun to talk about hoping to marry her.

Without any warning, Gamrah disappeared. All news of her suddenly ceased. So did the messages to Sultan, who went on writing e-mails full of desire and love and entreaty and conciliation for months, even though Gamrah did not respond, not even once.

28.

To: seerehwenfadha7et@yahoogroups.com
From: "seerehwenfadha7et"
Date: August 20, 2004
Subject: Had Matti Fallen for Her? And She for Him?

My reader Ibrahim advised me to create a Web site for myself (or he will create it for me) where I will publish my e-mails, starting with the very first one and going all the way through. Ibrahim says that this will protect them from literary theft or loss, and I can increase the number of visitors with some advertisements and I can make money if I agree to put links to other Web sites on my Web page. Ibrahim explained everything to me in detail.

I am most grateful to you, brother, for your kind offer and generous cooperation. But I don't know any more about designing Web sites than I do about stewing okra! And I can't possibly put such a burden on your shoulders, Ibrahim. So I will continue on in my own style, as outdated as it is, of sending weekly e-mails while waiting for a more tempting offer. A weekly newspaper column, maybe, or a radio or TV program all to myself, or any other proposition which your ingenious intellects can inundate me with, readers!

Matti had the power to make Michelle's life one long, totally cool adventure. He gave her practical help and moral support as she adjusted to her new life. He explained whatever she found difficult in her studies, whether in subjects he was teaching her or in other courses. He was vigilant about keeping up to date on how her dorm life was going, and he tried to help her solve any problem she encountered. She was enjoying her independent life and savoring the taste of a freedom she was experiencing for the first time in her life, but on a daily basis she still spent more time in her uncle's home than she did in her dorm.

After struggling through the challenges and strains of her first few months in San Francisco and getting used to the university routine, Michelle began getting involved in university activities, drawing in Cousin Matthew (that is, Matt or Matti), who in turn began to include her in his weekly pastimes, as did some of his friends.

There was a university-organized camping expedition to Yosemite one weekend. Matti went along because he was president of the university's Friends of Nature Club. Out there, in nature's enchanting embrace, amid beauties Michelle had never seen, Matti was the right companion in the right place at the right time. He would wake her up early for a hike to some small rock outcropping in some out-of-the-way spot where they perched to watch the sunrise. Sitting there, they saw the sun's rays break across the spray of the surging waterfall directly in front of them. They vied to see who could get the best shot in one captivating photo op after another. She roused his competitive zeal with a photo she took of a pair of lovebird squirrels kissing. A little later, he got her back with a picture of a deer blocking the disk of the sun with its head so that the rays appeared to be golden horns extending as far as the eye could see.

Another weekend—this time a long weekend—Matti took Michelle to the Napa Valley. He had been invited by one of his close friends, whose family owned a famous winery there. At the farm Michelle tasted truly superior freshly made jams, grilled meats and pasta made with grain grown on the farm, accompanied by some wonderful Chardonnays and Cabs.

Such were the weekend breaks. When they had longer vacations (but ones not long enough for her to travel home to Saudi Arabia)—Easter break, for instance—Matti would drive her to Las Vegas or Los Angeles. By San Francisco standards, her uncle would be considered, if not loaded, at least a member of the upper middle class. With Matti's monthly salary from the university and his father's help, in addition to what Michelle's father sent her each month, which was pretty substantial, they were able to come up with some totally satisfying plans for spending holidays in out-of-the-ordinary places.

In Las Vegas, he took her to a performance of the hit show *Lord of the Dance*. He surprised her with two tickets to the magnificent *"O"* show of the Cirque du Soleil. In LA, which she had visited before, they switched roles; she became the expedition organizer. She first took him to Rodeo Drive near Sunset Boulevard so that she could pursue her favorite passion: shopping! He began grumbling even before they got there. They spent the evening smoking hookahs at the Gypsy Café. The next day they walked along the beach at Santa Monica and spent the evening at the Byblos Restaurant. There she spotted lots of Saudi men with their Persian girlfriends. Staring at her, checking out her facial features, the Saudis suspected she might be one of them. They were disconcerted to see her there with someone who was obviously not Saudi. As they overheard her chatting with Matti, though, her perfect American accent chased away their misgivings; their eyes, so accustomed to stalking girls from the Gulf, stopped following her.

Back in San Francisco, Matti would take her to Chinatown, where they strolled among the tiny stores window-shopping and wandered into traditional Chinese restaurants. Each time they visited the Chinese neighborhood, they ordered the fruit juice "cocktail" thickened with tapioca, which turned the drink deliciously gluey and gummy.

In the spring they took excursions to Golden Gate Park to view the sunset. He played bewitching songs on his guitar as the sun biscuit dipped into the cup of sea. In winter, he often took her to drink hot cocoa at Ghirardelli overlooking the bay and the infamous island prison of Alcatraz. Sipping their hot drinks, they contemplated its tower in the distance, a notorious silhouette that conjured up a grim past of crime and violence in America.

What Michelle liked best about Matti was that he always showed respect for her opinions, however different they were from his views. Often, she noticed, she commanded sufficient authority to win him over to her way of seeing things. He always explained, though, that these disagreements didn't amount to much, just minor differences of opinion. It wasn't worth the effort to try to change each other's view just to march in lockstep in everything. In her own country, Michelle was used to pulling back from any conversation when disagreement threatened to boil over into hot verbal conflicts and an exchange of insults. She avoided expressing her opinions strongly except when she was with people she felt close to, such as her most intimate girlfriends. Public opinion in her country, she had become convinced, did not necessarily represent what people really thought. They were reluctant to offer their views on a particular issue because some prominent or important person, someone whose word was practically law, might step in and say a few words and then everyone would rush to support him. At home, public opinion coalesced around a single view—the view backed by the most powerful people.

Had Matti fallen for her? She didn't think so. So had she fallen for him? It was impossible to deny that spending so much time together for two years, together with all the interests they shared, made them very close. Nor could she deny that there were moments when she imagined herself truly loving him, especially after a poetic evening on the beach, or—more superficially—after she got a really good final grade in a difficult course in which Matti worked hard to tutor her. But deep in her heart, Faisal still lurked, a buried secret that she couldn't ever reveal to

Matti. Knowing nothing about Saudi Arabia, he couldn't begin to imagine the restrictions that had hindered her attachment to Faisal and had turned the story of her love for him into a tragic tale of loss.

Matti, who came from a country that breathed freedom, believed that love was an extraordinary force that could create miracles! When Michelle was first emerging from girlhood, she, too, had believed that. But that was before she returned from America to live in her own country, where she came to realize that love was treated like an inappropriate joke. A soccer ball to play with for a while, until *those in power* kicked it away.

29.

To: seerehwenfadha7et@yahoogroups.com
From: "seerehwenfadha7et"
Date: August 27, 2004
Subject: Firas Is Different

Nasser Al-Clubs wrote, inviting me to write for the magazine the *Diamond*, of the son of Al-Spades, whose editor-in-chief is Dr. Sharifa Al-Hearts.*

Now that I have discovered that the beggar may actually get what she wants when she sets her own conditions, I shall wait until I get an offer to anchor my own TV show just like Oprah or Barbara Walters!

And keep in mind that the better offers you have for me, the happier you make me, the longer e-mails you will be getting from me every week! So, what do you think?

Um Nuwayyir set down a platter of Kuwaiti tahini halvah** and a pot of tea in front of Sadeem, who poured them each a cup. They sipped their tea and nibbled pieces of the rich sesame dessert.

*Anonymous last names to protect the identities of those bold enough to offer a writing job to me!

**Tahini halvah: a type of dessert made of sesame paste.

"Can you believe it, Auntie, I didn't realize Waleed wasn't Mr. Right until I got to know Firas."

"I just hope the day doesn't come when you realize that Firas isn't Mr. Right until after you get to know the next one in line!"

"God forbid! I don't want anything from this world but Firas. Just Firas and that's it."

"You said exactly the same thing about Waleed, and soon a day will come when I have to remind you that you said that about Firas, too!"

"Ya, but just think about it—think about Firas and then picture Waleed, Auntie Um Nuwayyir. They're so different!"

"Both of them are losers! As the Egyptians say: Why compare flip-flops to wooden clogs!"*

"I do not get why you don't like Firas, even though he's so sweet and lovable. What's not to like?"

"I don't like men, period. You've totally forgotten the day when I told you I don't think much of Waleed. You weren't very happy to hear it then, either, and you have paid no attention to my concerns."

"I was kind of dumb and naïve. That sick bastard Waleed told me that he had spied on all the telephones in the house—landlines and cell phones both—before our engagement, that he got hold of telephone records and searched through them all, incoming calls and outgoing, for the past six months before his proposal to my father. He gave himself the right to search for anything that might suggest I had a relationship with any guy before him, and I was so brainless that I actually felt proud to know that I had passed *that* exam! What an idiot."

"Obstinate! That's what you were. At the time, I said to you this fellow has a real problem with jealousy, he's pretty sketchy himself. But you didn't believe me. You were absolutely blinded by love. I said to you: It's early days still, and look what's happening already. You'll never be rid of these tests he puts you through—it's not high school final exams, it's

---

*A saying used when you compare two things that are both worthless.

marriage! Do you know what that means? And what if you fail one of his 'trust checks'? What will happen to you? He's gonna leave you for sure! To hell with it. To hell with him!"

"But Firas is different, Auntie. I swear to God he's never put me through anything that suggests he does not trust me enough, he's never pestered me with questions like Waleed did. Firas has a good clean mind and he doesn't see everything through a veil of suspicion the way Waleed always did."

"But Saddoomah darling, it's not good to show Firas that he's everything in your life and that you'll do anything for his sake!"

"But Auntie, I can't help it! I'm deeply in love with him. I'm so used to having him around. His is the first voice I hear when I get up in the morning and the last voice I hear before I fall asleep at night. All day long he's with me wherever I am. He asks me about my exams before my father does, and he lists the things I have to do every day before I even realize them, and if I have a problem, he solves it for me in no time by using his connections. If I need anything, even a can of Coke in the middle of the night, he gets someone to bring it. Can you believe it, one time he went to the pharmacy at four in the morning to bring me a pack of sanitary pads because my driver was fast asleep! He went himself and bought it for me and dropped the plastic bag off at our front door! I mean, is it strange, Auntie, after the way he treats me and pampers me, for me to feel like he is everything in my life? I don't know, I don't even remember how I ever lived without him!"

"Oh, for God's sake! You are making him sound like Hussein Fahmi!* I ask God to give you the best out of him and spare you the worst. I'm just not very optimistic."

"But why? Tell me!"

"Well, if he loves you as you say he does, then why hasn't he proposed to you yet?"

---

*A handsome, well-known Egyptian actor who starred in many Arabic romantic films.

"This is exactly what I don't get, either, Auntie."

"Didn't you tell me you thought he changed after he found out that you had been previously married to Waleed?"

"He didn't change, really, but . . . well, uh, I sensed that he was a little different, maybe. There was the same caring and gentleness and worrying over me, but it's as if there's something inside of him that he doesn't show in front of me any longer. Maybe it's jealousy? Or anger that he's not the first person in my life, the way I'm the first girl in his."

"And who on earth is telling you that you're the first girl in his life?"

"It's just a feeling I have! My heart tells me I'm the only love he's known. Even if he got to know girls before me—and of course he did, given how old he is and all that time he lived abroad—I am sure he didn't actually really fall in love with anyone and become attached to her and get his life all entangled with hers like he has with me. A guy doesn't become so fond of someone and go to such trouble and devotion when he's this age unless he thinks that the one he loves is someone extraordinary! Someone who really suits him. He's not young anymore, and he doesn't see things the way a guy still in his twenties sees things. Men of this age, when they fall in love, right away they start thinking about settling down, about getting married. He's not just fooling around. There's none of this *C'mon, let's get to know each other* and *We'll see how it goes, let's go with the flow,* and all that little-boy stuff. And what proves it is that to this day he has never asked to see me, since those days in London, except that one time on our drive from Riyadh to Khobar in the eastern region."

"I don't understand how you dared let him drive right up to you in the next lane when you were riding with your father. You crazy girl! What if your father got suspicious? What if he saw the way that strange guy in the nearby car was looking at you and got furious? What would you have done then?"

"I wasn't being daring or anything. The whole thing was a coincidence. I was supposed to travel to the eastern province by car with my father to attend a funeral. Firas was going to spend the weekend with his parents like he always does and missed his plane, so he decided to go by car. My father left work early that day and wanted to set off right away. Firas, who was supposed to have left at noon, delayed until late afternoon because of his work. It happened that we were on the road at the same time! We were texting the whole time, asking each other, How many more kilometers till you get there? I was trying to convince him to stop typing on his cell phone while he was driving! Suddenly I found him saying to me, What does your father drive? I told him, A dark quartz Lexus, why? He said, Just look to the left in five seconds and you'll see me! Aah, Auntie! I can't begin to tell you what I felt the moment I saw him! I never imagined I would love someone so much. With that creep Waleed I felt I was ready to surrender, to give up anything, just so he'd be pleased with me. But with Firas I don't feel the need to make sacrifices. I feel I want to give without any limits. Give and give and give! Can you believe it, Aunt, sometimes I get thoughts I'm ashamed of."

"Like what?"

"I mean, like I imagine myself welcoming him home in the evening once we're married. And of course, he always comes home tired. I sit him down on the sofa and I sit on the floor in front of him. I imagine myself rubbing his feet under salted warm water and kissing them! Do you understand what this picture I have in my head does to me, Aunt? It drives me mad! I never imagined I could think things like that about any man, no matter who he was. Even when I loved Waleed, I was too proud to imagine such things! Do you see how this Firas has rocked all my thinking and left me loving him in a totally hopeless way?"

Um Nuwayyir took a long breath and let it out as a deep sigh. "Oh, my dear. I just don't want to see you get hurt again. That's all I'm saying. May God give you according to your good intentions, my darling, and keep evil away from you."

30.

To: seerehwenfadha7et@yahoogroups.com
From: "seerehwenfadha7et"
Date: September 3, 2004
Subject: Same Old Same Old Gamrah

> *And if Allah touches you with harm, there is no one who can remove*
> *it but He; and if He intends any good for you, there is none who can*
> *repel His Favor which He causes it to reach whomsoever of his slaves*
> *He wills.*
> —Qur'an, Surat Yunus
> (chapter of Jonah), verse 107

I'm getting many, many responses rebuking and insulting Um Nuwayyir, and censuring the families of my friends who have allowed their daughters to spend a single evening at the home of a divorced woman who lives alone. Wait a minute. Is divorce a major crime committed by the woman only? Why doesn't our society harass the divorced man the way it crushes the divorced woman? I know that you readers are always ready to dismiss and make light of these naïve questions of mine, but surely you can see that they are logical questions and they deserve some careful thought. We should defend Um Nuwayyir and Gamrah and other divorcées. Women like

them don't deserve to be looked down on by society, which only conde-
scends from time to time to throw them a few bones and expects them to
be happy with that. Meanwhile, divorced men go on to live fulfilling lives
without any suffering or blame.

G amrah's life didn't particularly change after the birth of her son,
since the real burden of caring for him fell onto the shoulders
of the Filipina babysitter whom Gamrah's mother had hired specifically
for the job. The mother knew how lazy her daughter was and how she
neglected even herself. How could she possibly look after a newborn?
Gamrah remained as she was. In fact, she reverted to what she had been
before she was married. She was busy enough tending to the profound
melancholy that had enveloped her after she cut herself off from chat.
She went on thinking about Sultan for quite a while. She often felt a
strong yearning to talk to him, but she always retreated as soon as she
recalled his situation and her state of affairs. Both would make it very
difficult for them to be together in any real sense of the word.

Every evening, her thoughts took her far away. Envisioning her three
friends, she compared her life with the lives they were leading. Here was
Sadeem, totally consumed with adoring (full-time) a successful politician
and a man about town, who might at any moment rise up to ask for her
hand in marriage. That image was based on what Sadeem was telling her
about their splendid love and how they saw absolutely eye to eye on everything. *Oh, how I envy Sadeem,* she thought. *She is lucky to get Firas instead
of Waleed! An older guy is a lot better than those amateurs who don't even know
what they want out of the world.*

Lamees was in her third year of university, and soon she would become a doctor and have the world at her feet! No problem if she was a
little late in getting married, since marriage later in life was common in
medical circles. In fact, it was so commonplace that one might even hear
murmurs of disapproval about the "early" marriage of a female medical
student. If a girl wanted to stay single without being labeled a spinster,

all she had to do was go into medicine or dentistry. It had a magic ability to turn away prying eyes. But for girls in liberal arts colleges or two-year diploma programs, not to mention those who didn't even go to a university, those eyes started staring and the fingers started pointing the moment they turned twenty.

Even more, Gamrah thought, *Lamees is so lucky with her mother, God protect her! Her mother is very smart and cultivated and she often sits and talks with Lamees, and with Tamadur, too, and they spill their hearts out to her freely because she's understanding. My poor little mama is so old-fashioned and unsophisticated. Every time we asked anything of her, all she ever answered was no! We shouldn't do this, we shouldn't say that! She always criticized everything. Like that day when Shahla went and bought a few thongs and sexy pajamas, saying all her friends had some. Mama really gave it to her. She grabbed it all and threw it in the garbage, screaming, "This is the last straw! You want to dress like a hussy and you haven't even gotten married!" She went straight to the old outdoors shops of Taiba and Owais* and bought her a dozen old-fashioned, matronly nightgowns and brought them home, insisting that Shahla was going to like them! She handed them over and said, "This is it for you, missy, and those other things you can have only when you're a married woman."*

Even Michelle, after Faisal dropped her, was luckier than I was, Gamrah thought. Michelle's family had let her study in America, while Gamrah wasn't even allowed to leave the house by herself. And in her rare visits to Sadeem's house, her mother insisted that one of her brothers deliver her in person and bring her back even though the driver was always around. *You're so lucky, Michelle. You can relax and live your life the way you want to! There's no one shadowing you and breathing down your neck, asking every minute where you're going and where you've been! You're free and you don't have to hear people's relentless gossip.*

Whenever she was with her three friends, Gamrah sensed an enormous gap that separated her from them, now that they had entered the university. What had happened to Lamees? She had changed. Why would

---

*Taiba and Owais is a massive outdoor flea market where cheap goods are sold.

she sign up for courses in self-defense and yoga? Ever since joining the lousy College of Medicine, she had been acting weird and had grown away from her old friends, especially in her way of thinking.

Meanwhile, Michelle had become truly frightening lately, the way she talked about freedom and women's rights, the bonds of religion, conventions imposed by society and her philosophy on relations between the sexes. She was continually advising Gamrah to become tougher and meaner in asserting herself and not to give an inch when it came to defending her own rights.

Sadeem was the one Gamrah felt closest to. She seemed to have gotten more mature since spending her summer break in England. Her self-confidence had been bolstered by traveling alone and working and reading, it seemed. Or, more likely, it came from being loved by a man with the status of Firas.

Gamrah felt that she was the only one who hadn't really changed since high school. Her concerns and interests were pretty much the same. Her ideas had not evolved and her old dreams had not given way to new ones. Her sole aspiration was still marriage to a man who would snatch her away from her solitude and make up for the hard times she had seen. How much she wished that she could draw strength from Michelle, intelligence from Sadeem and a measure of boldness from Lamees! How much she wanted to transform herself over into a personality as magnificent and vivacious as her friends. But, she despaired, as always she was just not able to keep up with them. God had created her with this weak personality, a character she herself scorned. She would always be a few steps behind. All her life.

She went in to have a quick look at Saleh before bed. Entering the room, walking toward his little crib, which lay next to his babysitter's bed. She crept up quietly so that she wouldn't wake either of them. And there were the baby's big brown eyes, wide open, turning innocently toward the source of the sound and light, gleaming at her from the darkness. She put her hands out to him and he clutched at them, as if to ask her to pick him up and hold him. Gathering him up, she felt his wet clothes and his moist thighs. She smelled a piercing odor coming from his tiny diaper. She took him into the bathroom. His bottom was completely wet and covered in diaper rash. Gamrah didn't know what she was supposed to do. Should she awaken her mother or Shahla? How much would Shahla know about babies, if she herself didn't know what to do? Should she rouse the babysitter? "God rid me of her!" Gamrah muttered. "It's all her fault. Look at her—she goes on sleeping while my son drowns in his own pee!" Washing his bottom under warm running water, she handed the baby his yellow rubber ducky and he played with it. He didn't show any sign of being upset or bothered. For Gamrah, though, this seemed more than a mere skin irritation and it was harder to bear.

Everything was hard on her. Rashid, her mother, her sister Hessah, Hessah's husband, Mudi, and even her best friends—all of them thought she was stupid and weak and ineffectual. Even the Filipina babysitter had begun to neglect her son after noticing how little the mother seemed to know. Life had taken everything from her and given nothing in return. It had robbed her of her youth and joy, replacing them with an emptiness and a child whose only sustenance in life was her—when she needed sustenance more than he did.

The rubber ducky fell from Saleh's hand when weeping Gamrah embraced him fiercely, with the force of all the oppression and regret and suffering that lay inside of her.

31.

To: seerehwenfadha7et@yahoogroups.com
From: "seerehwenfadha7et"
Date: September 10, 2004
Subject: Gossiping About MEN!

This story has become my life. Friday has become more sacred than ever. The PC room is now my home, the only place I feel safe. Now I just laugh whenever I feel annoyed by some stupid thing a professor or some girl in class says. These people make my blood boil but who cares! None of it means a thing compared to what I am doing. After all, those bossy teachers and arrogant classmates are glued to their computer screens every Friday just so they won't miss a syllable of what I write. So what if they annoy me every now and then? I'm plenty satisfied by the joy and pride I feel inside!

The four friends met at Gamrah's house on the last day of summer vacation. Each brought Saleh a toy or a piece of candy, dangling them in front of him as bait, trying to get him to walk toward them with his little stumbling steps and his cute plump legs.

Gamrah didn't waste any time, scolding Lamees for the bronzed skin she had acquired in the chalets of Jeddah.

"I swear by God, you are insane! These days, when everyone is going with whitening lotions, you have to go and burn yourself under the sun?"

"Oh, c'mon, guys! You don't appreciate a good tan! I find it so attractive!"

"Girls! Say something to her—this nut!" said Gamrah.

Michelle, home from San Francisco for the summer, had become accustomed to the healthy look of all the tan, sporty California girls. "Actually, I think it looks great," she said.

Gamrah erupted. She tried to get Sadeem to back her up. "Sadeem! Just look at these insane girls and what they are saying. Have you ever heard of any mother who wanted to find her son a black bride?"

"Oh, whatever! Everyone to their own tastes. How long are we going to keep doing whatever pleases these old ladies and their darling little boys? I say keep that up, Lamees—just do whatever you want to. And if you ever want to pour kerosene on your hair and set it on fire, go right ahead!"

Gamrah was left spluttering. "Thanks for the help, girl!"

"I mean, seriously," continued Sadeem, "I'm sick of how we let everyone else control us and lead us through this life. We can never do anything without the fear of being judged holding us back. Everyone steers us along according to what they want. What kind of life is that? We don't have a say about our own lives!"

"Saddoomah!" her friends all turned toward her and exclaimed. "What's the matter? Who has been bothering you?"

"Obviously, she's had a fight with Firas. It can't be anything else."

"What did that monkey do to you?"

"Did you see him in Paris?"

Sadeem tried to keep her voice calm, since her outburst had shocked her friends. Slowly, she began telling them what was bothering her. "I saw him once. I mean, he came to Paris for one day just to see me, and of course I couldn't say no. Okay. I'm not going to lie to you. Frankly, I was dying to see him, too! This whole entire year, I hadn't laid eyes on him because of my studies and his work, and because the two of us had an agreement not to meet in Riyadh. It's just too difficult, dangerous and awkward. It wouldn't be relaxing like it would be if we were abroad. Outside the country, you can loosen up, you can breathe without worrying who's watching you. Abroad I could meet him anywhere, in any public place, but here, no. In Paris, I met him at a cozy restaurant and we just sat there talking. It was nice."

"So far, so good," said Gamrah. "So where's the problem?"

"Of course," Michelle broke in, "right after it, *right* away, he asked you, 'How come you feel so comfortable and relaxed about going out with me?' Or he doesn't even ask; he just starts doubting you immediately, and by the next day he's already treating you differently. Different from when you had never agreed to meet him. After you meet a Saudi guy behind your family's back, behind the society's back, he loses his respect for you instead of appreciating your move! I know this stupid business *really* well; these hang-ups are built automatically into the messed-up heads of our guys. They are mentally twisted! Why do you think I left this country to live somewhere else?"

"No, not at all," replied Sadeem. "He's never treated me like that. Sure, I've noticed sometimes that he seems to have a little bit of this suspicion thing when he talks about girls in general. But he has never doubted me. Firas knows me really well and he trusts me very much."

"A guy's nature doesn't change," asserted Gamrah. "If he has that suspicion thing in him, then you will suffer from that one day, even if he tries to hide it in the beginning of your relationship."

"No, believe me, there wasn't any problem like this. The problem is that for a while now I've been noticing that he gives me these really strange hints about our relationship. One day he says to me that his family has found him a good bride, and another day he says, 'If a well-matched groom shows up for you, don't send him away!'

"How can his heart allow him to say things like that when he knows

I love him so much? At first I figured he was joking, just to torment me a bit. When I saw him in Paris, though, I told him that a friend of Papa's wants to marry me to his son. Really and truly, I wasn't lying about that. I figured that he would get upset and worried and would knock on my father's door the very same day. But what happened instead was that he gave me a smile as cold as the nighttime desert and asked me if the man was a good fellow. He said, 'Make sure your father asks around about him, and if he turns out to be okay, then put your trust in God and go ahead!' "

"He really said that?" asked Gamrah, her tone disbelieving.

"So what did you say when he said that?" asked Lamees impatiently.

"Nothing."

"Nothing?" All the girls spoke at once.

"My brain seized up! I couldn't get what he was saying! I just sat there staring at him. I couldn't say a word and I must have looked like a complete idiot. My eyes teared up and then I said, 'Sorry, I have to go.' "

"So what did he say?"

"He said, 'Don't be angry,' and he made me swear that I wouldn't leave! He said, 'Look, if you go now, I am not going to speak to you ever again.' "

"So you stayed?"

"Ya, I sat there until he finished eating and then we both got up and left the restaurant together. He then fetched me a taxi to the hotel."

"So are you guys still together?"

"Together, but nothing has improved since then. He is playing with my nerves and I don't know what to do to change him back to what he was before. Why is it always like this with me? Why do guys always change totally after they've been with me for a little while? There must be something about me! What seems clear is that the minute I start feeling comfortable with them they start getting really uncomfortable with me."

Men's insistence on calling the shots, Lamees believed, didn't just come about in a vacuum. It happened after a guy stumbled on a woman who really liked that kind of domineering behavior and encouraged it.

"I believe that men aren't scheming to tell lies or to deceive us," she said. "It's, like, they don't intentionally do that. It comes from their nature. They're just kind of wicked. A guy will begin backing off from a girl and even trying to escape as soon as she seems available. Because then he feels, *Okay, I don't have to do anything to get her. She is no longer a challenge.* He doesn't say this to her face. He doesn't let her figure out that he is in the wrong, no way! He makes her believe that she is the one who has problems, not him. Some of them give the girl hints, hoping she will end the relationship herself, but we stupid girls never pick up on them. We go on working on the relationship until it kills us, even if we're pretty sure from the start that it's a total disaster. That's why in the end we make fools of ourselves. We're the ones who don't hold on to our pride from the start to get out with our honor intact."

Next, Michelle gave Sadeem her own logical analysis of the situation. "Sweetie, this is the escape strategy of an immature little boy. You find that he has given it some thought and then tells himself, *So why should I take someone who is divorced when I haven't ever been married? Even divorced men are looking for girls who haven't been married, so why would I end up with a woman who has been previously married?* You'll find him weighing her in his mind and saying, *If I want to become a government minister or some other high official later on, I need to find a woman who will give me some standing, a woman to help me with her family name and her looks and her genealogy and her social position and wealth! I'm not going to take one who's flawed from the start cause she's been divorced, and then watch people devour me with their waspish tongues.* This is the way our men think, unfortunately. No matter how *impressive* he is or how refined his thinking is or how much in love he is, he still considers love something that can only happen in novels and films. He doesn't get it, he doesn't conceive of love as a foundation that builds a family. Maybe he's even a really cultured and highly educated guy who's been around. Maybe he knows deep down that love is a basic human need, that it isn't shameful for a man to choose his partner in life himself, as long as he's completely sure she's the right one. But he is still afraid. It worries him to even think about following a path different from the path his father followed, and his uncle, and his grandfather before them. And anyway, he'll think, *Those old men are still living with those shut-up women of theirs. So something must have gone right. What they did was successful. It's got to work because everyone else has done it.* So he follows their steps and doesn't go against their way of doing things. That way, no one can come along someday and rub it in that he failed because he strayed from the path of his ancestors. Our men are just too scared to pay for their own decisions in life. They want others to follow, others to blame."

Not one of the three other women had any idea where Michelle obtained her theories of how guys think. But they felt that her words evoked strong echoes in all of them. They didn't know how she had reached her conclusions, but they knew, in their hearts, that she was right.

32.

To: seerehwenfadha7et@yahoogroups.com
From: "seerehwenfadha7et"
Date: September 17, 2004
Subject: The Migrating Bird

To those who have totally annoyed me by declaring that I do not represent the girls of Saudi Arabia, I say: How many times do I have to repeat myself? I am not writing anything incredible or bizarre or so weird that you people absolutely do not relate to it or can say it's not true! Everything I say, the girls in my society know very well. Every week, every single one of them reads my e-mail and exclaims, "This is me!" And since I am writing to give a voice to those girls, I ask those who have nothing to do with what I say to quit sticking their snouts into what's not their business. And then, if they are so eager to offer a perspective other than mine, they're welcome to write their own e-mails. But don't ask ME to write only what YOU approve of!

Michelle discovered that the epidemic of contradictions in her country had gotten so out of control that it had even infected her parents. Her father, whom she had regarded as a rare symbol of the freedom in Saudi Arabia, had (himself!) now smashed the pedestal she had put him on, thereby proving the truth of the proverb: Anyone who lives with a people becomes one of them!

Her father exploded in a way she never would have anticipated, when he heard her suggest how much she liked her cousin Matti. Even her mother, who had only the one brother, Matti's father, and loved him devotedly, and considered his children as precious as her own limbs—even this woman was totally, shockingly upset by her daughter's unmistakable words.

Michelle would never have believed it of her parents, but there was undoubtedly a religious impulse behind their blowup. Her father had never been among the hard-liners when it came to religion. And her mother, who had become a Muslim after her daughter's birth, had never been one to strictly follow religious strictures. So why did they treat her so ferociously now, trying to force her to believe that Matti wasn't right for her? Her parents, it seemed, had absorbed their share from this garden of contradictions where they had put down roots in recent years.

What if Matti really did love her? She knew that was unlikely, but she couldn't help but think: was she going to give him up for the sake of her family, as Faisal had let her go for the sake of his family? Matti's problem was much more complex, because according to Islamic law, she couldn't marry Matti, since he wasn't a Muslim. Her dad, as a Muslim man, had been able to marry her Christian mother, but Muslim women weren't permitted to marry non-Muslim men. Could she marry him in a civil ceremony in America? She knew that her parents couldn't possibly agree to such a thing, no matter how liberated they were.

Anyway, praise be to God that Matti had never broached this subject of love. Perhaps his feelings toward her were no different from the customary affection between friends or between brothers and sisters. Especially since in America it wasn't generally accepted for first cousins to form romantic relationships. Perhaps her years in Saudi Arabia had so perverted her judgment in these matters that when a man was just being nice and kind to her, she misread it as LOVE.

Her parents decided to take the step they had been postponing until Michelle got her degree from UCSF. As a pretext for making that decision now instead of later, they insisted that with the situation being what it was in post-9/11 America, they were afraid for her to return there for her last two years of college. Michelle had a hunch, though, or more than a hunch, that what she had said about her relationship with Matti, as vague as it had been, was their real motive.

They would all move to Dubai! That was the decision the parents made once they became convinced they could no longer fit comfortably in the prim and prying Saudi society. Michelle had no choice in the matter. If she were to refuse to move with her parents and brother, the suspicions filling her father's head would only grow more intense. For her part, when she thought about her relationship with her cousin, she didn't believe he truly loved her. She felt he regarded her as a pampered younger sister whom he tried to make happy—the way he tried to make everyone happy, especially those nearest to him.

Their decision, coming after she completed only two years of her studies at the University of San Francisco, bewildered her. It was clear, though, that her parents had arranged everything in advance. She was to finish her studies in the Department of Visual Communications at the American University in Dubai so that the two years wouldn't go to waste, as had her first year of university when she moved from Riyadh to San Francisco. Little Meshaal, meanwhile, would enter a private school. Her father intended to make investments in Dubai as many of his friends were doing. Her mother would have more freedom and respect, which had mostly been denied to her in Saudi Arabia.

Even though Dubai was a lot closer than San Francisco, this move was much harder than the last one. This time she would have to say good-bye to her friends without the promise that she would see them again at the New Year's break. Their home in Riyadh would still nominally remain their home, yet Michelle was certain that she would return to it only if everyone in the family agreed. There would remain no ties to Riyadh except for the relatives who lived there, and her father and mother would not be interested in visiting them, anyway.

Lamees organized a big farewell party at her house. The girls gave Michelle an elegant diamond-studded watch. They cried remembering the days of their adolescence and young adulthood, which seemed to be vanishing with Michelle's departure from the *shillah*. Um Nuwayyir reminded her girls repeatedly that phone lines and Internet did exist! She pointed out that they could even converse daily, with picture and sound using a webcam and a microphone. That soothed them a little. Still, they worried that their relationship with Michelle would change once she moved to Dubai, just as it had when she went to America. This would be an even bigger change, for now the separation would be permanent, and so the ember of friendship that had remained constantly warm for years would be snuffed out, no matter how hard they all tried to preserve it.

Lamees was the most grief-stricken of all. Michelle's departure came at a trying time for her. She was suffering from an accumulation of things: difficulties at the university with some overbearing faculty members, plus her usual problems with Tamadur, who never tired of criticizing her and didn't conceal her envy whenever Lamees scored some success or other. There were also problems with Ahmad, who, Lamees had discovered, was repeating everything they discussed on the phone to his friends at the university—all those conversations that had nothing to do with their studies! He was passing on everything she told him for their amusement, including stories about her classmates, who then heard about it and got furious and stopped having anything to do with her.

In the last few years, Lamees had grown distant from Michelle. She had gone through a long period of uncertainty and conflicting feelings that came when she compared Michelle to her new, somewhat more sophisticated girlfriends at the College of Medicine. But on the day of the departure, Lamees had the sudden painful realization that Michelle alone understood her, really understood her. Michelle resembled her in so many ways and she had divined her true personality in a way that the others had not. Only she had unlocked her deepest secrets and could keep them safe. Yes, there had been problems. Michelle had put up with a lot; she had every right to feel hurt when Lamees neglected her at the university. But what was the point of dredging any of that up now? Michelle was about to leave and might never return, and so Lamees would lose forever the friend closest to her heart, whose worth she recognized only now.

33.

To: seerehwenfadha7et@yahoogroups.com

From: "seerehwenfadha7et"

Date: September 24, 2004

Subject: Abu Musa'ed and His Fine Print

> *The Prophet, God's blessings and peace be upon him, said: The virgin's agreement to a marriage must be sought by her guardian, but the widow or divorcee has more right to her own person than does her guardian.*
>
> —The hadith collection of Sahih Muslim, verse 3477

One of the guys reading my e-mails offered to collect them, once the last one appeared, and to organize them into chapters for a book to be published. That way everyone could read them.

Ya salam!* That's really something. For me to have a novel all my own! A book that would be displayed in bookstores and hidden in bedrooms. A book that some people would beg others to bring from oversees. (That's assuming that it would be banned here in Saudi.) And would I see my charming photo gracing its back cover—or defacing it!—just like other writers?

*Oh, wow!

I was astonished but also frightened at the suggestion. Astonished because I believe that no one is left in Saudi Arabia who hasn't received my e-mails. After all, I have been so diligent, using addresses of subscribers to Yahoo and Hotmail and other service providers, that I've sent them to all Internet subscribers who had Kingdom of Saudi Arabia mentioned in their online profiles. And after the first few e-mails, I have got thousands of new subscribers to my Yahoo group! And frightened because publishing a book would mean revealing my name, after keeping it hidden from all of you out there for these many months.

Here come the truly serious questions: Do my friends deserve to undergo such a sacrifice? Is it worth all the accusations that will be meted out to me and to them (in addition to those rebukes that have already been kindly sent my way) if my real name becomes known?

I am anxious to hear your views and advice. Write to me.

Gamrah's mother prodded her daughter to meet Abu Musa'ed, an army general and a longtime friend of her uncle's. This Abu Musa'ed was over forty. He had been married, but in the ten years he had spent with his wife, God had not blessed him with children. For some reason, everyone used to called him Ubo Musa'ed—father of Musa'ed—anyway. He had divorced his wife and was looking for another, younger one who would provide him with the son he was longing for. (Incidentally, just as he decided to marry again news reached him that his former wife had gotten pregnant by her second husband.) He put the troublesome issue of finding a fertile wife on the table for his friends to toss around. No sooner did his friend Abu Fahad, Gamrah's uncle on her mother's side, hear this than he nominated his sister's daughter. How utterly devoted he was to his niece's best interests, he thought triumphantly.

So here she was. When Abu Musa'ed came to call, Gamrah sat a little apart, but not too far away, and went about inspecting him with a scrutiny she had not practiced on Rashid when, three years before, he had presented himself as a suitable husband. She no longer was hampered by that old bashfulness of hers, nor was she in danger of tripping over her own feet.

The man wasn't as old as she had imagined; he looked to be in his late thirties. No gray in his mustache, but there were a few silver hairs along the temples, escaping from beneath his white *ghutra.**

Her uncle knew Abu Musa'ed very well and so her father's role in all of this seemed of little importance. Her father had every intention of getting up from his chair and disappearing for a few moments (as the mother had advised him to do) so that his daughter would have a chance to talk to this potential fiancé, an opportunity she had not been given in her first marriage. Her father was waiting for the uncle to rise. The uncle did not budge, however. He couldn't care less about any entreaties from his sister, who was waving furiously at him from behind the door. Gamrah's uncle simply stayed put, anxious and rigidly alert for the tiniest lapse, the slightest turn or look or whispered sign from Gamrah, that would allow him to vent his anger on her and on her mother, should Abu Musa'ed withdraw from the scene.

But Abu Musa'ed ignored Gamrah's presence entirely. He turned his attentions to her uncle, chatting with him about the latest share prices. His impolite attitude thoroughly disgusted Gamrah. It was all she could do not to walk out of the room even though she had made her entrance no more than a few moments before. But suddenly Abu Musa'ed set off a bomb that got her to stay long enough to see whether it would blow everything to smithereens.

"Now, as you know very well," he started in, talking to her uncle, "I'm a Bedouin and a soldier, and I ain't interested in makin' clever little chitchat with you fancy city folk. I heard your niece has a little boy from her first husband. So the fine print as I see it is, the boy stays here with his grandmother. To clarify, here, I am not gonna raise a kid who isn't my own, he is not welcome in my house."

*Male's head covering in Saudi. Similar to a *shimagh* but has a plain white color instead of red and white checks.

"But Abu Musa'ed," responded Gamrah's uncle, "the boy is still very young."

"Young or old, that doesn't matter to me! This is the fine print on the contract. I am just being frank about it and that shouldn't upset you or her father."

Her uncle tried to defuse the bomb, even if too late. "Be patient, Abu Musa'ed, and only good will come of your patience, God willing."

Gamrah was shifting her gaze from her father to her uncle to Abu Musa'ed. It hadn't occurred to any of these men to consult the person who had the biggest stake in this, and who happened to be sitting there in front of them, even if she was as silent and stiff as a wooden plank.

Gamrah stood up and left the room, but only after giving her uncle a scathing look.

In her own room, she found her mother waiting for her. Her mother had heard the whole conversation. Gamrah fumed about her uncle's coldness, her father's passive attitude, and the arrogance of this horrible man called Abu Musa'ed. Her mother made light of it all, though anxiously enough; Gamrah could hear the hard edge in her voice. She soothed her daughter with whatever words she could find, and then she sat silently, having calculated that it was best to remain quiet, now that she had once again bored herself and her daughter by saying the same old things. Gamrah was not to be placated. She went on ranting about this shameless man and his small print, this man who demanded so brazenly that she give up her little boy for his sake—even though the man was clearly not going to produce any children himself! How could he possibly dare to take away her only son? How could he demand that she make such a sacrifice? Who did he think he was, anyway, this Bedouin soldier, that he could speak to her uncle in such a conceited, self-important way? She had heard about those Bedouin men and their difficult natures, but never in her life had she had the bad luck to encounter someone as offensive as Abu Musa'ed.

After the man left the house, indignant that Gamrah had walked out of the room without bothering to come up with a polite excuse, her uncle, with her father behind him, came into her room. Just as her uncle had ignored her presence when they had all been sitting in there with the Bedouin, he ignored her presence now, addressing himself to her mother.

"Your girl has no shame, Um Mohammed! She is so spoiled. I say we go ahead and marry her to this man. There's nothing wrong with him, and praise be to God, the girl already has a son, that is, she isn't completely without children to fill her life. And we all know that leaving her here to sit around without a man to shield and protect her isn't a good thing. People are always talking, sister, and besides, we have other girls in the family who should not pay for what people say about your divorced daughter. God make your life—my dear sister—long for us, God let you raise your children and the children of your children. Gamrah's boy we can leave here to grow up in your house. His mama can come and see him whenever she wants to, and I don't think this man will forbid that. So what do you think, brother, what about it, Abu Mohammed?"

"Wallah, you know the man, and you've looked him over with your sharp eyes, and that's enough for me. If you don't see any problems in him, well, then, we shall rely on God and go ahead."

Having given his full and detailed opinion in a matter that was not his to decide, her uncle left. Her father also went out. Gamrah remained at home, able only to rant at her mother. Provoked and agitated, she flung her words into her mother's face. "Why? Why do I need a man to shield and protect me? Does your brother think I'm a disgrace, or I cannot protect my own self? You people do not realize that I am a grown woman now and I have a son! My word should count and I should be listened to! But no! You think absolutely the opposite from how any reasonable family would think. That's even worse than what you did to me in my engagement to Rashid! And what kind of a husband and father are *you* married to? He doesn't have even one word to say about his own daughter in front of your bossy brother? And this brother of yours, what do I have to do with his daughters whom he wants to marry off? He wants to dump me on that old defective junk of a man just so he can be rid of me and clear the way for good men to marry his own daughters? God willing, I hope they never get married! May he and every one of his daughters go to hell!"

"Shame, shame, Gamrah, dear! He is your uncle, after all, he is family. Don't worry about him now. Seek what is best for you and what the Lord has written will happen. Submit your life to Allah and rely on Him."

Her mother had not counseled her to seek "what is best" for her in her first marriage. Had Rashid come with such overwhelming qualities that seeking what is best wasn't called for then? That night, Gamrah performed the nightly prayer followed by the nonobligatory prayer for seeking guidance that Mudi had taught her. She unrolled her prayer rug and began praying.

"O Allah, I seek Your help in finding out the best thing to do about Ubo Musa'ed's proposal by invoking Your knowledge; I ask You to empower me, and I beseech Your favor. You alone have the absolute power, while I have no power. You alone know it all, while I do not. You are the One Who knows the hidden mysteries. O Allah, if You know that marrying Ubo Musa'ed is good for me in my religion, worldly life, and my ultimate destiny, then facilitate it for me, and then bless me in my action. If, on the other hand, You know this thing is detrimental for me in my religion, worldly life, and ultimate destiny, turn it away from me, and turn me away from it, and decree what is good for me, wherever it may be, and make me content with it."

Mudi informed her that she would not necessarily have a dream that would guide her to the right choice, as she had thought. It was by repeatedly seeking to do what was right that God would relieve her bosom of care and point the way to what was right; or He would make her chest seize up and she would know that this particular decision was not for her own good and then she would know to abandon it. Gamrah went on repeating the prayer for seeking what is right, time and time again, day after day after day, without finding herself really guided to a decision.

After ten days or so, one night when she had performed her ablutions and prayed and gone to bed, Gamrah dreamed that she was sleeping in a bed that was not hers. She was covered in a thick quilt with only her head and feet showing. In the dream, she was gazing at her own face, as if she were staring into the face of her friend Sadeem, except that she was absolutely certain that the sleeping body stretched out along the length of the bed was *her,* even though the facial features were strangely "Sadeem-morphed." The sleeping woman's hair had grayed to the point of white and she had a long white beard (and what was really strange was that during the dream, Gamrah didn't have any odd feelings about that beard on her face). Then she observed the scene, as if she were waking herself up, her sleeping self, by screaming at her. *Get up, get up, prayer time has come!* But she just tossed restlessly on her mattress until she woke up, in the dream and also in reality.

When she told her dream to Mudi, the woman contacted one of the sheikhs she knew who were expert in dream and vision interpretation. She wanted Gamrah to describe her dream to this specialist in her own words. The dream had come to her, Gamrah told him, when she was seeking God's guidance about a prospect who had proposed to her. The sheikh asked her if she had been married. "I was, sheikh, but then I was divorced." He asked her if she had children from that marriage, and she said, "I have a son."

"This sleeping girl is truly you and not your friend as it seemed to you in the dream," he told her. "I advise you, my daughter, before all else to strengthen your faith, in which is protection against every scourge and salvation from every evil. The blanket itself is the security and stability you had in your first marriage and appear to have lost. Seeing your hair as well as your head uncovered is a clear indication of your husband not returning to you. And that is better for you, because the gray hair tells us that he was an immoral person and a traitor who betrayed you. As for your beard, this gives you the good news that your son will be a man of weight and position, with God's leave, among his family and people. Not waking up in time for prayer means that there is a difficulty in the matter for which you sought guidance. I advise you not to accept this man who has come forth to ask for your hand. Good is in what God chooses and God is the most knowledgeable."

Gamrah began to tremble when she heard the sheikh's interpretation of her dream. Her whole body shook and she hurried to inform her mother, who told her brother, who made a scene and threatened them all. But Um Mohammed, with her long experience in such matters, just absorbed his anger until the whole thing was over and everyone had finally averted their eyes from this engagement whose conclusion, and consummation, God had not written and decreed.

34.

To: seerehwenfadha7et@yahoogroups.com
From: "seerehwenfadha7et"
Date: October 1, 2004
Subject: Mourning

The series of enticing offers continue, as do all sorts of propositions, and I cannot distinguish the sincere from the scam. One Saudi producer sent me a proposal to transform my e-mails into a Ramadan TV series of thirty episodes! Why not? If we were already talking about publishing it as a novel, why not film it for TV? I concur with our own Abdullah Al-Ghadhami,* that the literature of the written word is bourgeois while the image is democratic. I prefer the series to the novel, because I want the stories of my friends to reach everyone. This would certainly be a beginning.

But here the crucial question intrudes. Who will agree to act in my series? Must we rely on actresses from the neighboring Gulf states and lose the grand and refined Saudi accent of give and take that underlies the plot? Or will we disguise Saudi boys to take on the roles of young women,** and thereby lose the audience?

*Famous Saudi critic.
**It is generally frowned upon for young Saudi women to be actresses.

The home of Sadeem's senior uncle on her father's side filled with mourners. Sadeem's father, the much-respected Abdulmuhsin Al-Horaimli, had passed away in his midtown office following a sudden heart attack that did not allow him much time to linger on death's door.

In the most out-of-the-way corner of the reception room sat Sadeem. Gamrah and Lamees were on either side of her, trying to comfort her even though their tears were flowing more abundantly than hers. How would Sadeem live now, already without a mother and suddenly without a father to watch over her? How would she sleep at night when there was no one with her in the big house? How would she manage living under the care of her uncles, who without a doubt would force her to move into one of their households? These were questions they couldn't answer, even though, at this awful time, they could not help but ask them. Her mother had died before Sadeem could even know her, while her father had died when she was most in need of him. Verily, we are God's, and to God all must return, and to that there can be no resistance.

Um Nuwayyir stood beside the wives of Sadeem's paternal uncles and her maternal aunt, Badriyyah, to receive all the women who came to mourn. Frequently her eyes sought out Sadeem, wanting to see how she was bearing up under a trial that was enough to tear a person's heart in two.

Sorrowfully, Sadeem examined the women crowding the room. No signs of true sadness showed on any of their faces. Some had come made-up and dressed to the hilt. Some shamelessly lost themselves in meaningless chitchat. She could hear suppressed laughs coming from various parts of the room. Were these the people who had come to keep her company in her awful loss? Was she sitting there to receive the condolences of people who in fact had no sympathy for her at all, while others who felt her grief could not get close enough to embrace her?

Sadeem fled from this room where no one felt the pain squeezing her heart. The only person who understood her was her Firas. No one really perceived how strong her relationship with her father had been except Firas. He alone would be capable of lightening this awful load; he was all that was left to her after her father's departure. How much she needed him!

His text messages on her cell phone didn't stop. He tried regularly to make her feel his presence at her side and to remind her that he shared her grief and sense of loss. Her father was his father, and she was his soul, and he would not abandon her, no matter what.

In the late hours of the night, on the phone, Firas grasped hold of a book of prayers and began reciting to Sadeem, asking her to say Amen after him:

"God, may Abdulmuhsin Al-Horaimli be in your care . . ."

Firas recited the prayer for the dead in a hoarse voice, his heart breaking at the sobs of his Sadeem. But he did not despair of trying to save his beloved from her bereavement. He went on trying to console her with paternal tenderness and utter self-denial, as though he were exclusively there for her, a servant to her every need. Not for a moment did she sense his distance or any inability to truly embrace her.

Firas remained on call for his little Sadeem until she could swallow the first big bite of grief. After that he continued his support, helping her until she could stand on her own and get through the days of her suffering.

35.

To: seerehwenfadha7et@yahoogroups.com

From: "seerehwenfadha7et"

Date: October 8, 2004

Subject: The Aquarius

After my previous e-mail, let me take you away from your grief by invoking a blessing on you this week, on the occasion of the approach of the first day of Ramadan. God has given this blessed month to us yet again, to us and to all Muslims, as He has given us His aid that we may fast the daylight hours all through it and uphold it.

I ask your forgiveness in advance for not sending messages over the course of the coming month. I promise you that I will continue to follow the stories of my friends after the month of virtue comes to a close. I confess in advance that I will miss you. After Ramadan, I will return bearing truly weighty letters, by God's leave. Wait for me.

After finishing their fourth year at the university, Lamees and Tamadur decided to make the most of the summer break by training at one of the hospitals in Jeddah. Like all students attached to the hospital, female and male, they were not permitted to interact with the patients before they were licensed doctors. Their duties were limited to observing the resident physicians and consultants when they examined the sick and performed operations.

At the hospital with the twins were two male trainees from the College of Medicine and a few students, men and women, who were training in the hospital's dental unit.

At first, Tamadur felt downright mortified that she and her sister were the only young women among the medical students. She was so uncomfortable with this that in the mornings she made a point of getting to the hospital late, and later in the day she left before the shift officially ended. Lamees was exactly the opposite: precise in her appointments and eager that she should miss nothing in this new adventure.

The doctors and administrative personnel at the hospital were gracious and friendly with the two of them. But Tamadur felt too shy to sit with her two male colleagues in the single small room assigned to the students for relaxation. She kept her distance from them and even found it hard to get along with the female seniors. Lamees was just the opposite. She was bold and adjusted quickly. She angered her sister by making it obvious how quickly she was falling into a pleasant rhythm with everyone who worked in the hospital.

After about a week of summer training, Tamadur stopped going to the hospital. One of the male students also pulled out in order to travel abroad for the last couple of weeks before school resumed. Lamees was the only female medical student left, next to the only male medical student, Nizar. Lamees was immediately conscious of how much she preferred being with *one* male student instead of two. Before, whenever she had approached the pair of them, she felt she was intruding. But now Nizar was just as alone as she was. Neither of them had any other companion to while away the empty time between patient rounds and operations.

This unplanned proximity allowed Lamees some glimpses into Nizar's genteel personality. The way he behaved toward her was different from Ahmed or any other of her male friends on the Internet. He acted with a spontaneity that charmed her, even though she initially misunderstood his intentions. The day after his classmate left, for example, he invited her to have lunch with him in the hospital cafeteria. Lamees turned him down, saying that she was in the middle of reading a medical text and would wait a little while before eating. What he did was go to the buffet and return with two plates, one for him and the other for her! He handed hers over very politely, reminding her that the operation the two of them were to observe was going to begin in only an hour. Then he picked up the tray with his plate on it and went to a vacant patient's room to eat.

Lamees didn't need very long to get used to Nizar's impulsive ways and appreciate his well-mannered personality. Their conversations began to go beyond the confines of medicine and various treatments and the latest drugs and surgical techniques. They told each other their dreams and what they imagined life would be like after graduating. Eventually, they talked about their personal lives and families, how many brothers and sisters each had, their daily aggravations and other little tidbits that showed that the ice between them was now completely broken.

At a table in the cafeteria, Lamees pretended to be a seer to guess what astrological sign Nizar had been born under. He threw himself into the game.

"So you are definitely either a Sagittarius or an Aquarius. I expect it is Aquarius . . . no, no, Sagittarius! No, wait, Aquarius! Yes, definitely Aquarius. Has to be."

"Okay, so tell me, what is there about my personality that would make me Aquarius and what would make me Sagittarius?" And then, rather slyly, "So that I know which one to choose."

"No, no, it's not going to happen. Just tell me, tell me the truth, which sign are you?"

"Guess!"

"I told you already. Sagittarius or Aquarius. You don't give the impression of being a Virgo—men who are Virgo are really heavy going and hopelessly romantic. They make your blood pressure go up. You don't look like like a Taurus, either."

"How sweet of you, madame!"

"Maybe an Aries? Yes! You could be an Aries!"

"Aha? Keep going. What else could I be? There isn't a single sign you haven't mentioned. And the whole time, you're acting as though you know about sign-reading, but you're just faking it!"

"Okay, I've got it now, this is really *it*. You're either Aries or Sagittarius."

"This is really it? That's the final word?"

"Uh-huh."

"Hmmm, okayyy . . ."

"What do you mean, hmmm, okayyy?"

"I mean, I don't want to let you go down to defeat when I say that I'm an . . . Aquarius!"

"Ya! Really! From the very beginning I was saying Aquarius, but then it was you who got me all confused!"

"*I* got *you* confused! Wait a minute! Wasn't it you who kept changing your mind?"

"I hate you. C'mon, let's go. We've got a round to do."

"Fine, so when are you going to tell me what an Aquarius is supposed to be like?"

"Oh, I'll tell you right this minute. Aquarius men are really awful, they're snobbish and they think they're always cool. And the worst part is, some Libra girls make it easy for them!"

"So they're the lucky ones."

"Who? Aquarius men?"

"No! The ones they don't look so bad to. You lucky one!"

When she got home that day, the first thing Lamees did was search her horoscope books to discover the degree of compatibility between Libra and Aquarius. She found that in one book it reached 85 percent and in another it didn't get any better than 50 percent. She decided to put her faith in the first one. She came to a decision: this time around she would be smart and use her wiles. She would make Nizar fall into her trap. She would prove to Gamrah that it was possible for a girl to dream about the guy she wanted and then, with a little effort and patience, to get him.

That night she didn't sleep until after the dawn call to prayer, the first of the five prayers, sounded. She stayed up filling her journal with war plans and rules of engagement that she vowed not to break. She felt she needed them for the days to come in case that heart of hers threatened to stray off the path. That was her usual way: to write down her thoughts and ideas on paper so that she would stick to her decisions.

In her journal, she wrote down everything: her general observations about men; the various pitfalls and misfortunes suffered by herself and her girlfriends and relatives; and snippets of advice she had heard or read at some time or other that remained perched in her mind waiting for the right moment. All of her instructions to herself began with "I will not . . ."

- I will not allow myself to love him until I sense his love toward me.
- I will not become attached to him before he proposes!
- I will not let go of my guard and open up to him and I will not tell him about myself; I will stay vague and mysterious (men prefer that in women, an open-book girl is no challenge to them); and I will not let him feel that he is aware of every detail going on in my life no matter what the urge is to spill out *everything!*
- I will not be Sadeem. I will not be Gamrah. I will not even be Michelle.
- I will NEVER be the first to get in touch, and I will not answer too many of his phone calls.
- I will not dictate to him what he must do, the way every other woman does with every other man.

- I will not expect him to change for my sake, and I will not try to change him. If he doesn't appeal to me with all of his flaws, then there is no good reason for us to stay together.
- I will not give up any of my rights and I will not overlook anything wrong that he does (because he must not get used to that).
- I will not confess to him my love (if I fall in love with him) before he tells me he loves me first.
- I will not change myself for his sake.
- I will not shut my eyes or ears to any signs of danger.
- I will not live in a hopeless fantasy. If he does not tell me outright that he loves me within a period not to exceed three months, and give me very clear indications concerning the future of our relationship, I will end the relationship myself!

36.

To: seerehwenfadha7et@yahoogroups.com
From: "seerehwenfadha7et"
Date: November 12, 2004
Subject: Michelle Frees Herself of All Constraints

May God accept your fasting, your night prayers and all those good deeds you've been doing during the holy month of Ramadan. I missed all of you, my allies and my enemies, and I was touched by all the messages I got inquiring about me. They kept on coming right through the entire month of virtue. Here I am, I have returned to you like the fasting person returns to food in the month after Ramadan. Some of you thought that I would stop at this point and not continue the story after Ramadan. But friends and foes: I will carry on. The wick of confessions coils long. And the longer it burns, the more my writings blaze.

Michelle adapted to her new life more quickly than she had expected. She welcomed the fresh start and worked hard to put her former life behind her. It was true that all her deep anger and resentment at her world still lay crouched inside of her, but she was able to make enough peace with it so that she appeared undamaged to people around her. It helped that Dubai was prettier than she had expected, and that she and her family were treated far better by everyone there than she had anticipated.

At her new university, the American University at Dubai (AUD), she met an Emarati girl named Jumana who was about the same age and was also studying information technology. The two had several classes together, and each noticed the other's good looks and perfect American accent right away. Jumana's dad owned one of the biggest Arab satellite TV channels, and Michelle's father was delighted to find that his daughter had made friends with the daughter of one of the most successful men in the United Arab Emirates, if not the whole Gulf. Meshaal would tell Jumana every time she came to visit them that she was a carbon copy of his sister: same height, same figure, same hairstyle, even same taste in clothes, shoes and bags. Meshaal was absolutely right. The two girls also had the same outlook on many things, and that helped them become close quickly. Their similar attributes freed them from the nasty issue of jealousy between girls who feel inferior to each other.

At the beginning of the first year's summer break Jumana suggested to Michelle that she work with her at her father's TV station on a weekly TV youth program. Michelle agreed enthusiastically. Every day they surfed Arab and foreign Internet sites searching out breaking arts news, which they presented in a report to the program's producer. They were enthusiastic and thorough, and the producer gave them responsibility for handling the entire arts section on their own. As it happened, Jumana had planned to spend the rest of the vacation traveling with her family in Marbella, so the task fell on Michelle's shoulders alone.

Michelle threw herself into her new job and continued it even after her fall term started. The program reported news and gossip about Arab and foreign celebrities, so Michelle's job required her to contact PR managers around the Arab world to confirm this rumor or that or to schedule interviews. She got to know some of the people she reported on personally, and they began to include her in their plans when they visited Dubai. She got invitations to their parties regularly.

A few months later, Michelle was officially made a producer of the program. Then she got her own show to produce. They asked her to be the on-air presenter, but Michelle's father refused to allow her to host a show that would be broadcast in the homes of his relatives in Saudi Arabia. They ended up using a young Lebanese woman instead.

Working in the media opened up new horizons for Michelle, and for the first time she felt truly liberated from all the restrictions that had always been imposed on her. As she came to know different sorts of people and her network of friends and contacts grew, she began to feel increasingly confident and ambitious at work. Everyone there adored her, which motivated her to produce even better work. Jumana remained her close friend, but she wasn't particularly fond of the work, so after graduation she took an administrative job at the station.

37.

To: seerehwenfadha7et@yahoogroups.com

From: "seerehwenfadha7et"

Date: November 19, 2004

Subject: A Man Just Like Any Other?

Live your life fully, the sweet and the bitter,
and who knows? A new darling might come along
someone who would treat your sores
so your joy comes back
and you forget old love and me
and move outside the circle of my grief
  —Bader Bin Abdulmuhsin*

Brother Adel—who, I will hazard a guess, is a statistician—sent me a message criticizing my e-mails for being of varying lengths and not symmetrical like the hems of dresses in vogue this year. Adel says that in order for the lengths of my e-mails to be *even*, they must show evidence of natural distribution. According to him, natural distribution means that 95 percent

---

*Saudi prince and famous poet.

of the data contained therein will center around the mean (taking into consideration of course the standard deviation), while the percentage of data outside the area of normal distribution on both sides of the mean does not exceed 2.5 percent in either direction, such that the sum total of standard deviation is 5 percent.

Shoot me!

The inevitable finale that Sadeem had closed her eyes to for a full three and a half years finally arrived. A few days after her graduation, after Firas sent over the laptop he had always promised her as her graduation present, he told her in a whisper, the words dripping out slowly like drops of water from a leaky tap, that he had gotten engaged to a girl related to one of his sisters' husbands.

Sadeem let the telephone drop from her hands, ignoring Firas's pleas. She felt a violent whirling in her head that pulled her down, pulled her somewhere beneath the surface of the earth. Someplace where the dead lived: the dead whom at that moment she wanted to be among.

Was it possible for Firas to marry someone other than her? How could such a thing happen? After all this love and the years they had spent together? Did it make any sense that a man of Firas's strength and resourcefulness was unable to convince his family that he could marry a divorced woman? Or was it just that he was incapable of convincing himself of it? Had she failed, after all of her attempts, to reach the level of perfection befitting a man like Firas?

Firas simply could not be just another copy of Michelle's beloved Faisal! Sadeem saw Firas as greater and stronger and more noble and more decent than that pathetic, emasculated weakling who had abandoned her friend! But it appeared they were cut of the same cloth after all. Apparently, all men were the same. It was like God had given them different faces just so that women would be able to tell them apart.

Firas had called her on her cell phone twenty-three times within seven minutes, but the lump in Sadeem's throat was too painful to allow her to talk to him. For the first time ever, Sadeem did not pick up when Firas rang, even though she had always rushed to the phone the minute she heard the particular tune of his calls, the Kuwaiti song "I Found My Soul When I Found You." He started texting her, and she read his messages in spite of herself. He tried to explain his behavior, but her anger, far from dissipating, simply grew more intense with every letter she was reading.

How could he have hidden the news of his engagement from her for two entire weeks, the period over which she had taken her final exams? He had talked to her tens of times a day to make sure that her studying was going well, as if there were nothing out of the ordinary going on! Was this the reason he had stopped calling her on his private cell phone and had begun to use prepaid phone cards? So that his fiancée's family would not discover their relationship if they tried to get hold of his phone bills? So then he had been preparing for this for months!

He had been determined not to tell her, he wrote, before finding out for certain that she would graduate with honors. That was exactly what had happened: in her final term, she had received the highest grades it was possible to get, as she had generally done ever since she had known Firas.

Firas had considered himself responsible for her studies and her superior grades, and she had handed the reins over to him and contented herself—easily and happily—with obeying his commands, for they were always in her best interest. She had excelled in that term even despite her father's death just ten weeks before finals began. Sadeem wished now that she had not done so well, had not passed and had not graduated. If only she had flunked, she would not feel this heavy guilt about achieving honors when her father had so recently died, and Firas would not have been able to leave her in order to marry someone else for yet another semester!

Was Firas leaving her now forever, as her father had done a few weeks before? Once the two of them were gone, who would take care of her? Sadeem thought about how Abu Talib, Prophet Mohammed's—peace be upon him—uncle, and the Prophet's first wife, Khadija—may Allah be pleased with her—had died in the same year, which had then been named the Year of Grief. She asked God's forgiveness as she truly felt that her own sorrows this year equaled the sorrows of all humankind since the dawn of history.

She didn't eat for three days, and it was a full week before she could bear to leave her room—a tormented week that was spent in reaction to the news that had numbed her feelings, paralyzed her thoughts, reopened her wounds and left her, for the first time in years, having to make decisions without consulting the counselor Firas.

In his incessant text messages, he hinted to her that he was willing to remain her beloved for the rest of his life. That was what he wanted, in fact, but he would be forced to conceal it from his wife and family. He swore to her that the entire business was out of his hands; that circumstances were stronger than they were; and that he was in more pain at his family's decision than she was. But there was nothing that he could do. There was no path before them but patience.

He tried to convince her that no woman would ever be able to replace her in his heart. He told her that he pitied his fiancée because she was engaged to a man who had tasted perfection in another woman and that taste would remain forever on his tongue, making it impossible for any ordinary woman to erase it.

After years of effort on her part to attain a level of spiritual perfection worthy of a man like Firas, he was now kicking it away in favor of an ordinary woman and a banal relationship. To himself and to her, Firas acknowledged that she alone responded to every emotion and instinct within him. He tried to convince her—and, even more, to reassure himself—that this must be God's will, and they should be submissive to it even if they couldn't figure out the reasons behind it. All other women were peas in a pod to him now. In his eyes, it didn't matter who he married, if not Sadeem.

Sadeem responded to the initial shock by deciding to stay away from Firas altogether. For the first time in her life, she ended that conversation without even saying good-bye to him. She refused to answer his calls or acknowledge his imploring text messages, despite the truly demonic pain that had overcome her and that only he could relieve. She hid her grief over Firas inside her grief over her father, which had become fiercer after her breakup with the love of her life.

Sadeem made honest efforts to get beyond her heartbreak without help from Firas. But even the most innocuous events could send her spinning out of control. Sitting down at the dining table with her aunt Badriyyah, barely a moment would pass before she broke down in tears as she stared down at a plate of his favorite seafood dish or a bowl of sweet pudding that he liked. When watching television with her aunt, she would try to choke down the sobs that constantly threatened to escape, but they slipped out despite her best intentions.

Aunt Badriyyah, who had moved in with her after her father's death so that Sadeem could live at home while she got through her final exams, was insistent that Sadeem come to live with her in Khobar, but Sadeem refused. She would never move to Firas's native city, no matter what! She couldn't stand to live under the same sky as him after the wrong he had committed and the pain he had caused. But her aunt swore that she would absolutely not leave Sadeem on her own in Riyadh, no matter what she did and no matter what she said and no matter what excuse she came up with, in her father's house and among all of those memories that it would be so hard to part with.

Only a few days after the breakup Sadeem began to crave Firas with an intensity that surpassed mere yearning or longing. For years Firas had been the air that she breathed, and without him now she truly felt as if she were suffocating, deprived of oxygen. He was her saint and she used to tell him every detail of her life as elaborately as a sinner making confession. She had told him everything—so much that he used to tease her about her endless stories, and then they would laugh together as he reminded her of those long-ago days at the start of their relationship, when he literally had to drag each word out of her mouth.

38.

To: seerehwenfadha7et@yahoogroups.com

From: "seerehwenfadha7et"

Date: November 26, 2004

Subject: Patience Is the Key to Marriage

Some of you were saddened that Sadeem and Firas broke up. Others were glad that Firas chose a suitable & righteous wife instead of Sadeem, who would not have been a suitable & righteous mother to his children. One message contained the platitude that love after marriage is the only love that lasts, while premarital love is only frivolous play. Do you all really believe that?

Lamees would not have believed that her strategy of playing hard to get to conquer Nizar would demand so much patience! At first, she was convinced that three months would be time enough to ensnare him. It became clear, though, that this was a business that would require a great deal of savvy and patience. And as her admiration for Nizar grew, she found those two qualities diminishing.

She never called him and on the rare occasions that he called her, she tried to not always answer. But with every ring of her cell phone she would feel her usually unshakable resolve weaken. Her eyes would stay fixed on his number, glowing on the cell phone screen, until she picked up or the phone stopped ringing and her heart stopped its accelerated beating.

At first, the results were definitely satisfying. He showed an interest in her that indulged and gratified her vanity. From the start, she made it clear that their friendship did not mean he had the right to interfere or intrude in her life, asking her for an hour-by-hour rundown of her daily schedule. And so he was constantly apologizing to her, justifying his concern about knowing when she was free by saying he wanted to be certain of not bothering her while she was busy. She also never returned his text messages. She informed him that she didn't like to write messages, as she found that a waste of time and effort she didn't have to spare. (Of course, had her cell phone fallen into his hands he would have found it crammed with text messages, sent and received, from her girlfriends and relatives, but he didn't really need to know that!)

Gradually his obvious interest in her began to lessen, alarming her. His calls decreased noticeably, and his conversation became more serious and formal, as if he were beginning to set new limits on their relationship. Perhaps the time had come, Lamees thought, to ditch her plan. But she was afraid that she might regret her hastiness later on. After all, she was the one who always criticized her girlfriends for their naïveté and lack of patience when it came to men. She comforted herself with the thought that Nazir wasn't the easy type—one of the main reasons she was attracted to him. She would be filled with pride if she was the one who ultimately captured his heart.

She tried to maintain her optimism throughout the three-month period that she had set to get the relationship on track. She reminded herself how much Nizar had seemed to like her, thinking hard to recall every single moment or gesture indicating his admiration. It seemed so easy the first month that she was back in Riyadh, when everything that had transpired in Jeddah was still fresh in her mind. He seemed to enjoy anything she said and did even if it was really silly or trivial, like telling a dumb joke or having to brew two cups of coffee first thing every morning. Even their phone conversations during the first month after classes began to imply some lingering, hidden affection, for even though she was often standoffish and disagreed with him openly on many things, he was always the first to call, and to apologize if need be.

As the second month went by, she started thinking about the moments with him that she hadn't much noticed at the time, but that on deep reflection seemed meaningful. For instance, there was the memory of her last day at the hospital in Jeddah, when they had lunch together in the cafeteria. He pulled out a chair for her, something he had never done. And then he sat in the chair closest to hers, rather than across the table as usual, as if the chair across the table were farther away than he could be on the day of their farewell. And there was the way he so often tried to lure her into saying certain words that he liked to hear from her because of her particular way of saying them, like the word *water,* since she pronounced the *t* like a *d,* sounding just like the Americans. And the way he imitated the way she pronounced the word *exactly* in her Americanized accent: egg-zak-lee!

As the third month rolled around, Lamees counted two entire weeks since the last time they had been in touch. Two weeks in which she had gotten totally fed up with optimism and strict tactics and strategies, which only someone completely without a heart would stick to, right? But she was still afraid of relenting. After all, looking back, she had covered pretty impressive ground, when you calculated the amount of time actually spent in carrying out her policy. She convinced herself that Nizar would be back on her radar one of these days. But only if he was really meant for her.

Fate didn't disappoint her. In fact, the plan she was intending to cut short succeeded. He came to her father to officially ask for her hand. Three entire weeks before her absolute drop-dead deadline!

39.

To: seerehwenfadha7et@yahoogroups.com
From: "seerehwenfadha7et"
Date: December 3, 2004
Subject: Pages from the Sky-Blue Scrapbook

Don't wake up a woman in love. Let her dream, so that she does not weep when she returns to her bitter reality.
    —Mark Twain

My friend Bandar, from Riyadh, is totally exasperated. He is furious with me because my intent, as he sees it, is to portray men coming from Jeddah (the west coast) as angels who do no wrong, not to mention their being courteous, refined and witty. Meanwhile, rages Bandar, I am portraying Bedouins and men from the interior and east of the country as vulgar and savage in the way they treat women. I also depict the girls of Riyadh as being miserable head-cases while Jeddah girls are up to their ears in bliss which they procure with the flick of a finger!

Hey, Bandar. This has nothing to do with geography. This is a story I am telling just as it happened. And anyway, one can never generalize these things. All kinds of people exist everywhere: this variety is a natural feature of humankind and we can't deny it.

On a page in her sky-blue scrapbook, where she used to paste the photos of Firas that she collected so carefully from newspapers and magazines, Sadeem wrote:

Ahh, the blemish of my heart, and my only love;
To whom I gave my life past and what's ahead.
What makes the body stand tall when the heart's pierced through?
With you gone, I've no sense, no sight and nothing said!
O God, O Merciful One—You wouldn't return him,
But You needn't make him happy! Or loving her instead!
Make him taste grot and jealousy like me
And go on loving me!
God is generous,
He'll repay me for the one who sold me off and fled.

Sadeem had never been in the habit of writing down her thoughts. When she met Firas she was inspired to write a series of love letters, which she read to him from time to time (feeding his arrogance so much that he would strut around afterward like a peacock spreading his tail feathers). After Firas's engagement, though, she found herself spilling out lines of poetry in the silence of the night, during those hours which for the last three and a half years had been devoted to speaking to him on the telephone.

To my best friend, most cherished of mine,
To the star that one day fell down into my palms,
You were so near yet so far, so oppressed, so divine.
The Fates burst us apart! that we meet once again ...
My friend, we will become the heroes of tales
We spin for our children, false names assign'd,

The internal struggle Sadeem lived in that period—the way her emotions zinged back and forth between extremes of rage and forgiveness—made her life a nightmare. She was incapable of discerning her own true feelings: she would curse Firas and spit at every picture of him that she could find, only to leap back and plant a kiss tenderly on each photograph as she begged it for forgiveness. She would recall how, through all those years, he had seemed to stand by her, and it would make her cry, but then she would remember the day years ago when he had alluded to broaching with his parents the subject of his attaching himself to a divorcée, and their response, which had hurt her so deeply that she had intentionally "forgotten" it (exactly what Michelle and Lamees warned her not to do). And that would make her cry even more bitterly over the lost years of her life, and wish all kinds of horrible fates for Waleed, who was the true reason behind all of her troubles.

Gamrah, Lamees and Um Nuwayyir began to notice that Sadeem had started to become careless, even neglectful, about performing her prayers. They also observed that she was exposing some of her hair when she threw on her hair cover, which was supposed to leave only her face visible. Sadeem's religiosity seemed to be in direct proportion to her relationship with Firas. Her anger at him made her angry at everything that reminded her of him, and that included religious duties.

Throughout Sadeem's whole ordeal, her aunt Badriyyah had been traveling back and forth between Riyadh and Khobar, all the while keeping up her relentless campaign to convince Sadeem to move out east to live with her and her family permanently, or at least until her "fated share" would come to her.

When she saw the daughter of her only sister in such a severe state of depression and still firmly refusing to go to Khobar, Aunt Badriyyah decided to broach the subject of Sadeem's getting married to her son—Sadeem's cousin Tariq. Aunt Badriyyah had intended to instill in Sadeem a sense of security and the possibility of some future happiness for her, but she only succeeded in making Sadeem all the more upset and embittered.

So they wanted to marry her off to that adolescent dental student who was only a year older than she was? If they knew her Firas, they would never have dared to make such a proposition! They were exploiting the fact that she was now alone in this world and needed a home she could live in securely without having to face people's scrutiny and their inevitable gossip about her living alone after her father's death. Even Aunt Badriyyah wanted to ensure that Sadeem would remain under her supervision by marrying her to her own son. And who knew? Maybe Tariq was already thinking about the money and property she would inherit from her father and was planning how to get his hands on it. Maybe his mother—her own aunt!—was even encouraging him.

It was out of the question. She would not marry Tariq or anyone else. She would shut herself up like a monk in her father's house. If Aunt Badriyyah didn't let up in her insistence about not leaving her alone, and didn't allow her to live in the family home in Riyadh, then she would consent reluctantly to live with them in Khobar. But she would dictate her own terms. She would not allow anyone ever again to take her for granted, as Firas had done.

40.

To: seerehwenfadha7et@yahoogroups.com
From: "seerehwenfadha7et"
Date: December 10, 2004
Subject: Hamdan, the Cute Guy with the Pipe

Nothing is harder than the life of a woman who finds herself torn between a man who loves her and a man she loves.
   —Khalil Gibran

Whenever I start thinking about the shape my life will take when I bring this story to a close, it stresses me out. What will I do then, having gotten so used to finding all of these messages from you folks out there, e-mails in my mailbox that fill the emptiness of my days? Who will call me every bad name in the book, and who will be there to pat me on the shoulder? Who will even remember me at all? Will I be capable of adjusting to life in the shadows after becoming so accustomed to the glare of publicity, to my role as the spark that sets off the arguments that flare up whenever people in this country get together now?

Even just thinking about what it will be like is upsetting. It's true that I began with the simple intention of trying to reveal a few of life's daily realities that pass so many of you unobservant people by. But I've become so invested in this story! And I also find myself waiting eagerly—impatiently!—for your readerly responses. I get irritated if I don't get as many e-mails with feedback as I want; and I'm ecstatic whenever I read about ME in a newspaper or magazine or on a Web page. I'm going to miss all of this attention, there's no doubt about that. In fact, I might find myself pining for it so fiercely that I don't have any choice but to start writing again. In that case, what do you all want me to write? I'm standing by, readers, ready and willing: what should be the topic of my next exposé?

M ichelle couldn't believe that her friend Sadeem considered Saudi Arabia to be the sole Islamic country in the world! In Michelle's opinion, United Arab Emirates was just as Islamic, even though its people were allowed a lot of latitude in their social behavior, and were even allowed to practice other religions. In Michelle's opinion, UAE was going about it in a much better way. Sadeem tried to make it clear to her that just because a country was "Muslim" did not necessarily mean that it was also an "Islamic country." Saudi Arabia was the only country ruled solely and completely by the law derived from the Qur'an and the way of the Prophet, peace be upon him, applying that law—the Shari'ah—in all spheres of life. Other Muslim nations might draw on the Islamic Shari'ah for their basic principles and outlook, but as society changed and new needs arose, they left specific rulings to human-made law. Michelle could see the gap between her and her friends widening to the point where at times she wondered how it was that she ever fit in their scene at all—their world didn't accord in any way with her own ideas about life or the ambitions she had.

And what were those ambitions? Michelle felt she had found her calling working in the media, and she planned to make it to the top. She was going all the way. She dreamed of one day seeing her portrait on the cover of a magazine, standing next to Brad Pitt or Johnny Depp. She fantasized about magazines and radio channels and TV stations vying with each other to get her exclusive scoop interviews with celebrities. She imagined the invitations to attend the Oscars, Emmys and Grammys that would surely come her way, just as the invitations to the Arab awards ceremonies already had. Never mind that her father had not let her attend even one of them—she would convince him with time. It would be over Michelle's dead body that she would be reduced to the circumstances her poor miserable friends found themselves in: a prisoner of the house (Gamrah), a prisoner of a man (Sadeem) or a prisoner of her vanity (Lamees).

The safest route, Michelle determined, was to stay away from entanglements with men altogether—if her experience with Faisal and her sort-of experience with Matti had taught her anything, it had taught her that. There would be no man at all, not even if that man was as sweet and cultivated as Hamdan, the young producer who was now directing her weekly program and who had studied media production at Tufts University in Boston . . .

Michelle had to admit to herself that she had been attracted to Hamdan from the start. He had a natural gift for making everyone gather around him as soon as he showed up at a shoot, making one of his usual loud appearances. And whenever he was around, the laughs and excitement level in the air seemed to climb up a notch.

Michelle and Jumana had watched Hamdan from a distance as he was smoking his *midwakh** pipe on one of their first days on the job, and Jumana had commented on how attractive he was. But Jumana was in love with one of her relatives whom she intended to marry as soon as he finished his MA in England and returned home, so she had been trying to set Hamdan up with her friend Michelle instead. But Hamdan beat her to it. When he made his interest in her obvious, Michelle wasn't surprised. After all, out of everyone in the crew it was clear that she and Hamdan seemed to agree on things the most and to be the most in sync. They seemed to be a natural match.

*A type of tobacco pipe popular in the UAE.

Hamdan was twenty-eight. The most handsome thing about him was his nose, as sharp and fine as an unsheathed sword. He had a trim, light beard and a truly infectious laugh. He was as stylishly turned out as Michelle always was. Usually, he wore a nice pair of jeans and a name-brand T-shirt to work, but sometimes he showed up in his white *kandurah** and *isamah*.** Even though he was relentless about keeping up his urbane appearance, he could never endure having his head wrapped up for more than an hour at the very most. So he would inevitably yank off the carefully wound turban, revealing his hair, which was longer than Michelle's, since she had gotten her hair cut short like Halle Berry's—a style Faisal forbade her to adopt because he didn't want to lose her lovely long hair with its delicate soft curls which he loved to wrap around his fingers.

Hamdan and Michelle had long conversations about all kinds of things, not least the TV program and their goals at the station. Because their work demanded it, they began going out to various places together—restaurants, cafés, shops and local events. Hamdan often invited her to go out hunting with him or on fishing trips in his speedboat (the one thing he was even more infatuated with than his Hummer automobile). Though Michelle enjoyed these kinds of expeditions, she always declined his invitations, limiting herself to looking at his photographs and listening to him as he talked about his adventures.

---

*Male garment in UAE, similar to the Saudi *thobe*.
**Turban.

41.

To: seerehwenfadha7et@yahoogroups.com

From: "seerehwenfadha7et"

Date: December 17, 2004

Subject: A Message for "F"

Anyone can become angry—that is easy. But to be angry with the right person, to the right degree, at the right time, with the right purpose, and in the right way, that is not easy.
    —Aristotle

A lot of people have written to me asking to know more about Sadeem's sky-blue scrapbook that I mentioned a couple of e-mails ago. Some have asked how it is that I managed to see what Sadeem wrote in it (and of course the subtext here is: if you aren't Sadeem, that is.). They're just DYING to figure out if she and I are one and the same. Others are just curious about what is written in that scrapbook.

To the curious ones out there, I say: I will read to you, and with you, more of Sadeem's musings from her sky-blue scrapbook. To those who are nosy and have made it their business to "out" me, I say: Just drop it.

When she couldn't seem to find an appropriate job after graduating, Sadeem decided to start a business with a portion of her inheritance. She had for some time been thinking about becoming a party and wedding planner, since there certainly was a demand for it—hardly a week would go by without her receiving an invitation to someone or other's wedding or dinner party or reception. During summer—the high season—it was not uncommon for her to get invitations to two or three different occasions on a single evening. She and many girls her age, whenever they felt bored or cooped up, would arrange to get invited to a wedding—it didn't matter whose. They could dress up and deck themselves out and put on heavy makeup and spend the evening dancing to music played by live bands or DJs. It was the closest you could get to an evening in a nightclub, albeit a very respectable and entirely female nightclub.

Sadeem's idea was to start by arranging small get-togethers for her relatives and friends and then to gradually expand until she got good enough to organize weddings. For years she had noticed that the party-organizing sector was pretty much a monopoly held by a small group of women, all Lebanese, Egyptian or Moroccan, who demanded enormous sums of money but did not provide excellent service in return. Sadeem was electrified at the thought of having the opportunity to plan every detail of an event herself, from A to Z, and modifying the plans to fit the type of occasion and the budget. She already knew the restaurants, florists, furniture shops and clothes makers that she would want to work with.

Sadeem proposed to Um Nuwayyir that the older woman take charge of the Riyadh office, with Gamrah as her assistant. Sadeem would assume control of the eastern region, where she was about to move, and Lamees, if she wanted, could set up an office in Jeddah, where she would be moving with her husband, Nizar, after her graduation. They could even arrange with Michelle over in Dubai to hire some singers who would make special recordings of songs suitable for wedding processions or graduation parties.

Um Nuwayyir welcomed the idea. It would fill the hours of loneliness she faced daily when she got home from work, which would be lonelier still after Sadeem's departure. Gamrah was very enthusiastic as well. She and Sadeem began setting up small gatherings to which they invited their acquaintances. Tariq, Sadeem's cousin, helped them take care of official tasks, obtaining a commercial license and other necessary documents. Since women are not always permitted to take care of legal matters with banks and other offices themselves, Sadeem made him their official agent for legal affairs.

The evening before Sadeem left for the eastern province, Gamrah produced invitations to the wedding celebration of a relative of a friend of her sister Hessah, and so Gamrah, Lamees and Sadeem went along with Hessah to the wedding. Hessah took her seat at the table reserved for the bride's friends, while the three girlfriends sat up on the dance floor. That was where all young single girls customarily sat, magnets for the roving eyes of matrons who were mothers of eligible young men.

When the *tagagga* crooned into the microphone, the three girls stood up, ready to dance to the familiar Saudi ballad. All of the girls sitting on the raised space started to move as the drumbeats began to throb. The sound roused the entire hall as the *taggaga*'s voice soared.

Sadeem was dancing in place, shaking her shoulders softly and moving her head from side to side with her eyes closed as she drummed her fingers in time to the song. Gamrah was moving her arms and legs in a random rhythm that had no relation to the beat, her eyes staring upward. Lamees shook her hips as if she were belly dancing, singing the song lyrics along with the singer, as opposed to Gamrah, who did not memorize song lyrics, and Sadeem, who considered showing off how in tune you were with the music while you danced to be a bit overdone.

When the song was over, Lamees went off to chat with an old friend from her school days that she had happened to bump into. The friend had been recently married and Lamees wanted to ask her how she was finding marriage so far, and what the wedding night was like and what kinds of birth control she had tried, and other such particulars that were concerning her now that her own wedding had been booked for the midyear break.

Sadeem remained with Gamrah on the dance floor to dance to a song she loved by Talal Maddah:*

I love you even if you love another
and forget me and stay far away
because my heart's only wish
is to see you happy, every day

The gentle words and mournful tune pierced straight through Sadeem's heart. The image of Firas clouded over her mind, and though she was surrounded by people on the dance floor, she danced as if it were only Firas who was watching her.

When it was time for dinner, they all filled their plates from the buffet and started talking about Sadeem's departure the next day. Sadeem was feeling so sad that her chest was constricted in sorrow, and she did not know how she would ever emerge from the ordeal whole again. As they talked and ate, one of the cell phones lying on the table beeped twice, indicating that a text message had been received. Every one of the girls dove for her phone, hoping that she would be the one who got the text from someone who had remembered her at that particular moment. Lamees was the lucky one. Knowing that his darling was attending a wedding party, Nizar had written from home saying: "May *our* wedding be the next, *habibti!*"**

*Old and famous Saudi singer.
**My love.

HOURS LATER, Sadeem stared at the suitcases and boxes that filled her room, ready to be shipped to Khobar. She felt a lump rise in her throat as she traced the scratching she had made on the edge of her desk as a child and gazed at the magazine pictures of celebrities and her friends' photos plastered on her closet door. She picked up her sky-blue scrapbook and pencil, and wrote.

Letter to F: It is now 3:45 a.m., local kingdom time.

In a few minutes the dawn call to prayer will echo through the city of Riyadh. You must be on your way to the mosque at this very moment, since your prayers in the eastern region start a little earlier than ours do here. Or are you in Riyadh right now? I don't even know whether the two of you are living here or there.

Do you still always go to the Friday prayer service? Or has the pleasure of sleeping at her side made you lazy about getting up and performing what is due to God?

I'm dying to hear your voice. If only I could wake you up right now! Without you, the world is a gloomy place. The night is darker than it should be. The silence is worse, and lonelier.

Oh, God . . . how much I love you!

Do you remember when you called me from your private jet as you were on your way to Cairo? I don't remember the reason we argued that day, but I do remember how depressed I was that you were traveling somewhere when I was still so upset.

About half an hour after I got your text message saying good-bye from the airport, I got a call from a long and unfamiliar phone number. It didn't occur to me that it could be you. I screamed when I heard your darling voice, I was so happy! Your voice washed my heart clean of whatever pain was there. *Firas, my love!* I yelled. *Didn't you leave?*

You told me that your body was up in the air but your heart was on the ground with me, trying to soothe me. You went on teasing me and flirting with me for a whole half hour. I practically melted away, I was so madly in love with you!

I wish you were with me right now.

Today, I went to a wedding party. I danced there imagining you standing in front of me, and I reached out to you but of course you weren't there.

I lament you at night like twenty death rites, while you're by her side,

May God not forgive you, nor forgive her through life,

Nor bring you back to me, nor give her bliss

I love you . . .

My love who I HATE!

Did I tell you that I am traveling to *you* tomorrow?

Finally, in Khobar, I will live by your side. That city has brought us together again: me and you, and now Madame Wife, too!

How am I going to drive down that road, all the time remembering when you went by, on the same road, three years ago, beside my car, guarding me from afar? I can't imagine myself on the highway heading east without you. No, it's more. I can't imagine myself in any place without you. I can't imagine that I will be able to go on in this life without you. It's all because of him! God punish you, Waleed, who ruined my life! God get my revenge on you.

42.

To: seerehw enfadha7et@yahoogroups.com
From: "seerehwenfadha7et"
Date: December 24, 2004
Subject: Lamees Marries the First and Only Love of Her Life

From a sensitive woman's heart springs the happiness of mankind.
—Khalil Gibran

One reader—she didn't give her name—tells me she doesn't know how I can be so naïve as to exalt love. And how can I be so proud of my clueless friends who go on pursuing this hopeless quest and probably will do so for the rest of their lives? There is nothing better, she proclaims, than a respectable fiancé who, as they say, "walks in through the front door." The two families already know each other, there are solid ties and since it's all done through family channels the bride is certified as a good girl and everyone agrees on everything. There is no room for nonsense or deception as there is with this "love match" thing. This method is beneficial to the girl, since it guarantees that the guy won't have any suspicions as to her past, which might well happen if they had had any sort of relationship before marriage. How could any rational girl kick away an opportunity like that and run after something not guaranteed?

Your opinion, my friend, is one I respect. But if we lose faith in love, ev-erything in this world will lose its pleasure. Songs will lose their sweetness, flowers their fragrance, and life its joy and fun. When love has been in your life you see that the only true, real pleasure of life is love. Every other thrill arises from that basic source of pleasure. The most meaningful songs are those your lover hums in your presence, the prettiest blossoms are the ones he offers and the only praise that counts is your beloved's. In a word or two, life only goes Technicolor in the very moment love's fingers caress it!

O God, we—the Girls of Riyadh—have been forbidden many things. Do not take the blessing of love away from us, too!

After a three-week engagement and after waiting four months after the contract-signing ceremony, Lamees's wedding day arrived.* It was the first wedding to be planned by Sadeem, Gamrah and Um Nuwayyir, in collaboration with Michelle, who had come from Dubai especially to attend her friend's wedding on the fifth of the month of Shawwal, the month after Ramadan, when the marriage busi-ness booms.

Preparations were in full swing all through Ramadan. The biggest share of the burden fell on Um Nuwayyir and Gamrah, since they were the only ones in Riyadh, where the wedding would take place. Sadeem took on some light duties such as ordering the chocolates from France, while Michelle was responsible for using her connections to record a CD of songs written by some of the famous singers she knew personally. A custom-made CD for Lamees and Nizar to play during the party, and then copies could be handed out afterward to the guests as a keepsake.

*Many native Hijazis prefer to shorten the engagement period and lengthen the time between the marriage contract-signing and the wedding, i.e., the *milkah* period. Unlike Najdis, who would not mind a long engagement period but do not like a long *milkah* period, when the couple are considered officially married and have the right to meet and go out even before the wedding ceremony takes place.

Gamrah would begin working every night after she performed the evening Ramadan prayers at the huge mosque downtown. Shopping malls rarely open in the daytime during Ramadan, but they make up for it at night, opening until three or four in the morning throughout the holy month.

She always brought Saleh with her to the mosque when she went to pray—she wanted to be sure to inculcate in her little boy, who was now three years old, a sense of religious devotion early on. Saleh was happy to come, and would throw on his miniature black woman's *abaya,* which Gamrah had cut and hemmed to his size after he demanded that she buy him one exactly like hers. He wouldn't be put off about the *abaya,* and so she had relented, shrugging off Um Nuwayyir's repeated warnings about giving in to his desires. Gamrah would remind Um Nuwayyir that Saleh was growing up in different circumstances than those in which her Nuri had been raised. Her little Salluhi was growing up among all his uncles, and so there was no cause to fear that he would lack adequate male role models just because his father wasn't around. Anyway, he looked so cute, gathering the folds and ends of the voluminous black *abaya* around his little-boy clothes, his head covered all the while in a traditional *shimagh.*

During the prayers, Saleh would stand next to her imitating every one of her moves, from the very beginning with saying "Allah Akbar"* to reciting to bending down and prostrating himself on the carpet-covered floor. When he got bored with imitating her, he would twist his head and contort his upper body toward her as she bent and knelt, trying to peer into her eyes and those of the rest of the grown-ups lined up for prayer, seeing if he could make them laugh. Kneeling in front of them, he would lean so far forward that he would topple over on his face, and then he would roll over onto his back, still grinning his wide grin and waiting for someone to smile back, any one of those gloomy-looking

*God is Great. The starting line in every prayer.

women in the row who tried to avoid meeting his gaze and keep their concentration on the prayer. Losing hope, he would take the opportunity of their kneeling and bending to the ground in prayer to give every one of those frowning women a little pat on her rear end, before going back to stretch out on his back in front of them, laughing and totally proud of his achievement!

The women complained about his naughty behavior and ordered Gamrah to send him over to the men's section to pray. Gamrah found his little antics adorable but would try to reprimand her son in front of the other ladies, fighting to keep from laughing. Saleh would give her one of his cute smiles, encouraging her to let out the laughter she was suppressing, as if he knew that she didn't mean to scold him.

Riyadh Tarawih prayers* usually ended around eight-thirty or nine P.M. and the shops opened their doors right after that. Gamrah would make her rounds, from the seamstress who was sewing the tablecloths and chair coverings for the wedding hall to the restaurant where she tasted new dishes every evening in order to select what pleased her most for the wedding buffet. She had visits to the florist and the printer who was doing the invitations, and many others, in addition to her many trips to the mall with Lamees to get whatever Lamees was still lacking for her trousseau.

Gamrah wouldn't get home before two or three in the morning, although during the final third of the month she would return an hour or two earlier, in time to do the Qiyam prayers** at the mosque with her mother and sisters. At first, Gamrah's mother wouldn't let her go out on these work missions alone, but she began going easier on her daughter when she noticed how seriously Gamrah took it all. What most

---

*Nonobligatory prayers held right after Isha prayers during the whole month of Ramadan.
**Nonobligatory prayers held in the last third of night during the last ten days of Ramadan.

impressed Um Gamrah was when she saw her daughter make her first profit—for arranging a dinner party in the home of one of Sadeem's professors at the university—and hand it over to her father, who finally was persuaded of the suitability of his daughter's odd work. Her mother had tried to force her sons to accompany their sister in her nightly outdoor activities, but they refused, one and all, and she eventually let it drop. So Gamrah was free to go about her work, sometimes in the company of her sister Shahla, or with Um Nuwayyir, or—most of the time—with Saleh and no one else.

On the long-awaited day, Lamees looked more gorgeous than ever. Her long chocolate-brown hair flowed down her back in pretty waves. Her mother-of-pearl-studded gown dropped softly from her shoulders, draping gracefully in front and revealing her upper back before widening gradually until it reached the ground. Her tulle veil flowed from her head down her bare back. One hand held a bouquet of lilies and the other clasped Nizar's hand. He was softly invoking God's name over her before every step and helping her lift the long train of her gown.

Lamees's friends could see the unadulterated joy in her eyes as she danced with Nizar after the procession, amid a circle of women, his relatives and hers. Their friend Lamees was the only one who had fulfilled the dream they all had, the dream of marrying the first love of their lives.

> **GAMRAH:** May God's generosity put us there next! Just look at those two blissed-out faces out there on the dance floor! Ah, how lucky is the girl who gets a Hijazi man! Where are *our* men when it comes to these romantic gazes of Nizar toward his bride? I swear to God, a Najdi would kill you if you said to him, sitting up there on the bridal dais, "Just turn toward me a little, and smile, for God's sake! Instead of sitting there frowning as if somebody had dragged you here against your will!"

SADEEM: Remember how Rashid reacted when we told him to kiss you during the wedding? And look at this Nizar, all he does is kiss Lamees's forehead every couple of minutes, and then her hands and her cheeks. You're right, men from Jeddah are a different species.

GAMRAH: And look how considerate he is, he's happy to let her stay in Riyadh while he's in Jeddah, until she graduates and can move there. I swear to God he's a real man, God bless both of them and make them happy.

MICHELLE: But isn't that the way it should be? Or did you think he was not going to let her finish her studies, or that he would force her to finish in Jeddah because he's there? This is *her* life, and she's free to run it as she wants, just as he's free to run his as he wants. Our problem *here* is that we let men be bigger deals than they really are. We need to realize—assume, even—right from the start that things like letting us graduate are not even optional, it's just what makes sense, and our eyes should not fly out of our heads if one of these men actually does something right!

SADEEM: Shut up, both of you. You two are giving me a headache! Let's just watch those lovebirds over there. They look so *cute* when they're dancing together. Just look at how he looks at her! His eyes are glazing and he looks like he's going to die of happiness. Oh, my poor heart! That's what I call *love*.

GAMRAH: Poor Tamadur. Don't you think she must be jealous because her twin sister got married before she did?

SADEEM: Why should she be jealous? Tomorrow her own luck and fate will show up. And by the way, have you noticed how well groomed these Hijaz guys are? Nizar is positively glistening, he's so clean and tidy! Just look how perfectly trimmed his goatee is. Every Hijazi bridegroom I've ever seen has a goatee precisely that shape, and not too heavy. You'd think they all go to the same barber!

MICHELLE: Those guys get a scrubbing, a Turkish bath and facial threading so they won't be too hairy, plucking and a pedicure and sometimes even a waxing. Not like the guys from Riyadh, where the groom looks just like all the guests except for the color of his *bisht*.*

SADEEM: I couldn't care less whether a guy is well groomed or not. In fact, I prefer a man who is a little untidy. It's so much more masculine—he doesn't have the time or the vanity to dress up and buy the latest fashions and act like a teenager who has nothing better to do.

UM NUWAYYIR: God have mercy on the old days! The days when you used to fall all over yourself when it came to good-looking men. Even Waleed, how your eyes were full of him!

SADEEM: True, but after Waleed I got Firas, the untidy devil who filled my eyes with nothing in the world but him.

GAMRAH: Basically I'd take any guy, whoever he is, clean or filthy, tidy or messy. Who cares? As long as he's there. I'm ready to be happy with any man. I'm so bored, girls! I'm fed up and I can't stand it. A little more of this and I'll go insane.

When it was time for the bouquet toss, the young single ladies lined up behind the bride, eager to find out who would get to board the sparkling marriage train next. Lamees's and Nizar's relatives crowded in, mixing with the rest of her friends. After her mother insisted, Tamadur sulkily joined them. Sadeem and Michelle stood front and center, and were hurriedly joined by Gamrah, who was quick to comply with Um Nuwayyir's encouragement to stand among the young bachelorettes; even if she was married before, she was technically single at the moment of the bouquet toss and more than ready to remarry again.

*Traditional black cloak that men wear on top of their *thobes* for important occasions or events.

Lamees turned her back to the girls, having earlier agreed with her three friends that she would try to throw the bouquet in their direction. She tossed it high in the air and the crowd of girls surged to grab it. After a lot of pushing and shoving and kicking and hitting, Gamrah got hold of what was left of Lamees's bouquet, a few green leaves tied with a strip of white lace. She raised it high, giggling ecstatically. "I caught the bouquet! I caught the bouquet!"

43.

To: seerehwenfadha7et@yahoogroups.com
From: "seerehwenfadha7et"
Date: December 31, 2004
Subject: Today He's Back

Today he's back
as if nothing happened
and with an artless child's eyes
he's come back to tell me
I'm his life companion,
his one and only love
He came bearing flowers,
how can I say no,
my youth sketched on his lips
I remember still, flames through my blood,
taking refuge in his arms
I hid my head within his chest
like a child returned to his parents . . .
        —Nizar Qabbani

Happy New Year! I don't feel like writing any little introduction this week.
I'm going to let events speak for themselves.

Firas came back!

When Sadeem heard from Firas again, she tore out that day's page from her little daily diary and enclosed it gently in her sky-blue scrapbook, where it nestled among the pages so full of his photos and interviews.

Firas came back to her, only two days after she had longed for him at the wedding. He came back, a few days after his marriage contract was signed and a few weeks before his wedding was to take place.

Sadeem was in Khobar. After spending the evening at a relative's wedding, she had returned to her room at Aunt Badriyyah's, and was unable to sleep. The air of Firas's city polluted her lungs and the glaring streetlamps that lit the road blinded her eyes, and it seemed as if Firas was everywhere—as if he had spread out his black *bisht,* the cloak he wore on top of his *thobe,* in most of the official photographs, over the entire city, so that everything underneath it was cast in his shadow.

Sadeem had been lying in bed awake, sighing deeply, at four A.M when a text message appeared on her cell phone, which had all but died since Firas had gone away:

> I am suffering enormously, and have been ever since you went out of my life. I see now that I will suffer for a long time. A very long time. I deleted all your pictures, e-mails and text messages and burned all your letters so that you wouldn't have to worry that they were around. I was in pain as I hit the delete button and as I watched the fire eat my treasure, but your face and your voice and the memories are engraved in my heart and can never be wiped out. With this message I'm not trying to get back together. I'm not even asking you to write back. I just want you to know how it is with me. I'm in bad shape without you, Sadeem. Really bad . . .

Sadeem couldn't even read it clearly. Tears had filled her eyes, blurring her vision, the minute she read the sender's nickname, which she had been too weak to delete from her phone: Firasi Taj Rasi. My Firas, my Crown.

She barely knew what she was doing as she pressed the button to call the sender's number. Her Firas answered! Firas, her darling and brother and father and friend. He didn't say anything, but just hearing his breathing on the other end of the connection was enough to make her weep.

He stayed silent, not knowing what to say. The sound of his car motor partly concealed the tightness in his breathing, as Sadeem went on sobbing in wordless rebuke of what he had done, releasing all that had been packed inside of her, waiting to be unloaded, swelling and growing until it filled her completely. He listened and listened to her painful gasps for breath as he murmured into his cell phone for her to imagine his planting one kiss after another on her forehead.

In one fell swoop he destroyed all the fortifications the resistance forces possessed.

He couldn't believe it when she told him she was living with her aunt in Khobar, just a few kilometers away from his home! He kept her talking on the phone as he made his way toward her neighborhood. He didn't know the house she was in, and he didn't ask her. He told her that he was getting closer to her than she could imagine.

That was a dawn never to be forgotten! Birds cheerfully engaged in their early morning flutter, and a lone car roaming one of the quarters of the city of Khobar, driven by a man worn down by desire and longing for his sweetheart's eyes. The two lovers lost the last of their reservations after what had seemed a lifetime of denial. Now fate, with the tender love of a father who cannot bear to see his children in torment, gripped their hands and led each to the other.

Sadeem went over to her window and looked out onto the street. She began describing the houses nearby to Firas, since she didn't know the number of her aunt's house or its exact location. All she knew was that it had a huge glass front door and on either side of the large door were a few untrimmed trees.

She caught sight of the lights of his car in the distance and felt as though she were floating in a warm ocean of bliss. He saw her at the window, her ash-brown hair tumbling across her shoulders and the creamy skin that he dreamed of kissing. "You're cream and honey!" he would say to her whenever he stared at her pictures.

He shut off the car engine in front of the house, not far from Sadeem's window on the second floor. She begged him to move farther off before one of the neighbors coming back from the nearby mosque after Fajr prayer saw him by her window at this early time of the day! He couldn't care less. He started teasing and flirting with her, singing to her:

Be patient a moment, let my eyes feast!
I'm thirsty for you—melting of desire
Oh you little devil, you are prettier than you ever were then!
*But your eyes remained the way I love them.**

*By Nabil Shu'ail, a Kuwaiti singer.

44.

To: seerehwenfadha7et@yahoogroups.com
From: "seerehwenfadha7et"
Date: January 7, 2005
Subject: Life after Lamees's Marriage

Readers were divided—as usual—between those who supported Sadeem's return to Firas and those who opposed it. But everyone did agree this time—unusually—that come what may, the extraordinary love between these two demands an extraordinary ending to their story.

The hints about the benefits of attachment and stability Michelle heard from Hamdan came in a variety of shapes. He told her his dream was to marry a girl who would be his *best friend,* and that he was hoping he would find a girl who had exactly *her* grasp of things and *her* openness toward the world. (Michelle smiled as she heard him praise her openness, the very same quality she'd heard so much criticism of in her own country.) He was always complimenting her on her elegance, and he noticed the tiniest changes she made to her appearance from one day to the next.

Michelle admitted to herself now (having come to depend, in her new life in Dubai, on the principle of being frank with herself) that she could see one of two possibilities. Either she admired Hamdan very much or she loved him very little. His presence left her feeling happy—it was happier than she had felt in Matti's pleasant company but much less happy than she had felt when she was with Faisal. She was quite sure that Hamdan carried in his heart stronger feelings for her than she had for him, and so she deliberately missed his hints and tried to get him to sense her hesitation about taking their relationship further than friendship. She was able to do it without completely severing the strands of his hopes (and hers) for the future. Hamdan gracefully accepted that Michelle wasn't yet ready to talk about commitment.

He was perceptive enough to know that talking may be the best way to express what is in one's mind, but expressing what is in the heart is more eloquently done in other ways. He knew from his university studies in nonverbal communication that when a person's words conflict with tone of voice or gestures, the truth almost always lies in the way words are said rather than in what is said.

That he was free of the mental complexes that usually cripple men's brains was one huge attraction for Michelle. Even though he possessed many of the qualities that seemed to make other men self-obsessed—he was handsome and had strong principles and was materially and socially successful—he appeared to her to be amazingly well balanced. She found him intellectually stimulating, engaging, sophisticated and emotionally enlightened.

And even so, even with all of this, Michelle realized that she could not really love him. Or maybe she was unable to allow herself to try. She had had two tries already, and that was plenty for her. If her family was going to refuse her relationship with her American relative because *he* wasn't one of *them,* and the people of Saudi Arabia were refusing one of *their* own sons to her because *she* wasn't one of *them,* what was there to guarantee that this run of misfortune would be broken now with Hamdan the Emarati guy? After the first experience, she had fled to America, and after the second, she had immigrated against her will to Dubai. Where would she be exiled if she were to fail for a third time?

Everything in her life seemed to be going brilliantly except when it came to love and marriage. Michelle did not believe that she and destiny would ever agree on a suitable man, for Michelle had been quarreling with her destiny for time immemorial. If she found a man she liked, destiny plucked him away from her; and if she detested him, destiny threw him at her feet.

LAMEES ANNOUNCED that she would officially start wearing the *hijab* after returning from her honeymoon. In Saudi, as everyone knows, women have to wear some form of *hijab*—some kind of head cover to conceal their hair and neck—but women have the choice to take it off, even in front of unknown men, within the confines of houses and as soon as they cross the country borders. Lamees decided that she would start to wear it whenever non-Muhram* men were around, following the rules of Islam. She would wear it in front of her cousins and coworkers and whenever she traveled outside of the kingdom. Her friends all congratulated her on this bold spiritual step—except for Michelle, who tried to dissuade her from her decision, reminding her how hideous *hijab*-wearing women usually looked and how the *hijab* restricted a girl from being fashionable because it also required covering her arms with long sleeves and her legs with long pants or skirts. But Lamees had made her mind up absolutely, and she had done so before seeking anyone else's thoughts on the matter, including Nizar's. Lamees felt that she had had all the liberation she wanted before her marriage and during her honeymoon. Now it was time to pay her dues to God, especially after He had granted her such a wonderful husband, one who was just right for her and whom she had dreamed of finding, and whose love and tenderness toward her made her the envy of all her friends.

Lamees's life with Nizar was truly a picture of married bliss. They

---

*Muhram men are men whom a woman is allowed to go without *hijab* in front of; e.g., male members of her immediate family.

were in greater agreement about everything and more in tune with each other's needs than any of the married couples around them. They were totally complementary. For example, it was really difficult to get Nizar upset about anything; Lamees, on the other hand, was highly strung and sensitive. But she was more judicious and more patient than he was when it came to anything related to home or budget. So Nizar relied on her to take care of all household affairs, while always lending a hand, every day, in cleaning and washing and cooking and ironing. As long as they had no babies, they both preferred not to have a maid.

Lamees was very attentive to her relationship with her husband's family. She worked hard to please them, especially his mother, whom she called Mama—something none of her Najdi friends would ever do.* The excellent relationship between Lamees and Um Nizar strengthened Nizar's attachment to his wife even more as time went on.

Nizar would randomly bring home a bunch of red roses for Lamees for no special occasion. He posted little love letters on the fridge door before going off to his on-call shifts at the hospital. When he was about to take his rest break there, he always called her before going to bed. And when he returned home, he would take her out to a restaurant or shopping without the slightest anxiety or embarrassment about the possibility of running into one of his friends while his wife was at his side (a hang-up many Saudi men have). She made him sandwiches and salads, leaving them in the fridge when she set off to do her own hospital rounds. He waited impatiently for her to be finished so that they could spend the rest of their day together, like newlyweds still on their honeymoon.

THERE WAS a question haunting Sadeem that no one could answer to her satisfaction. She put her question regularly to Gamrah and Um Nu-wayyir, leaving them feeling at a complete loss as to how to help their

---

*While Hijazi girls call their mothers-in-law Mama, Najdi girls find that disrespectful to their own mothers, so they call the husbands' mothers Aunt.

Sadeem. Is it a blessing or a curse for a woman to have knowledge? she wanted to know—referring to both academic knowledge and the practical experiences of everyday life.

Sadeem had observed that despite human progress and a general refinement of society's ideas about life, when it came down to searching for a suitable bride, young and naïve girls tended to hold more of an attraction than girls who had attained an advanced level of knowledge and had a more sophisticated understanding of the world. The fact that it was extremely unusual for a female doctor to be married was a case in point. Men who came from this part of the world, Sadeem decided, were by nature proud and jealous creatures. They sensed danger when face to face with females who might present a challenge to their capabilities. Naturally, such men would prefer to marry a woman with only a very modest education, someone feeble and helpless, like a bird with a broken wing, and without any experience of the world. That way the man could assume the position of the teacher, who takes on the job of forming his pupil into whatever he wishes. Even if many men admired strong women, Sadeem pondered, they did not *marry* them! So the ignorant girl was in hot demand while the smart and savvy one watched helplessly as her name became slowly etched in a giant plaque in commemoration of spinsters, a virtual list that was growing longer every day to accommodate the requirements of all the insecure men who didn't actually know what they wanted and so refused to attach themselves to a woman who knew absolutely what she wanted.

45.

To: seerehwenfadha7et@yahoogroups.com

From: "seerehwenfadha7et"

Date: January 14, 2005

Subject: Sadeem's Addiction

A man who signed as "Son of the Sheikhs"* is furious. He doesn't under-stand why I criticized proud and jealous Saudi men in my last e-mail. (The ones who wouldn't like to expose their wives to strange men, even their own friends, by walking down a shopping mall next to them or dining out in a restaurant with them.) "Son of the Sheikhs" explains this behavior by informing me that it is more embarrassing if a friend sees your wife than if a stranger sees her, because a stranger would not know who the husband is, but the friend will carry your wife's picture engraved in his head and can call it up whenever he sees you! Brother "Son of the Sheikhs" sums it up with this: A man who is not jealous is not a man. Furthermore (he adds), it is perfectly natural for a man to choose a woman who is inferior to him (especially since all women, in his view, are one level below men in the

*Here, *Sheikh* refers to the patriarch of an Arabian tribe or family.

hierarchy of organisms anyway!). But according to our guy's reasoning, "a man needs to feel the weight of his own superiority and masculinity when he is with a woman. Otherwise, what would prevent him from marrying someone just like him—another man?"

Um, no comment . . .

T he Sadeem who came back to Riyadh to visit her friends over the weekend was very different from the Sadeem who had left for Khobar in such misery a few weeks earlier. Gamrah was sitting in Sadeem's old home, watching her friend closely. She didn't doubt for a moment that Firas had something to do with Sadeem's sparkling eyes and rosy cheeks; and the smile sketched across her face contained an adorable element of complete inanity: here were the well-known symptoms of love. "You cannot be balanced when it comes to expressing emotions, can you! It's either a frown down to the ground or a smile that splits your face!" said Gamrah.

Sadeem's return to Firas, or her acceptance of his return to her, wasn't something that had been carefully considered and worked out. There were no documents containing clauses of agreement or compensation stipulations, not even a prenup. This was not one of Sadeem's clever schemes. It was simply the insane, bell-pealing spontaneity of love. The rapture that held the two of them in thrall after their return to each other was epic, and it was more powerful than the sting of guilt he felt from time to time, or the sting to her dignity that she experienced whenever she thought about what he had done.

But Sadeem's happiness did not stretch so far as to include forgetting and forgiving the past. Hers was a joy whose brittle edges had become curled from cruelty, a sweetness masking a bitter core. Feelings of pain and abandonment still haunted her, lurking deep inside, ready to leap out and announce their presence at any moment. By allowing Firas to come back to her, Sadeem was conceding a large part of her honor and self-respect. But, like so many women before her, she did it because she loved him.

Neither Sadeem nor Firas wanted to spend whatever time there was left before his wedding apart from each other. It was as if they had been told he had a fatal disease, with only a few more days to live, and they were determined to live their final moments in pleasure. They decided that they would remain together until the date of the wedding, which would take place in less than two months. It was a strange agreement, but they clung to it.

His love for her, which had not subsided in the least, was what compelled him to call her the moment he finished speaking to his fiancée on the telephone. Her love for him was what allowed her to wait until after he was done flirting with his fiancée on the telephone every night, so that he would be free to flirt with her.

He refused to talk about his fiancée in front of her. He refused even to mention her name or to give any hints about her personality, just as he refused to inform Sadeem exactly what the date of the wedding was. Every time it came up she would blow up at him, quieting down after he soothed and calmed and comforted her—a job he was becoming very skilled at performing.

Every few days—during his *milkah* period—he would visit his fiancée, who was already his legal wife, since the contract had been signed. Sadeem would discover these visits despite his attempts to hide them from her, and then her last remaining shreds of dignity would fall from her, permanently, it seemed.

Sadeem's jealousy of Firas's unknown wife grew deeper and stronger. Firas, who used to be able to melt her with his sweet words, now made her neck burn as if slapped with his coarse and insolent comments. "What's the matter with you? Why are you in such a bad temper all the time? Must be *that* time of month!" Firas, who used to moan in pain at seeing a single tear drop from the eye of his Sadeem, began listening unmoved every night as she hemorrhaged her wounded pride in tears that dripped into the phone. *"Ma shaa Allah,* Sadeem!" he said to her one night, his voice rough and derisive. "Those tears of yours never quit, do they? They're always ready, at any minute and at any word!"

How had he come to speak to her in such a way? Once she had returned to him, once she had accepted the tainted relationship he offered, did he suddenly see her as third-rate goods? And how had she gotten to such a low point that she had accepted this situation in the first place? How had she come to accept Firas's love when he was bound to another woman?

One night he told her smugly that his mind was completely at rest about the wife his family had chosen for him. She had all the qualifications he required. The only thing she lacked, Firas said, was that he didn't love her as he loved Sadeem. But that love, he went on, might show up after marriage; after all, that's what had happened to all of the men whose advice he had sought. They had all counseled him to drop Sadeem despite his feelings for her and take the more rational, prudent road. He told her he forgave her for not understanding his predicament, for after all, she was a woman, and women think with their hearts, not their minds, in such matters. He kept telling her the advice he received from various relatives and friends who were devoid of compassion and understanding of what prompts a human being to love. She asked herself, if someone doesn't believe in love, can you expect that person to grasp other high virtues such as nobility and responsibility toward others and loyalty to someone who spent years waiting to marry the person she loves?

Every one of those self-appointed muftis* listened to Firas and then gave him a considered opinion designed to agree with what he was already thinking. They knew he didn't really want to hear something that contradicted what he was coming to on his own. No, he only asked for advice to shore up his resolve. So they worked hard to bolster his spirits, reassure him and soothe his conscience. They went so far as to warn him to stay away from that young woman who had bewitched him.

*Jurists.

"They warned you against me? *Me?* Are you serious? How do they presume to know me? These guys know *nothing* about me, or us, and they warn you to stay away from me? And you actually *listen* to them! So when did you start listening to everyone who came and gave you a fatwa,* a piece of advice as ugly as his face? Or do you just like hearing that you're not wrong, and that you're the best, and that this girl you happened to get to know is the one who's wrong, and that you should leave her because she's not good enough for you? You, you . . . who deserve the best! You who have no shame! You come and tell me this stuff after everything I've done for you? You bastard, you stupid coward, you ass!"

This time it was Sadeem who broke up with Firas, a mere five days after they got back together. She had no regrets this time, now that she had told him exactly what she thought of him. It was the first time Sadeem had ever raised her voice to Firas, and of course it was the first (and the last) time that she swore at him and insulted him—at least to his face.

There were no tears, no hunger strike, no sad songs—not this time. The end of the long tragic story of forbidden love and loss was more stupid and banal than she could have imagined. Sadeem realized that her love for Firas had far surpassed his love for her. She was embarrassed to remember that she had once imagined that theirs would be among the most heartbreaking and legendary love stories in history.

That night, in her sky-blue scrapbook she wrote:

Can a woman love a man for whom she has lost respect? How many love stories like mine ended after years, in a single night, because the woman suddenly saw the man for what he was?

Men don't necessarily love the ones they respect, and women are the opposite. They respect only the ones they love!

*A legal opinion or ruling.

In the same sky-blue scrapbook that witnessed the blossom of her love for Firas, she wrote down her last-ever poem about him:

What shall I say of the strongest of men
when he's a little silent drum in his mom's and dad's hands?
On his quiet hide they beat the anthem of their tribe
because he's hollow! He's empty as the sands
though he had the love that only an ingrate would refuse,
God's graces be upon him in all the far-off lands!
Then he tells me, I'm a man!
The mind gives me counsel and I've listened to it.
So I say to him, and I'm a woman!
I sought my heart's wisdom, and in the heart I trust!

Sadeem felt for the first time in four years that she no longer needed Firas to survive. He was no longer her air and water. Reuniting with him was no longer the one dream and the hope that kept her alive. That evening was the first, since their initial separation, that she did not pray in the silence of her bedroom for his return. She felt no grief about leaving him. She only felt regret for wasting four years of her life running after the mirage called love.

On the last page of the sky-blue scrapbook, she wrote:

I wanted my love for Firas to continue no matter what, and then with the days passing this love became my whole life, and I started to feel afraid about what would happen if he left, that my life would leave with him. That's all.

Sadeem realized that she bore a major part of the responsibility—and guilt—because she had refused to receive Firas's hidden messages, as Lamees had called them. She hadn't allowed herself to understand the true reason that he avoided real attachment to her all those years. She refused to let her heart perceive how little Firas valued her and how ready he was to forsake her. She had committed the cardinal mistake of the lover, tying her mind and heart in blindfolds so that they could not see unwanted messages from the beloved.

Sadeem was finally cured of her love addiction. But it was a harsh experience that caused her to lose her respect for all men, beginning with Firas and, before him, Waleed, and every man alive after that.

46.

To: seerehwenfadha7et@yahoogroups.com

From: "seerehwenfadha7et"

Date: January 21, 2005

Subject: And Now . . . Welcome Tariq the Lover

Those who want us, our souls resent them
And those whom we want, fate refuses to give to us.
   —Norah Al-Hawshan*

Many happy returns on the occasion of the blessed Festival after Pilgrimage, Eid Al-Adha. Since I might not be with you during the next festival, in 12 months from now, let me say it now for always: I extend my best wishes for all of your days to come. May God make all your days, and mine as well, full of goodness, health and love.

When Sadeem moved into her aunt Badriyyah's home, the person who was happiest about the new arrangement was Tariq, her aunt's son. From the very first day, he decided that he would be in

---

*A female Saudi poet.

charge of assuring her comfort in her new home, and he took to the task with an almost alarming dedication. He committed himself to fulfilling every one of Sadeem's needs. And since Sadeem did not actually demand anything, Tariq tried to offer his services as best he could in other ways, like surprising her with her favorite order from Burger King so the two of them could have their dinner together. Sadeem sensed Tariq's interest in her, but she couldn't respond to him in the way he hoped. In fact, she felt uneasy whenever he was in the room, since he never lifted his eyes from her. It began to get increasingly difficult for her to live in the same household with him.

Tariq was one year older than Sadeem. He had gone to elementary and middle school in Riyadh, as his father was working as a civil servant in one of the Saudi ministries at the time. But after retirement his father had moved the family to Khobar so that he could be near his siblings, and Tariq had gone to high school there. Tariq had returned to Riyadh to attend the College of Dentistry at King Saud University, because there were no dental schools in the eastern province at that time.

Sadeem first noticed Tariq's interest in her when he was a dental student and used to visit them at home on weekends, since he did not generally travel all the way to his own family in the eastern province. She could tell that his admiration had grown stronger over time, but she always knew that she didn't reciprocate his feelings. Even though Tariq was perfectly pleasant, and even though he spoiled and indulged her every time he came to visit them, and singled her out for attention in his words and glances, there wasn't anything about him that could make her heart soar the way it had with Firas. Her feelings for him hadn't changed from the sisterly affection she had developed for him long ago when the two of them had shared toys and games in their grandfather's Riyadh home.

Only Gamrah knew about the lovesick cousin whom her friend sometimes joked about, though fondly, in her presence. But Sadeem had not mentioned him for a long time, not since her engagement to Waleed. And during her long drawn-out relationship with Firas, Sadeem had actively tried to avoid seeing Tariq. Every time he visited them he would find only his uncle at home. After a few visits when Sadeem was never in the room—on the pretext that she was busy studying upstairs—Tariq had stopped visiting. On the few special occasions when Sadeem had to go to Khobar, Tariq avoided seeing her then as well, and Sadeem appreciated that.

In Sadeem's eyes, Tariq's problem was that he was way too simple and straightforward. She was amazed that he would let his feelings toward her show in such a straightforward and artless manner. To her, Tariq did not seem more than a big kid, with his baby face, so like their Syrian grandmother's, his slightly fleshy body and his guileless smile. None of this was really a failing, but altogether these impressions added up so that she couldn't conceive of him as a real man she could have a serious relationship with.

One evening after everyone else had gone to bed, the two of them were left in the living room, in their PJs, watching a film on one of the satellite channels. When the film ended—and poor Tariq hadn't taken any of it in, since he was so engrossed in what he intended to say to Sadeem—he turned to her, whispering the name by which he was accustomed to call her.

"Demi?"

"Yes?"

"There's something I want to talk to you about, but I don't know how to start."

"Why don't you know how to start? Nothing's wrong, is it? I hope not."

"Well, for me it's all good, but I don't know what you will think about it."

"I hope it's good. Just spell it out and get it over with. There are no formalities between us, right?"

"Okay. I'll just say it straight out, and God give me strength. Demi, we've known each other for a very long time, haven't we? Since we were little, when you used to visit us on holidays, I always looked at you, a lot, and what I saw was the lovely girl with soft hair and pink hair band.

The little girl who dressed prettier than any other girl and didn't want to play with boys. Do you remember how I used to fight with the other kids when they annoyed you? And if I went to the grocery shop I wouldn't take any girl with me except you so I could buy you what you wanted? We were still kids, I know, but by God I loved you even then!

"When we got a little older, I loved being around you and my sisters whenever you came to visit us, even though I was always the only boy sitting with your small group of girls. I know it didn't look so great, my being there, but the only thing I cared about was being near you in the hours you spent with us! Can you believe it? I wouldn't bring my sisters ice cream unless you were there! My sisters got to the point where if they wanted me to bring them something they would say to me, 'Hmm, we wonder if Sadeem is coming tonight!'

"All this and I knew that you didn't love me the way I loved you. Maybe you played along a little bit to be nice to me, and maybe you were happy that I was interested in you, and you had the right to feel that way, of course. I would say to myself, *She's got every reason! And what would she love in you anyway? Not handsome, no degree, no money, chubby figure, there's nothing in you that would attract her, except the fact that you're crazy about her.*

"The day they accepted me in the College of Dentistry in Riyadh, I was in ecstasy! Do you know why? First, because you might respect me more if I became a doctor, a dentist in fact, and second, because I was going to live in Riyadh, where you lived. I could visit you and I could get to know your dad better, so that maybe he would invite me over every day and I could see you.

"When Waleed asked for your hand, I felt like everything collapsed at once! I couldn't propose to you like he did because I was still a student with no income. My mother told me your father would never turn down the son of Al-Shari in favor of me, the kid son of your aunt, who hadn't even finished college. Your engagement and *milkah* periods were absolutely the most horrible times in my life. I felt I had lost every single dream that I've had for myself. And then, after you split up with Waleed, the world smiled at me again! I wanted to open the subject with you quickly. I intended to propose to you as soon as possible, but I couldn't, because right away you went off to London."

Sadeem's face was fixed in astonishment as Tariq went on. "When you came back, I noticed you were avoiding me whenever I came to visit, and you wouldn't answer my phone calls. When I saw that, I said to myself: *This girl clearly doesn't love you. She can't even stand you! Stay away from her and leave her alone.*

"And I really did stay away. But, and God is witness to my words, I didn't forget you for a single day. You were always on my mind and I resolved to wait for fate to bring us together.

"After your father died, I felt I wanted to be at your side, but I couldn't. I knew that my mother wanted to bring you here and that you didn't agree. There was something inside me telling me that the real reason you were refusing to move here was me.

"The day you came, I vowed to myself that I was not going to bother you. I was going to do whatever it takes to cheer you up, but keeping my distance so that you wouldn't feel like I was exploiting your presence in my home in order to win you over. Even my mother—I warned her not to talk to you about my feelings. She knows how much I love you and she has always longed to get us engaged, sooner rather than later. But I wanted to make sure you'd agree first so I wouldn't embarrass her in front of you or you in front of her.

"Now it's been a year and a half that we've been here together. I graduated—you know all of that—and finished my internship and I've submitted my papers and I'm waiting for a job or a scholarship to specialize abroad. To tell you the truth, my university professors have offered me a teaching assistant position in one of their divisions, but the problem is that if I take it I'll be sent abroad within a few months, and I just can't go away until I know what my fate is with you. If we get engaged, I have to get your agreement about this business of traveling, especially since you're working here and I don't know if you would want to come with me or not.

"So what I mean is, if travel doesn't suit you, I can get a job here in any hospital or dental office and drop the idea of doing my residency abroad. But if you are not meant to be mine, I will take that job offer. With me away you won't have to feel any embarrassment or unease about turning me down; I'll be away for three, maybe four years, and by the time I get back I'm sure you will be married to somebody else. Demi, I want to be sure you understand that my request isn't going to affect your living in this house or feeling settled here. I'm not pressuring you, sweetie. It's up to you, and you have complete freedom to make whatever decision you want to."

Finally Sadeem was able to say something:

"But Tariq. Sure, we are close, but we were never close in a way that would mean I could make a decision like this! There are a lot of things you don't know about me, and there's a lot I don't know about you."

"Sadeem, it's impossible that anything could change the love that's been in my heart since I was little. But, of course, you have the right to know whatever you want about me. Ask me all the questions you want answered and I'll give you the answers, about anything at all!"

"You don't want to know, for instance, the reason behind the breakup between Waleed and me? Or the reason I didn't pay a lot of attention to you, specially in the last four years?"

"The reason behind the breakup between Waleed and you was that he's completely *insane!* Is there anyone with a brain who would sacrifice Sadeem Al-Horaimli for any reason? Demi, I know you, and I know your roots and how you were raised, and that's enough for me to trust you. If you want to tell me the reason, that's up to you, but demanding it is not my right, not at all. You didn't have any obligation to me in your life before, so that I have no right to ask you about anything that happened then; even those years when you were avoiding me, when I figured you probably had a relationship with someone—they don't mean a thing to me. What's important to me is our life together from now on, I mean *if* God has decreed it. About myself, I'm prepared to sit and tell you everything that has happened in my life since the day I was born until this morning! Although there isn't much to say. But I will tell you, for instance, which ones do I prefer, the girls of the eastern region or the girls of Najd. The girls of Khobar or the girls of Riyadh."

"Oh, really! So you've got experience with both!"

"Just a few girls that I and my friends managed to 'number' in malls as teenagers. If you want their names and phone numbers, I'll give them to you!"

"No, thanks. Well, I have to say that you caught me totally off guard. Give me a little time to think and give you an answer."

"I'm going to Riyadh tomorrow. I have some people to see there, and I'll stay a few days so that you can think in peace."

47.

To: seerehwenfadha7et@yahoogroups.com
From: "seerehwenfadha7et"
Date: January 28, 2005
Subject: The Best Closure Ever

To listen to the song, <u>click here</u>

Why does the first love refuse to let go?
It comes back right away and awakens us to the past.
It grows as we do, yet returns us to the old days.
With insistent reminders, we're thrown to its flames.
With its fire, it burns us, it burns to the core.
Why does the first love refuse to let go?
　　—Julia Boutros*

The story has almost reached its end. But my friends are still candles that life sets aflame. They melt down, burned away by love and giving. I took you by the hands, my dear readers, to lead you on a weekly tour of these

---

*A Lebanese singer.

scented candles, flickering desperately. I wanted you to breathe in their fragrances yourselves. I wanted you to stretch out your hands to catch a few dissolving drops of wax so that you would feel their hot sting. So that you would understand the pain they had been through and the fires that lie behind that sting.

I plant a kiss, now, on every candle that has been lit and melted away but in so doing has lighted a way for others—making for them a path that is a little less dark, contains a few less obstacles and is filled with a little more freedom.

When Michelle woke up after the first night she had spent in Riyadh after more than two years away, she did not know that she had come back to the city at just the right time to witness an important event—a very important event indeed in a life that was already full of changes and quick reverses.

Her day began with a surprise phone call from Lamees. "Go into the bathroom and wash your face with a little cold water," her friend advised her, so that she could absorb the full impact of what she was about to tell her.

"What's wrong? Why did you have to wake me up so early?"

"Michelle. Today is Faisal's wedding."

Silence from the other end of the line.

"Michelle! Are you there?"

"I'm here."

"Are you okay?"

"What Faisal? My Faisal?"

"Yes, girl, Faisal the scumbag, no one else!"

"Did he tell you himself or what?"

"Here's the next whammy—it turns out Nizar is friends with the bride's brother."

"Your husband Nizar? Knows the brother of Faisal's bride? Why didn't you tell me the minute you heard about that?"

"Are you crazy, to ask me that? I swear I only found out about this today. I came from Jeddah to Riyadh yesterday to attend the wedding of one of Nizar's sisters. I was really eager to come so that I could see you on the same trip. Nizar told me about the wedding a week ago, but I just got the invitation card today, and when I opened it, my eyes just about flew out of my head. I read the groom's name maybe one hundred times to be sure it was really the same Faisal."

". . . When did he get engaged?"

"I swear to God, I have no idea, and unfortunately I can't ask Nizar to ask his friend about it because they are not really close buddies. They just know each other from work. Looks like they probably had a bunch of extra invitations, so they invited me. I don't expect Nizar knows anything more than I do."

"So who is this girl he's marrying?"

"Her last name rings no bell. Nothing impressive."

"Lamees . . ."

"Yes, darling?"

"I want you to fix me up with an invite. I'm coming with you."

"*What?* No, c'mon, you must be kidding. You going to Faisal's wedding, are you out of your mind? How would you get through it?"

"Don't worry about me. I can do it."

"Michelle, honey, I'm scared. What are you thinking? There's no reason for you to go and make things harder on yourself."

"I won't. In fact, I'll be giving myself the best closure ever."

Lamees convinced her husband that she had a splitting headache and couldn't go to the wedding. She told him she would give her invitation to Michelle, who could go in her place.

Michelle turned the invitation card over and over in her hands as the hairdresser worked on her hair: **Announcing the Wedding of our Daughter Shaikhah to our Son Faisal.** *So this is what it comes to, Faisal? A girl named Shaikhah? What a silly, very silly name!*

She did her own makeup and put on a gorgeous Roberto Cavalli gown. It was slinky enough to show off her body perfectly.

At the entrance to the hall, she contemplated the photos of the bride and groom that formed a dazzling display on a table near the door. She studied his expression, trying to gauge how he felt about the woman standing beside him. She happily noted that Shaikhah was totally not his type! She was of a large build, when what he adored was petite women. Her hair wasn't black—which he preferred—but dyed a range of tints to the point where it looked like a disco globe reflecting a prism of colors. She had a big nose and a mouth with thin lips. What did they have in common with Michelle's cute nose and seductive lips?

Michelle paid her respects, in the way one does, to his mother, whom she was able to single out after hearing one of the greeters call her "mother of the groom." She congratulated Um Faisal on the marriage of her son. Faisal's scent seemed to waft from this woman who had given him birth.

She found a seat near the entrance where the bridal pair would emerge, at the end of the hall facing the dais. She chose her spot carefully, for this evening she had an important and historic mission to accomplish.

She moved her eyes among his sisters, assigning the names she had heard to them. This one looked the oldest, so it must be Norah. That was definitely Sarah, the loud one. This young-looking one over here was apparently Nujud, the prettiest of the bunch, as he always described her. And there was the mother again.

This time, observing his mother from a distance, Michelle remembered her overbearing power and dictatorial ways and also Faisal's abjectness before her. Michelle would have expected to feel disgust and hate for this woman, and to wish her the worst that life could give, but in fact she found herself respecting her and feeling scorn for her weak son. She noticed that Um Faisal was examining her from afar and seemed to like what she saw. She imagined this woman considering trying to get her for Faisal's younger brother who hadn't gotten married yet, or maybe for one of her nephews! Ah, could fate be that twisted?

Michelle had decided that today she would announce her victory over all men. She would rid herself once and for all of whatever bits of Faisal remained in her heart and soul. She found herself heading for the long corridor of people preparing to dance. This was definitely a first: swirling around the dance floor on the day her true love married someone else.

It wasn't as difficult as she had imagined. She had the sensation that she had lived these moments before in her mind, time and time again— so that this was merely a déjà vu. She felt relaxed and happy. That night she danced and sang as if she were the only person in that enormous hall. It was her own special celebration—a celebration in her honor—to acknowledge her survival and endurance despite everything. It marked her liberation from the slavery of deep-seated traditions, which had sub-jugated all the other miserable, pitiful women in the dance hall.

She imagined Faisal in bed that night with his bride, dreaming of reaching out to touch his love Michelle, while Shaikhah crouched on his chest with her large body, her folds of fat keeping him from moving and breathing.

The lights were dimmed in the other parts of the hall, leaving one strong beam spotlighting the entry. The bride crossed it, heading toward the dais, flashing smiles at the invited women, and even at Michelle, who quietly followed her progress from nearby. Michelle was filled with confidence, seeing the bride's large body stuffed into the wedding gown, which was stretched tightly around her body unappealingly, creating un-sightly folds of skin at her armpits.

When it was announced that the men were about to come in, a truly devilish idea occurred to Michelle and she didn't waste any time acting on it. She sent a short message from her mobile phone to Faisal's: *Congratulations, bridegroom! Don't be shy. Come on in. I am waiting.*

After her message, the men's entrance was delayed by almost an hour. The hall was awash in the whispers and mutterings of the women guests, and the poor bride was in a state of confusion. Should she go out? Or stay where she was and wait for her groom who refused to come in? After what seemed an eternity the groom appeared, surrounded by his father, the bride's father and her three brothers. He came in so quickly that no one could really see him. From afar Michelle smiled. Her plan had worked.

A few minutes later, as the photographer was taking photos of the bride with her groom and the family on the dais, Michelle rose, heading toward the exit, intending to leave. But she made very sure that Faisal would see her, more glorious than he had ever seen her before. She looked at his beard, which had altered the face she was accustomed to. He turned toward her, with a desperate look in his eyes, as if begging her to go away. She raised one eyebrow in challenge, not caring in the slightest about any of the women who were looking at her, and she went on standing there in front of the entryway, playing with strands of her short hair as if to annoy him with her new haircut before turning her face away in obvious disgust and making her way toward the door.

After getting into her car, behind the Ethiopian driver, she could not keep back her laughter as she imagined how the wedding night would go for Faisal after seeing her there. It would be a "night cursed by sixty curses," as Lamees would have said. And that was the point.

Upon reaching the house, she realized that this was the first wedding since her separation from Faisal where her eyes had not become blurry with tears seeing the bride happy with her groom on the dais. Michelle knew now that behind their smiles, many of those brides and grooms were concealing their own sad and yearning hearts because they had been kept from choosing their life's partner. If she had any tears to shed this evening, they should be for that poor bride whom circumstances would unite tonight, and all the rest of her nights, with a man forced to marry her, a man whose heart and mind were with that other woman, the one who had danced with such abandon at his wedding.

48.

To: seerehwenfadha7et@yahoogroups.com
From: "seerehwenfadha7et"
Date: February 4, 2005
Subject: The "Getting Over Them" Phase

A woman is like a tea bag. You never know how strong she is until she's dropped into hot water.
—Eleanor Roosevelt

Now, be honest. Haven't you had enough of me after a year of e-mails? I've had enough of myself!

O ne day Sadeem read a news item on the society page, congratulating Dr. Firas Al-Sharqawi on the occasion of the birth of his first son, Rayyan. It had now been more than fifteen months since she and Firas had parted for the last time. Sadeem tried to think about their relationship, over nearly four years, compared to an engagement, contract-signing, wedding, pregnancy and birth with another woman that had occurred all in a little over a year. It seemed to confirm that

Firas was not the extraordinary and discriminating person she had once imagined him to be, but just another ordinary boy, much like Waleed and Faisal and Rashid and countless others. Those claims he used to make about holding his life partner to absolute criteria were nothing more than a ridiculous attempt to flex muscles that were pretty weak in the first place. Or maybe they didn't even exist at all.

Sadeem was in Riyadh for the celebration of Michelle's and Lamees's graduation, and the four girls gathered at Sadeem's old home. As usual, they launched into their various complaints on the woes of lost love.

"Sadeem!" said Lamees, "how could you have accepted—even run after—a sweetheart who tramples you underfoot? You know what your problem is? Your problem is that when you fall in love, you lose your mind! You allow the one you love to humiliate you and you let him get away with it! No, even worse, you say to him, I like it, baby, give me more! This is the truth, unfortunately, and if it wasn't, you wouldn't have stayed with Firas all those years when you knew he had no intention of marrying you."

Everyone was hard on her these days. They were blaming her for getting into a relationship that was bound to fail from the start. At the time none of them predicted that her relationship with Firas would end as it did; they had been as optimistic, basically, as she was. But now, naturally, all of them claimed to have known it all along! She had no recourse but to remain silent. At one point Michelle, who had gone through a similar thing a few years before, shot her a wink. Michelle, of course, had taken a firm and severe decision to walk away from Faisal the moment he revealed his parents' position on their relationship. And so she had sidestepped the agony and humiliation Sadeem endured up until the bitter end, when her love finally drowned itself in a sea of emotional mendacity.

Sadeem did wish Firas had proven his superiority to the passive Faisal. She had wanted to demonstrate to Michelle that Michelle had made a mistake in letting Faisal go. She wanted to prove that *she,* Sadeem, a believer in the power of love who upheld the principle that she had a right to marry the person she loved, would end up smarter, more successful and happier.

It hadn't worked out that way. Having refused to sacrifice her love, she had received the stunning blow that her beloved had sacrificed her. And Firas's deception had run deep: he had hung hope's sparkling pendant around her lovely neck and taught her to recite love's anthem of struggle and persistence long after he himself had stopped reciting it.

"The luck you've had, Michelle—you don't have to constantly see a photo or read an article in some newspaper about the guy you were in love with. The worst thing is for a girl to fall in love with someone famous, because no matter how hard she tries to forget him, the whole world keeps reminding her of him! You know what I wish sometimes, Michelle? I wish I could have been the man in this relationship. I wouldn't have let go of Firas, I swear I wouldn't have let go."

"See? So you haven't lost a *real man,* have you?"

Her friend's sarcastic comment made Sadeem more disgusted than ever with Firas. Did that selfish man even realize the rough treatment she had received from society, on top of the way he had mistreated her and then had abused her further by walking out?

"Sadeem, I didn't drop Faisal because I was no longer in love with him, as you imagine. I was crazy about that guy! But everyone here was entirely against him and against me. I have complete confidence in myself, and I know I can face whatever hassles stand in my way, but frankly I don't have the same confidence in Faisal or in any other guy in our sick society. For our relationship to have succeeded, we would have had to be strong. Both of us. I couldn't have done it all on my own. And even though Faisal went on pursuing me and every so often I got an e-mail or a text message begging me to come back to him, I knew it was only one side of him—the weak side—talking. I knew he hadn't come up with a solution to our problem. That's why I went on refusing him and denying my feelings and not letting myself be sucked into his weakness. One of us had to be the strong one. I decided it was going to be me. You can be sure, Sadeem, that Firas and Faisal—even though there's a big difference in age—are stamped out of the same mold: passive and weak. They are slaves to reactionary customs and ancient traditions even if their enlightened minds pretend to reject such things! That's the mold for all men in this society. They're just pawns their families move around on the chessboard! I could have challenged the whole world if my love had been from somewhere else, not a crooked society that raises children on contradictions and double standards. A society where one guy divorces his wife because she's not responsive enough in bed to arouse him, while the other divorces his wife because she doesn't hide from him how much she likes it!"

"Who told you about *that?* Gamrah?" Sadeem asked, aghast.

"Sadeem, you know I'm the last person in the world to even think about gossiping about my friends. Don't be afraid of me, because I wasn't raised in this society which doesn't know how to discuss anything except who said this and who that."

"If what you're saying is true, if your refusals only have to do with our young men, then why didn't you defy everyone and marry Matti or Hamdan?" Sadeem countered.

"Simple. Anyone who has gone through love and knows how far it can go can never ever be satisfied with a love that's just so-so. Now I can't settle for less. *I just can't!* My love for Faisal—that was the love of my life. Look, even though I threw him out of my life, he still stands there inside my mind like a statue that I measure every man up against, and unfortunately, they all come out short. And of course I'm the one who really loses after such comparison."

"I wanted a number one, Michelle. The way I saw it was, like, I don't deserve anything less than Firas. But my number one was satisfied to be with someone less than me, and so now I'm forced to be satisfied with something less than him."

"I don't agree with you there, Sadeem. For me, my number one is gone, but someone who's even better will come along! I will never sell myself short and I can never be satisfied with the crumbs."

49.

To: seerehwenfadha7et@yahoogroups.com

From: "seerehwenfadha7et"

Date: February 11, 2005

Subject: Graduation Ceremony

If only I had known how very dangerous love was, I wouldn't
   have loved
If only I had known how very deep the sea was, I wouldn't have set sail
If only I had known my very own ending, I wouldn't have begun.
   —Nizar Qabbani

A bittersweet fact. The story that began nearly six years ago is coming up to the present time, and so the end of my e-mails is drawing near.

In one of Riyadh's grand hotels, a dinner was held to honor the graduates, Lamees and Tamadur Jeddawi and Mashael Al-Abdulrahman. The guest list was restricted to the three of them, plus Gamrah and Sadeem, Gamrah's sisters and Um Nuwayyir.

Lamees was the unchallenged star of the party with her expanding belly; the fetus was in the twenty-eighth week. Lamees's rosy cheeks and confident smile announced to her friends that hope still existed somewhere in this troubled business of life. Everything about her, on this graduation day, showed them that at least one of them was a young woman bursting with happiness. Even her fellow graduates, Tamadur and Michelle, didn't have a quarter of her joy. And why shouldn't she celebrate and exude all this radiant pleasure? As Michelle said, "She's got it all!" A successful marriage, a diploma with honors, the promise of a professional future. She alone among her friends had not suffered for trying to obtain what she longed for.

A few moments before leaving the hotel, Gamrah and Sadeem ran into Sattam, the obliging bank employee whom they had met through Tariq. He had worked out the bank transactions for their party-planning business and they had conferred with him a few times after that at the bank. Sattam came into the restaurant with a group of businessmen. He smiled and nodded from a distance, but of course he couldn't come over to greet them in the company of all those men, nor could the two young women return his greetings when they were in a group of women or, to be exact, when they were in the presence of Gamrah's sisters, spies who loved nothing more than to snitch on inappropriate behavior.

At the men's table, Firas asked his friend Sattam in a low voice about the women who had just gotten up from the table not too far away, and whether he knew them. He had caught a whiff of a certain rare *dehn oud** that he was very familiar with coming from their direction. Sattam informed him that two of the women were regular clients of the bank and successful businesswomen, even though they were so young. Firas felt his heart tighten sharply when he heard Sattam mention the name of Sadeem Al-Horaimli.

If only he could have searched their faces and not have averted his gaze, he would have noticed that his Saddoomah was among them! His Saddoomah. Could she possibly be his after all he'd done? Sadly he let

*Expensive oil perfume that is extracted from trees in limited parts of Asia.

his eyes follow the backs of their *abayas* as they moved farther away, his imagination sketching a beautiful innocent face so dear to his heart.

No one knows what went through Firas's mind that night after the brush with Sadeem. What is certain, though, is that his thoughts ran on for hours as her fragrance continued to tickle his nose. Did it confirm for him that she still loved him, if she was still using the scented oil he had given her two years before?

Firas had never experienced such a wealth of feeling for any woman except Sadeem. His wife, who loved him very much, wasn't able to make him happy as his Sadeem naturally had. Firas made a sudden decision that night, while he was lying in his marriage bed, next to his wife—the mother of his first son and now pregnant with his second.

50.

To: seerehwenfadha7et@yahoogroups.com
From: "seerehwenfadha7et"
Date: February 18, 2005
Subject: Advice Spun from Gold: Take the One Who Loves You, Not the
One You Love!

<u>Click here</u> to listen to the song

> *So you ask: What's new? . . .*
> *Nothing has changed, ever since you left me.*
> *Are you happy to hear that?*
> *Nothing has changed, alas,*
> *To this day I'm in your hands.*
> —Thikra

I confess that my immersion in the story of my friends for an entire year has
made me one of those women who know exactly what they want.

I want a love that fills the heart forever like the love of Faisal and Michelle. I want a man who is tender and cares for me the way Firas took care
of Sadeem. I want our relationship after we marry to be rich and strong like
the relationship Nizar and Lamees have. I want to have healthy children like

Gamrah's child, and to love them, not just because they are my children, but because they are a part of him, my love. That is how I want my life to be.

Two days after the graduation party, Sadeem returned to Khobar and invited Tariq to have coffee with her in his house, on an evening in which she pretended to be sick so she wouldn't have to go with her aunt and her daughters to a dinner party at the home of a relative. For the first time ever, she found herself completely paralyzed about what to wear in his presence! She stood in front of her mirror for hours and changed her outfit and put her hair up and let it down twenty times. The whole time, she was still trying to figure out what to say to him. He had spent more than two weeks in Riyadh waiting for her to make up her mind about his proposal. Not wanting to rush her by coming back before she was ready. She had begun to feel very embarrassed about how long she was taking, and so she asked him to come back to Khobar, without telling him that she still hadn't made up her mind.

Sadeem remembered Gamrah's advice, which Gamrah would give her over and over whenever they were together. "Take the one who loves you, not the one you love. The one who loves you will always have you in his eyes, and he'll make you happy. But the one you love will knock you around and torment you and make you run after him all the time."

But then Sadeem would recall what Michelle had said about how true love can never be made up for with any ordinary, run-of-the-mill love. And then the image of Lamees laughing happily at her wedding would come into her mind and confuse her even more. At that point, Um Nuwayyir's prayer for her would ring in her ears: "May Allah give you everything you deserve." Then she would calm down a little bit and feel a little reassured. She was sure she deserved a lot and she was sure that Um Nuwayyir was a good person and that God must give her what she was praying for.

When she greeted Tariq, he kept her hand in his longer than usual, trying to read in her eyes the answer she would give to his request. She led him toward the reception room, chuckling at the scene he made behind her as he tried to get rid of his little brother Hani, who was insisting on fleeing from the nanny and going into the living room with them.

This meeting wasn't like any of the times they'd been together years before. They didn't play Monopoly or Uno, and they didn't quarrel over who had the right to have the remote as they sat in front of the TV. They even looked different. Sadeem was wearing a brown knee-length chamois-cloth skirt with a sleeveless light blue silk blouse. Around one ankle she wore a silver anklet and on her feet were high-heel sandals that allowed her carefully trimmed nails and French pedicure to show. Tariq was wearing a *shimagh* and a *thobe,* though he never put on this traditional wear unless it was a religious holiday. One thing had not changed: Tariq had not forgotten to bring her the Burger King double Whopper meal she liked.

They had their dinner in silence, each of them immersed in private thoughts. Sadeem was having a dialogue with herself, a bit mournfully.

This isn't the one I have dreamed of all my life. Tariq is not the person who will make me cry for joy the day the contract is signed. He is a sweet and nice person, in a very ordinary and normal way. Marrying Tariq doesn't require anything more than a beautiful wedding gown, the usual trousseau and a wedding party in some lavish hall. There won't be any real happiness or even any sadness about it. Everything will be ordinary and normal, just like my love for him and every day of our future life together. Poor Tariq. I won't thank the Lord every single morning when I find you next to me in bed. I won't feel butterflies in my stomach every time you look at me. It's so sad. It's so ordinary. It's nothing.

After they had finished eating, she tried to think of something else to do other than talk about what he really wanted to hear. "Can I get you something to drink, Tariq? Tea? Coffee? A cold drink?"

Her mobile phone, which was on the low marble table in front of them, rang. Sadeem's eyes widened with astonishment and her heart jumped into her throat when she read the number of the sender there plainly on the screen. It was Firas's number. She had erased his name from her phone directory since their "last" separation.

She jumped up and left the room to answer this unexpected phone call, particularly sudden and unexpected right at this moment. Had Firas somehow learned about Tariq and called to influence her decision? How did Firas always seem to know everything and show up at crucial times?

"Saddoomah. What's new with you?"

"What's new with me?"

At the sound of his voice, which she had not heard for quite a long time, her heart plunged. She expected him to ask her about Tariq, but he didn't. Instead, he began telling her about seeing her two days before in the hotel with her friends. She watched Tariq rubbing his palms together anxiously, waiting for her.

"So, are you calling me right now in order to tell me you happened to see me the other day?"

"No . . . to be honest, I am calling to say to you, um, I have discovered . . . I feel that—"

"Hurry up. My battery's low."

"Sadeem! In one phone call you make me happier than I've felt all the time I've lived with my wife, from the day we got married!"

There were a few seconds of silence, then Sadeem said in a taunting tone, "I warned you, but you were the one who said you could live this kind of life, because you're strong, and because you're a man. You think with your head and not your heart, remember?"

"My Saddoomah, darling, I want you, I miss you. And I need you. I need your love."

"You need me? What do you mean? Do you really think I'm going to be willing to come back to you and be your lover, just like before, now when you are married?"

"I know that's impossible. So . . . I'm calling to ask you . . . will you marry me?"

SADEEM HUNG UP on Firas for the third time. The triumphant tone of his voice had made it clear that he was expecting her to crumple at his feet that second with a grateful "Yes" at his generous offer to make her his second wife. She turned to Tariq. He had thrown off his *shimagh* and the *eqal* that kept it in place on his head. The *shimagh* sat untidily on the arm of the sofa. Tariq had begun to rub his hair wildly with both hands. She smiled. She went into the kitchen to make him the loveliest surprise of his life.

She came back in carrying a tray with two glasses of cranberry juice on it. He lifted his head to look at her. She lowered her head and smiled with feigned embarrassment exactly like in the old black-and-white movies they had watched together. In imitation of the classic scene when the girl signals that her suitor's marriage proposal has been accepted, she put the tray down in front of him and offered him a drink. Tariq began laughing and kissing her hands. He repeated over and over, in utter happiness, "If only this phone call had come a long time ago!"

Between You and Me

I do not claim that I have uttered all of the truth here,
but I hope that everything I have said is true.
　　—GHAZI AL-QUSAIBI

The girls of Riyadh went on with their lives. Lamees (who you will recall actually has a different name in reality, along with the rest of my friends) got in touch with me after the fourth e-mail. She wrote from Canada, where she and Nizar are doing their graduate studies, to congratulate me on the wild and crazy idea of writing these e-mails. Lamees laughed and laughed at the name I had chosen for her sister, "Tamadur," since I knew in advance that her sister despised this name and that Lamees called her by it whenever she wanted to irk her.

Lammoosah told me that she is very happy with Nizar and that she has given birth to a beautiful baby girl named after me. She added, "I just hope the girl doesn't turn out to be as crazy as you are!"

Michelle was really bowled over and told me she had no idea that

I had such a knack for storytelling. She often helped me recall certain events and she corrected details I remembered unclearly, even though she didn't understand some of my classical Arabic words and was always asking me to use more English, at least in the e-mails that were about her, so that she could understand them.

Sadeem didn't divulge her true feelings to me at first, and that made me think I had lost her as a friend after telling her story in my e-mails. But she surprised me one day (after my thirty-seventh e-mail) with a really precious gift, which was her sky-blue scrapbook. I never would have known about it if she hadn't given it to me. She handed it over before signing the marriage contract with Tariq. She gave it to me to keep and told me that I could disclose all that she felt in that painful period of her life. May God bless her marriage and make it a union that erases all of the sadness and misery that came before.

Gamrah heard about the e-mails from one of her sisters, who realized from the very beginning that Gamrah was the intended double of this character, but she didn't know which one of Gamrah's friends I was. Gamrah blew up at me and threatened to cut off all ties if I didn't stop talking about her. I tried to convince her—Michelle and I both tried—but she was afraid people would find out things she and her family didn't want them to know. She said some really hurtful things to me the last time we spoke. She told me that I am taking away all that might be left of her chances—marriage chances, I presume. And after that she cut off every link she had with me despite my many pleas and apologies.

Um Nuwayyir's house still serves as a safe haven for the girls. The girls had their last meeting there during the New Year's break when Lamees came from Canada and Michelle from Dubai to attend Sadeem and Tariq's wedding. Sadeem insisted on having it in her father's house in Riyadh. Um Nuwayyir planned the wedding with Gamrah.

As for love, it still might always struggle to come out into the light of day in Saudi Arabia. You can sense that in the sighs of bored men sitting alone at cafés, in the shining eyes of veiled women walking down the streets, in the phone lines that spring to life after midnight, and in the heartbroken songs and poems, too numerous to count, written by the victims of love unsanctioned by family, by tradition, by the city: Riyadh.

ACKNOWLEDGMENTS

I would like to express my deepest gratitude toward everyone who has helped me edit the English counterpart of my Arabic novel (*Banat Al-Riyadh*): my dear eldest brother Nasser, my best friend Aceel, my sister/ my rock Rasha and my wonderful editor at The Penguin Press in New York, Liza Darnton, who all tried their best so that my novel does not get *lost in translation*.

I would also like to express my deepest appreciation to my role model, Dr. Ghazi Al-Gosaibi, former Saudi ambassador to Britain, current minister of labor and brilliant poet and novelist, for his unflagging support.

Last but not least, I would like to remember the man who taught me how to write, my father, Abdullah Alsanea, may he rest in peace. I hope I would have made him proud.

GLOSSARY OF NAMES

The number 7 refers to an Arabic letter similar to the letter *H* in English. Arabs use numbers like 7, 3, 5, 6 to refer to certain Arabic letters that have no counterparts on an English keyboard. This is called the Internet language and is also used in cell phone text messages as well.

Seerehwenfadha7et: the name of the mail group created by the narrator. *Seereh* means memoirs or story; *wenfadha7et, wenfadhahet* means disclosed or exposed. The name was taken from a Lebanese talk show called *SeerehWenfatahet*. It means "a story told" but the name got changed to *wenfadhahet* to reflect more of a scandalous scene.

I chose the characters' last names to show where they come from. Just like any other place in the world, in Saudi Arabia you can tell a lot from where the man or the woman comes from.

P.S. *Al* means *the.*

Sadeem Al-Horaimli: of or relating to Horaimla, a city within Najd, the center of Saudi Arabia.

Gamrah Al-Qusmanji: of or relating to Qasim, a city within Najd, the center of Saudi Arabia.

Lamees and Tamadur Jeddawi: of or relating to Jeddah, a city within Hijaz, the west coast.

Glossary

Mashael and Meshaal Al-Abdulrahman: a random name that can belong to any family with unknown roots (i.e., from an untraceable tribe).

Firas Al-Shargawi: of or relating to Sharqiyah, the east coast of Saudi Arabia.

The following family names are Arabic adjectives to describe the personality of each:

Rashid Al-Tanbal: the bonehead.

Faisal Al-Batran: the wellborn.

Waleed Al-Shari: the buyer, the purchaser.

Fadwa Al-Hasudi: she who hates to see other people more happy or successful than her.

Sultan Al-Internetti: of or relating to the Internet.